THE

# JUDAS
## *Hoard*

# THE
# JUDAS
## *Hoard*

BARBARA ERLICHMAN

# THE JUDAS HOARD

iUniverse books may be ordered through booksellers or by contacting:

iUniverse
1663 Liberty Drive
Bloomington, IN 47403
www.iuniverse.com
1-800-Authors (1-800-288-4677)

ISBN: 978-1-5320-1954-8 (sc)
ISBN: 978-1-5320-1955-5 (e)

Library of Congress Control Number: 2017903686

Print information available on the last page.

iUniverse rev. date: 04/04/2017

# Acknowledgements

I want to take a moment to thank all the people who have given me so much encouragement and support, especially Susan Forman and Brenda Sorg for their editing, insights and suggestions. And also to my cheering section — Barb G, Chadda, Chellie and Mary F. Thanks for always being there for me.

And, of course, thanks to my wonderful husband, Jay, who's always making sure my writing is the best it can be.

To all of you, thanks for everything.

# Chapter 1

Linden thought her head was about to explode. *This*, she decided, *is absolutely, positively the last time I'll attend a frat party.*

Except . . . she wasn't a student anymore. She distinctly remembered graduating from the Rhode Island School of Design, could recall the photograph of herself in cap and gown, flanked by her Aunt Helena and Uncle George, both smiling proudly. *So why the monster hangover?*

As if on cue, a bell rang, intensifying the drumbeat inside her skull. Swallowing a wave of nausea, she opened her eyes to a murky gloom that still felt bright. Peering around the sparsely-furnished room, she realized one thing: she hadn't a clue where she was. The ringing stopped, only to resume seconds later. A flashing red light caught her attention, and stumbling toward it, she snatched up the phone.

"I started to think you were dead," a metallic voice mocked.

"Who is this?" she mumbled.

"Shut up and put on the TV."

Spotting a remote control on the coffee table, Linden pushed the power button. A wall-mounted TV lit up, with a photograph of her uncle filling the screen. It was the formal portrait that his PR department always used for official shots.

". . . tributes continue to pour in following the news of George Lambert's passing," intoned the newscaster. "One of New York City's most respected real estate developers, Mr. Lambert died suddenly last night. In related news, his home was also the scene of a multimillion dollar theft, and local law enforcement officers have been at the house for several hours. A source tells me that his niece, Linden Travers, visited him last night and she hasn't been seen or heard from since."

Stunned, Linden changed the channel only to be confronted by a live shot of Laurel Court, as a reporter emoted, ". . . behind me is the Lambert home where the robbery took place. The police are anxious to speak with his niece, Linden Travers. If anyone has seen her, please contact Detective Gorton at the number below."

A third click brought another channel with Linden's own face on the screen. The image was from a photo taken at her cousin's birthday party a month earlier. The voice-over belonged to Tom Blair, the family lawyer and George Lambert's best friend since college.

"Linden, please call me," he implored. "You know I'll help you get through this."

Once again, she fought back nausea as her fingers found the remote's "off" button. The phone by her ear crackled, but the distorted voice speaking was impossible to identify.

"The law may say you're innocent until proven guilty, but the police and your family don't seem to see it that way, do they?"

"Who are you?" she demanded.

No answer came—just the silence of a disconnected call.

Collapsing against the back of the sofa, Linden tried to remember the previous night, but she had no recollection of being anywhere or talking to anyone. Monday night was a complete blank.

Memories fluttered around before taking on substance. She had called the house late Monday morning but her aunt said Uncle George's condition remained unchanged, and she didn't think a visit to Radford was necessary. So Linden stayed in Manhattan and tried to distract herself by polishing her presentation for Tuesday's client meeting. By mid-afternoon she needed a break, and leaving her home office, she'd gone out to Central Park for a three-mile run. Her memory ended there.

Eyes flying open, she examined her clothes. The black slacks, silk blouse and low-heeled pumps proved she'd returned home after her run, although she couldn't recall dressing to go out. Given the magnitude of her hangover, she knew she over drank. Yet one thing was for sure—no matter how upset she was, she would never go to a bar alone. So who was with her? A more important question: how did she get from there to this room?

The urgent need for water stilled all questions. Her parched throat felt glued shut. With effort, she staggered out of the den into a silent, shadowy foyer. A staircase led to the second floor, but Linden ignored it and opened the nearest door. Inside was a powder room, where she took care of her other urgent need.

As she dried her hands on the neatly-folded hand towel, morbid curiosity drew her gaze to the mirror above the washbasin. Stringy blonde hair drooped around her head, while her eyes, which normally glowed like polished amber, stared back with the empty gaze of a zombie.

Returning to the foyer, she tiptoed down the hallway in search of the kitchen. Window shades kept the room in semidarkness, but Linden spotted goblets in a glass-fronted cabinet. Filling one with tap water, she gulped down the tepid liquid as she crossed the kitchen to the back door, only to find it locked. The windows were similarly secured, as was the front door. Both the entry and exit required a key. For added security, a keypad on the wall blinked, an obvious warning that an alarm would sound if she were to open the door. And even if the noise didn't rouse the neighborhood, it would ring somewhere, alerting someone that she was leaving.

Across from the keypad, an archway opened onto the living room. Furnished with two drab sofas and an empty wall unit, the room appeared unused, but the windows interested her. Again, a key was needed to unlock the frames, and the square panes of glass were too small to squeeze through. A rapid check of the upper floor revealed additional locked windows. Back in the den, her worst fears were confirmed. Not only was the patio door locked, but the windows were alarmed. She was a prisoner in a house that was as secure as Fort Knox.

Anger surged through her veins, adding fuel to her pain, but she pushed it back. Self-pity could come later. It was time for action. Grabbing the TV remote, she flicked through the stations to the Weather Channel. According to the local forecast, the noontime temperature was 68 degrees and the region could expect seasonable weather for early June. She also learned one other thing; she was somewhere in Nassau County, NY. It was welcome news, since she was still in New York State, but she could not pinpoint her exact location.

On the other hand, local transportation was available in most of Nassau County, which was essential if she was ever to escape her jail. Although where would she go? And why was she so reluctant to contact the police? Her family? Was she guilty of a multimillion dollar theft? Linden didn't *need* to steal anything, and why would she *do* it anyway? George Lambert had been like a father to her—no, much more than that. He'd replaced the father she could barely remember. So what was the story with Monday night?

As if in answer, a memory surfaced. She was standing in a shaft of light, a leather box in her hands, its top flipped open. Dark shadows obscured the rest of the room, but not the bulky figure looming over her.

"There's only the goddamn letter."

The whispered words held the same quality as a scream—agonized and angry.

"All this for nothing? Where is it?"

"I don't know."

"Bullshit. You were involved in this."

Coupled with unnaturally broad shoulders, the furious voice increased Linden's sense of menace.

"It's exactly the sort of stunt your uncle would pull. You're the only person he'd tell, and now you're going to tell me. By the time I've finished with you, I'll know everything!"

The memory ended, and Linden found herself staring at the TV screen, which still showed the map of Nassau County. She replayed the scene in her mind, hoping to identify the man, but he remained a mystery. The room, though, seemed familiar. *Okay,* she thought. *I don't know what I've done, where I am. But staying here isn't an option. I need to find a way out.*

Slumped on the sofa, she massaged her aching head, but pain wasn't her only problem. Her skin crawled. She felt as if she was being watched, but when she looked out of the window, no one was in sight. As she studied the room, she noticed something next to the cable box—a tiny camera.

Switching off the television set, she limped into the foyer and grabbed the banister, her eyes scanning the room. Attached to the light fixture, a second camera faced the front door. Back in the kitchen, Linden refilled her glass and leaned against one of the granite counters. As she sipped the water, she checked the room and finally spotted the camera, perched atop the fridge with a view of the back door. She was under constant surveillance, she realized, which meant her best defense was to appear clueless.

Walking back to the foyer, Linden went up the stairs to the second floor where she checked the hallway and three bedrooms. She didn't believe there would be any cameras upstairs because the windows were locked, but escape still seemed impossible.

Or *was* it? What about the attic space between the bedroom ceilings and roof? Maybe someone had added windows for ventilation. Head tilted back, she walked along the hallway and spotted it—a square panel outside the smallest bedroom. Since no one had come to the house so far, she assumed that whoever was watching was far away, unable to react quickly. Even so, there was no time to waste.

Remembering the armchair in the master bedroom, she dragged it to the hallway and positioned it under the panel. Armed with a couple of coat hangers, she jabbed at the panel until it slid to the side, exposing a retractable metal ladder. Seconds later, she was inside an unfinished attic with windows at each end. Relief surged through her. Not only was the nearest one unlocked, the backyard was surrounded by trees and their canopy would conceal her escape.

Escape. Right . . . she was three flights up. There was no way she was about to jump. But maybe the linen closet would provide a solution. It was equipped with sheets and towels that she could tie together. In less than five minutes she'd fashioned a primitive rope, which she secured to the top rung of the ladder. The knots only needed to hold for a few minutes, and then she'd be free. But free to go where? Good question. And how was she going to get there? An even *better* question.

Returning to the first floor, a thorough search of the den proved useless. The purse she always carried was nowhere to be found.

She flashed back to her sixteenth birthday and her aunt's words of caution.

"Even if you have friends old enough to drive you to places, they may not be around when it's time to leave. Always have money for cab fare, and make sure it stays with you."

To Aunt Helena that meant tucking it in her bra. Linden felt for the tiny inside pocket and took out the wad of paper money within. Unfurling it, she counted ninety dollars. Had she been expecting trouble? She'd figure that out later, but for the moment, she just wanted to get back to New York, the city where she'd lived since college graduation—and the best place in the world to disappear.

# Chapter 2

Alex Blair's new office was a cleared out storage room in his uncle's Nassau County law practice, just outside New York City. Hands clasped behind his head, feet on the desk, Alex studied his new quarters. The room was barely large enough to hold the nicked desk, but size didn't matter. He didn't plan on spending much time inside anyway. Hired to find Linden Travers, he knew he needed to be out and about, talking to people, following up every tip.

A few hours earlier, his uncle, who had been the Lambert family lawyer for decades, called with the news of George Lambert's passing.

"Sorry to hear that," Alex responded. "What was the cause of death?"

"Heart failure," Tom said. "At first the police thought they were dealing with murder but there was nothing to support the theory. George had been terminally ill so his death was not unexpected."

The older man paused.

"Ever heard of the Judas Hoard?"

Alex thought for a moment.

"Seems to ring a bell. Lambert's *coin* collection?"

"Right. It was George's pride and joy. And considered priceless, although everything has a price. Well, it's disappeared, along with his niece. Both have vanished without a trace."

"Do you think the niece was involved?"

"No one's seen her since she left her uncle's home last night, which does raise questions. As for the Judas Hoard: that was last seen several weeks ago. It was stored in a bank vault, but George decided he wanted to keep it in his home safe, and Linden was supposed to have put the coins away. This morning the safe was found unlocked and the coins were missing."

"Could be a coincidence. What does Mrs. Lambert think?"

"She doesn't know what to think. However, she no longer wants the police and FBI involved, and asked me to hire a private investigator. Interested?"

"You bet."

"Some people won't be happy that I've recommended you, but they'll just have to get over it. You're the best."

After hearing about Alex's credentials, Helena Lambert agreed that he was the best. Based in Boston, Alex specialized in finding people who didn't want to be found: runaway adolescents, disgraced financiers, fugitives trying to evade paying alimony/child support/financial settlements—he'd encountered them all during the last ten years. Impressed with his success rate, Helena called a couple of his references and hired him, sight unseen.

By lunchtime, Alex was in his new office ready to review the stack of notes, files, and videotapes related to the case. Several hours later, he felt confident enough to form an opinion. Because her fingerprints were all over the safe and there was no explanation for her disappearance, Linden appeared to be guilty as hell. Everyone agreed she was devoted to her aunt and uncle and conceded that hurting them would be out of character. Yet they also admitted that she was certainly smart enough to pull off such a stunt.

As he became familiar with the basics of the case, Alex was more than eager to visit the crime scene while everyone's memories were still fresh. He set off on the five-mile drive to the Lambert home in his rented Ford Taurus, the GPS dictating the route.

Before that morning, there was little to distinguish the town of Radford from any other exclusive Nassau County community. Life-changing events, such as births, marriages and deaths were announced in *The New York Times*, and the media invasion generated by George Lambert's death had outraged Radford's residents. As a result of their calls, the local police swiftly erected barricades outside Laurel Court, the secluded cul-de-sac where George had lived for most of his married life. Protected by thick woods, the ten multimillion dollar mansions were further shielded from prying eyes and uninvited guests by iron gates and seven-foot high hedges.

A police officer guarded the entrance to Laurel Court, and producing his ID, Alex waited while the officer reviewed the list of approved visitors. Finally allowed into the cul-de-sac, Alex drove up to the gate outside the Lambert home and identified himself over the intercom, tapping his steering wheel impatiently until a car-wide gap opened. The gate slammed shut the instant he cleared the space.

A half-timbered house stood at the end of the driveway. With its pitched roof and diamond-shaped window panes it could have been a transplant from Tudor England. Parked in front were a red Audi, a blue Mercedes and a white Porsche. Alex left his Hertz rental behind the Porsche and followed the slate path to the house.

Three shallow steps led to the front door, a forbidding slab of dark oak with a brass knocker shaped like a sphinx.

Careful not to burnish the brilliant shine, Alex knocked, and the door swung open to reveal a man in a black suit with the rigid spine of a drill sergeant. Although he appeared to be in his mid-sixties, the only gray in his dark hair was at the temples.

"Good afternoon, Mr. Blair. We were told to expect you," the man said, with the precise diction of an ex-pat Briton. "I'm Brunnings, the Lamberts' butler. Please come with me."

The butler gave Alex no time to check out the paneled entrance hall as he led the way to a spacious kitchen at the rear of the house. Seated at the table in front of the picture window, a white-haired woman dabbed at her cheeks, grief accentuating the furrows in her face.

"My wife," Brunnings acknowledged. "This is Alex Blair, the private investigator Mrs. Lambert hired."

Like her handshake, the offer of coffee was perfunctory but Alex was quick to accept a cup.

"Thanks for seeing me," he began, taking a seat at the table. "I know this must be a very difficult time for you. You've been here what . . . nearly thirty years?"

"That's right, and a nicer family you couldn't wish to meet," Mrs. Brunnings declared, setting down Alex's cup with more force than necessary.

In response to Alex's questions, the couple confirmed that George Lambert's two children, their spouses and his niece had all been at the house Monday evening, even though Lambert's condition had remained unchanged. Everyone had made the trip to Radford on impulse, with Linden being the last to leave around eleven p.m.

Alex also learned that she had been a frequent visitor since the onset of her uncle's illness, rearranging her life in order to spend as much time as possible with him. When Alex observed that she was fortunate to have such flexibility, Mrs. Brunnings responded that Linden brought work with her.

"She's a freelancer," Mrs. Brunnings explained. "Designs office space and exhibits. Mr. Lambert was very proud of her and loved to watch as she sketched out ideas for her latest commission."

Deciding he'd heard enough about the saintly Linden Travers, Alex brought up the subject of the theft.

"According to your statement, Mr. Brunnings, you were the one to discover the Judas Hoard was missing around six a.m. Had something alerted you to the fact that the coins had been stolen?"

"No, I'd been up for about an hour. Matt, the night nurse, woke us at five o'clock with the news of Mr. Lambert's passing. My wife went to tell Mrs. Lambert and I called the doctor and your uncle."

"Mrs. Lambert wasn't *with* her husband?" asked Alex, surprised.

Brunnings shook his head.

"He wanted it that way. Wouldn't permit the family to keep a deathwatch. Matt told us Mr. Lambert just slipped away."

Alex nodded, adding information to his notes.

"After making your phone calls, what did you do?"

"Checked the first floor rooms to make sure everything was in order. I do it every morning. The minute I entered Mr. Lambert's study, I knew something was terribly wrong."

Brunnings stood, refilling his coffee cup.

Alex tried to remain patient. "Why?"

The butler heaved a deep sigh as he sat again.

"Mr. Lambert's safe is hidden behind a painting, and the frame wasn't flush against the wall. On closer inspection, I found the safe door to be slightly open and discovered the Judas Hoard was gone."

"Do you know why the coins were here and not in Mr. Lambert's safety deposit box?"

"He insisted on having them brought to the house a few

weeks ago," the butler answered. "The chauffeur was ill that day so I drove Mrs. Lambert and Linden to the bank. I have a pistol permit and Mrs. Lambert wanted me along for security."

"When you got back here, what happened?"

"Linden put the coins in the safe in his study."

"Did you see her *do* it?"

"If Linden was asked to put away those coins, then that's what she did." Mrs. Brunnings' voice left no room for argument. "And she didn't steal them either. I don't know what happened to her but I just hope she's all right. She adored her aunt and uncle. She'd never do anything to upset or hurt them . . . or anyone. You couldn't meet a nicer girl."

"I agree with my wife," Brunnings said, although less emphatic. "Linden would never go anywhere without telling someone. It just isn't her nature to disappear like this."

"No matter how well you think you know someone, you never know what's going on inside their head," Alex pointed out. "Whose idea was it to report the missing coins?"

"Mr. Lambert's son—Roger," the butler answered. "Mrs. Lambert called him and he and his wife arrived here within the hour. When they heard the coins were missing, Roger contacted the police. He and his wife also felt their cousin was somehow involved in Mr. Lambert's death. That's why we're dealing with a media circus."

He continued, his voice tinged with distaste, "Once the TV stations heard about Linden, the reporters invented their own scenarios."

"The doctor was adamant Mr. Lambert died of natural causes," Alex stated, "and the police haven't revealed that the Judas Hoard is missing—just that a theft took place. We want to keep it that way."

A trace of anger flickered on Brunnings' face. "Neither my wife nor I indulge in gossip."

"I know you don't. Your loyalty to the family is very obvious," said Alex, getting to his feet. "I don't have any more questions for now, but I'd like to see Mr. Lambert's study."

With its carved desk and floor-to-ceiling bookcases jammed with books of all shapes and sizes, the study was a comfortable retreat. Two hunter green armchairs and a matching leather sofa were grouped in front of a massive stone fireplace, the blackened hearth large enough to roast a pig. An oil painting of two greyhounds hung on the adjacent wall, its gilt frame marred by fingerprints outlined in black powder.

"The safe's behind here," said Brunnings, nudging the edge of the painting. "While I could see immediately that it was slightly out of position, someone else might not have realized it."

After studying the slight angle, Alex swung the painting out further to reveal a metal door sunk into the wall. More black smudges covered both the door and the knob in the center. "Who knows the combination to this?"

"Just the family," Brunnings answered, his voice expressionless. "Not even *I* was privy to that information."

Walking over to the French door, Alex looked out across a rolling lawn that was bordered on both sides by glossy rhododendron bushes. No other houses were visible. The property ended in a forest, and Alex stared at the old-growth trees for a moment while absently rubbing the brass loop around the hunter green drape.

Turning back to face the room, he asked, "So this is exactly how you found it?"

Brunnings nodded. "Except for two things. The French door was open and the alarm was turned off."

Realizing the butler did not intend to volunteer anything, Alex asked to inspect the house's alarm system. As he walked through the first floor with Brunnings, he saw the system followed basic wiring and zoning protocols—apart from Lambert's study which was on a separate line. Lambert often stayed up late, Brunnings explained, and had requested a separate alarm with its own keypad. Although the butler swore every alarm was set Monday night, he couldn't deny that family and staff all knew the codes.

Alex next asked to meet Lambert's children. Brunnings returned several minutes later to say that they were too upset to speak with him, but they would see him the next day. Taking advantage of being at the Lambert mansion, Alex checked out the apartment where Mr. and Mrs. Brunnings lived. It was located over the three-car garage and totally private, so it was unlikely that anyone inside would hear or see anything unusual from there.

Walking down the drive to the gates, Alex studied the cameras mounted on the top of each sandstone pillar. Monitors inside the house provided a clear image of all arriving and departing vehicles—even those owned by the family—and the electronically-controlled gates weren't opened until visitors identified themselves over the intercom. Alex couldn't fault the positioning of the cameras, but their only purpose was gate surveillance—not to monitor activity outside in Laurel Court.

As Alex hurried back to the house, he experienced the familiar rush of adrenalin he always felt at the start of a new case. Finding Linden would be a challenge, but ordinary people rarely managed to drop out of sight for long. Even with time to prepare, they invariably tripped themselves up with dumb mistakes.

In addition to the APB issued for Linden's car, the police were also watching her bank accounts and credit cards. Over time, the tips would start to trickle in, resulting in the inevitable tightening of the noose. And that's where Alex got his real high—pursuing every lead, no matter how insignificant. No one *ever* outsmarted him.

# Chapter 3

"Never do anything unless you've thought it through."

George Lambert's frequent advice boomed inside Linden's head as she prepared to climb down the makeshift rope. Glancing over to her right shoulder, she half expected to see her uncle's hand there.

Just what was her plan when she reached terra firma? Thanks to TV's insatiable appetite for breaking news, she probably had the most famous face in America. She needed a disguise, and the most obvious was a baseball hat. Although her earlier search through the closets and drawers revealed only empty space, she checked again more carefully. And poking around the closet in the smallest bedroom she hit pay dirt—a Yankee cap. While not the greatest camouflage in the world, at least it would hide some of her face and hair.

At the top of the stairs, she stood and listened, praying the silence was a good sign. Hopefully "The Voice," as she now thought of him, figured she was either in the shower or taking a nap.

Refusing to spend another second in her prison, she scrambled up the ladder to the third floor. Gripping the sheet with both hands, she took a deep breath and climbed out the window.

The sheets held until she was four feet from the ground when the top knot uncoiled and she landed on the slate patio with a thud that jarred her spine. Rubbing her back, she looked around. The large yard was even more secluded at ground level, as all signs of surrounding houses were blocked out by towering swamp maples and thick shrubbery.

Concerned The Voice might have accomplices posted on the street, Linden stayed in the back yard and raced from bush to bush to the boxwood hedge that marked the rear property line. Forcing her way through a gap in the foliage, she stumbled into the neighboring yard, jagged nerves calming when the silence remained unbroken. Cautiously, she headed to the front of the house and down a black-topped driveway. A mailbox at the end had the name "Lawton" stenciled next to the number twelve, details that she absently noted as she entered the tree-lined street beyond.

Ignoring the urge to run, she walked to the right, keeping her pace to an easy stroll until she reached the end of the block. The street signs showed she was leaving Mulberry Lane and entering Arbor Drive. Four blocks down, traffic lights indicated a major highway.

Instead of being relieved, Linden felt the earth start to spin, and she slumped against the nearest tree. Eyes closed against the dazzling sunshine, she wondered where she'd find the energy to move again. But she had no choice, and straightening up, she took a few unsteady steps. Telling herself just to keep putting one foot in front of the other, she trudged forward.

She was less than a hundred yards from the traffic lights when the vehicle pulled up beside her.

"You okay?"

Heart pounding, Linden looked at the truck. White

lettering on the door advertised *Carlin's Landscaping*, which was confirmed by the gardening tools in the rear. The name was also embroidered on the navy baseball hat perched atop the driver's head. Shoulder-length auburn hair gave him a boyish look, but laughter lines etched around his eyes put him around forty.

Mouth painfully dry, she swallowed. "Sure. Just felt like some exercise."

"Not too many people walk around here. Want a lift?"

Although her aunt had always warned about accepting rides from strangers, Linden was *desperate*. "Thanks. I'm headed into town."

"Sorry. I'm going to Syosset," he said.

Opening the passenger door, Linden slid into the seat.

"That works."

As the man pulled away from the curb, he asked, "Visiting someone?"

"Yes. My boyfriend. He had to go to work today, but I told him I'd be fine by myself. It's my first time here, and I didn't realize how much you need a car to get around."

"Guess you're a city person."

"Totally. Boston. Great subway system."

"If you say so. Never been there myself."

Linden let out a mental sigh of relief. Despite visiting Boston several times while a student in Rhode Island, she wasn't an expert on the city.

"Nice place. You should try to get there."

"Can't say the same about Syosset. Not much to see."

Unexpected hunger pangs pierced Linden's numbness. "Just so long as there's a coffee shop where I can get some lunch."

"There are plenty of those, but they don't serve what you'd call gourmet food."

The man's phone rang, and the ensuing conversation

claimed his attention for the rest of the ten-minute journey. Navigating a network of traffic lights with practiced ease, he entered Main Street where a sign pointed to the train station. Spotting it, Linden sent up a silent prayer of gratitude. She knew the name of the town where she was. It was the name of the town she had left that remained a mystery.

Stopping in front of a bank, the driver said, "As promised, downtown Syosett. Hope it satisfies all your needs."

"I'm sure it will. I'll get a cab back to . . . would you believe I've drawn a mental blank on the name of the town?"

Sounding surprised, the driver said, "It was Ashton."

"Right. Ashton. Had a senior moment just then." Linden forced a smile. "Thanks for the lift."

Leaving the truck, Linden headed straight for the drugstore across the street. Inside, she grabbed a pair of sunglasses, found a small notebook and pen in the stationery department, and added a packet of aspirin when she reached the display at the checkout counter. The teenaged cashier rang up the items with a palpable lack of interest while darting glances at her smart phone.

At the train station, the departure board showed the two o'clock train to New York was due in ten minutes, giving Linden enough time to buy coffee and a cranberry muffin from a nearby Dunkin' Donuts. Once seated in the middle of a half-empty train car, she washed down two aspirins with a slug of coffee. For a moment she experienced a sense of security until the memory of her uncle's death caught her unawares. But grief was a luxury she couldn't afford just then: she needed a game plan. Since the police would already have the names of her friends, her Number One priority was to come up with someone who would be under the radar. Pushing back her heartbreak for another time, she spent the trip considering who that someone might be.

Forty minutes later she was at Penn Station, just another unremarkable arrival in the press of harried travelers. Her first stop was the phone store across from the ticket windows. Given her financial situation, buying a burner phone was a huge extravagance, but she couldn't function without one.

Although the station bustled with activity, she found a spot away from the crowd and called Information. She needed the number for Anderson & Wood, one of New York's most prestigious interior design companies. Its current star was Julia van Oppen—and her one-time best friend. Roommates since their first day at RISD, she and Julia had shared everything for four years. On graduation day she discovered that they also shared the same boyfriend. When confronted, Dave chose Julia. Tempers flared and words best left unsaid were hurled like javelins, piercing each other with a hundred different hurts.

Although it was six years since they last spoke, Linden had kept track of her friend through social media. She had even dialed Julia's phone number once in a while, but always lost her nerve before the call was connected. She missed Julia—and now it was time to see how deep their friendship had really been.

Holding her breath, Linden dialed the number.

"Julia van Oppen." The voice was achingly familiar.

Linden was reluctant to say too much over the phone.

"It's Linden. From Phi Beta."

After a moment's shocked silence, the line went dead.

Linden redialed, but the call went straight to Julia's voice mail.

"Please help me," she begged. "I'm in trouble and there's no one else I can turn to. Please call me."

Leaving her number, Linden disconnected and stared at her phone. Ten minutes crawled by before she gave up waiting for a response. She couldn't stay in the station all day, and across the concourse two police officers seemed to be discussing her. Clutching her phone, she merged into the crowd and headed for the nearest exit.

Despite her sunglasses, Linden cringed when she emerged into the daylight, half-blinded by the sun's glare. Her wrinkled silk blouse and pants added to her discomfort, but a nearby K-Mart offered a solution, and she joined a group of tourists as they entered the store. Picking out the cheapest tote bag, she stuck in a package of underwear, several tee-shirts, a brush and a small shoulder bag.

As she looked around for a checkout counter, her phone rang. Uncaring about the lack of privacy, she answered it.

"Where are you?"

Although Julia didn't sound overly friendly, at least she'd called back.

"Near Penn Station."

"Meet me in Bryant Park in fifteen minutes. There's a patio near Sixth Avenue and 42$^{nd}$ Street. It's close to my office and it will be crowded, even now."

"Thank you," Linden whispered. "I'll be there. I'm wearing a Yankee baseball hat."

"You used to hate the Yankees."

"I still do, but it was all I could find."

Hanging up, Linden called Information for the number of the Sheraton Hotel on Seventh Avenue. Located just a few blocks from Times Square, the streets around the tourist mecca were always busy, making the hotel a perfect place to hide out. Within minutes she had made a reservation in Julia's name.

After paying for her purchases, she pulled on one of her new tee-shirts to cover her wrinkled blouse. Feeling less conspicuous, she left the store and set off for Bryant Park.

The sun beat down on the crowded streets, and short-fused office workers were forced to slow down to the leisurely pace favored by shoppers and sightseers. At Bryant Park, Linden bought a bottle of water and snagged two chairs by the edge of the patio. Slouched in hers, she scanned the ever-changing flow of people until she spotted her friend's flame-colored hair. Although a sleek bob replaced the unruly mass of ringlets of their college years, the face was almost the same. Catching sight of Linden, Julia hurried over, her body stiff with tension as she sat on the adjacent chair.

"What's going on?" she demanded. "You're all over the Internet. Something about a giant heist."

"I wish I knew. I woke up a few hours ago on Long Island, in a house I've never seen before. The house phone was ringing and the caller told me to switch on the TV. That's how I discovered Uncle George was . . . what had happened."

Julia's face remained tight with anger.

"Who called?"

"I've no idea. The caller used one of those voice changers, but I have the feeling he was male. In my mind, I just think of him as The Voice and he practically accused me of stealing whatever it is that's gone."

"Why not go to the police?"

"Because last night's a total blank." Linden fought back tears. "I blacked out."

"What's the last thing you *do* remember?" asked Julia in a softer tone.

"Going for an afternoon run in Central Park. Since I woke up with the mother of all hangovers, I must've gone home to change and then went out drinking."

"Unless you've undergone a major personality change in the last six years, you were with someone." Julia's tone was very definite. "The Linden I knew would never drink alone."

"It had to be The Voice," Linden choked. "How else would he know where to find me?"

"Could he be a boyfriend?" There was no trace of Julia's earlier fury—only interest. "Are you dating?"

"No one special," Linden answered. "And I can't imagine it's one of them."

"Yeah. This takes a special type of creep," Julia observed. "I thought we'd left them all behind after college."

"Me, too. Even with the creeps, though, they were fun years."

"A lot of fun." Eyes glistening, Julia caught Linden's hands in hers. "I missed you."

"I nearly called you a million times to apologize," Linden admitted.

"I nearly called you a million times to tell you that Dave and I were through by Christmas," Julia confessed. "It didn't take me long to discover he was a world class jerk."

The tension between the two women disappeared, and they hugged each other, erasing any leftover resentment. Pulling away, Julia looked at Linden with a sympathetic expression.

"I'm so sorry about your uncle. I know he was like a father to you."

As Linden's grief resurfaced, tears streamed down her face. "That's why this situation is so unreal. I'd never do anything to hurt him or Helena . . . Aunt Heni."

Delving into her leather tote bag, Julia pulled out a package of tissues, which she handed to Linden. "And that's why I'm here to help. What do you need?"

"Money," Linden sniffled, wiping her eyes.

"No problem. First stop will be an ATM. What else?"

"A hotel room, since my apartment's probably under surveillance. Anyway, I don't have a key. My purse disappeared along with last night's memory. I've made a reservation in your name at the Sheraton on Seventh Avenue. Will you check in for me?"

"Sure, but you know you can stay with me."

23

"Your name's bound to come up eventually, and then the police will be all over you. The last thing I want is for you to be in even more trouble."

"I can handle any trouble, but the Sheraton's probably a better choice because it's so huge. It should be easy to get lost in the crowd."

"You're amazing," Linden said. "And I'll repay you as soon as I get my old life back. I'm good for it."

"Don't worry about it." Julia seemed suddenly fascinated by the slender gold chain around her wrist. "Money's the reason Dave chose me. Figured he'd live off me for a few years and then walk off with half our assets after we married."

Linden knew all about her friend's financial situation. "He must have been shocked to discover that your parents were funding you only until you found a job."

"That's an understatement," said Julia. "But my parents still help out, so we'll have enough money to find out what's going on here. Any ideas?"

Linden shook her head. "*None.*"

Glancing at her watch, Julia said, "Time's moving on. Let's get you checked into the Sheraton."

Linden handed over her tote bag. "Your luggage. No respectable woman checks into a hotel without something."

Fifteen minutes later, Linden was in the Sheraton's elevator heading up to the tenth floor. The door to room 1012 was ajar and as Linden stepped inside, Julia spoke.

"Here it is. Home sweet home. For a while."

"Thanks, Jules. I don't know how I'll ever pay you back. And I'm not talking about money."

"Just having you back in my life is payment enough. The room's charged to my AMEX card and set up for express checkout, so you don't need to sign when you leave. Order up room service. Clothes. Whatever."

Handing over a slip of paper, Julia said, "This is a copy of my signature plus all my phone numbers. Work. Home. Cell. Call anytime if you need anything."

"And to keep you updated," Linden promised, hugging her friend.

When they separated, Julia she forced a smile. "We'll find out who's behind this, and exactly what you're accused of stealing. I promise."

Linden's pleasure from the reunion evaporated the instant Julia walked out of the room. Loneliness enveloped her, and she felt like a traveler on a trip to nowhere, intensifying her depression. An air of impermanence cloaked the room, which even the cheery pink and green color scheme couldn't disguise. Although waves of exhaustion rolled over her, she stripped off her clothes and stepped into the shower. She stood under the hot spray for a long time, but the water's healing properties didn't reveal any answers.

While drying her left arm, a jolt of pain made Linden look at the spot in surprise. It reminded her of last year's flu shot when the injection site remained tender for several days. She inspected the area, but no needle mark was visible.

*You're crazy*, she taunted herself. *Why would anyone inject you with some sort of substance?*

But . . . maybe it was still worth getting a blood sample. Her eyes fell on the little basket on the vanity. Nestled amongst the miniature bottles was a sewing kit. Taking out the needle, she pricked her finger, blotting the spot of blood with a tissue. Should it ever become an issue, today's high tech equipment would detect anything of interest.

# Chapter 4

As arranged, Alex was back at the Lambert mansion on Wednesday morning to meet with the family. He was almost at the front door when Brunnings opened it. Neither Roger Lambert nor his mother was available, the butler informed Alex, but Roger's sister would see him.

Brunnings marched across the entrance hall like a soldier on parade, stopping at a set of double doors. Holding one open, he waved Alex into a cavernous room with a vaulted ceiling and several Impressionist paintings on the walls. A French door opened onto a paved patio, and waiting beside it was a man whose well-defined muscles could only be the result of daily workouts.

"I'm Gerry Hammond," he bristled. "My wife's devastated by her father's death. Just remember that."

His animosity continued as he led Alex outside to where Melanie Lambert Wentworth Hammond stood next to a glass-topped table. Waves of Titian hair framed her oval face, and although her perfect features were pinched with grief, she was still a beautiful woman.

"I'm so sorry for your loss," said Alex. "It's good of you to see me."

"My mother made me." The harsh voice was a dramatic contrast to her appearance. "Gerry, we need some coffee."

With the grace of a born athlete, Gerry retreated back inside the house while Melanie collapsed into a wicker armchair. As she dabbed at her sapphire blue eyes, Alex settled in the adjacent chair.

"When you left Ms. Travers on Monday night, how did she seem?" he eventually asked.

"Very upset. Like the rest of us."

"Did you get the impression your cousin was going to disappear?"

Melanie shook her head. "Absolutely not. Her last words to me were that she'd call me tomorrow. That would be yesterday. Tuesday."

"What about the last few weeks? Anything unusual happen?"

"No, she was still the same old Linden. Devoted to her work. I was always fixing her up with guys but nothing ever happened. They all said she was too intense."

"That means she refused to join them in their favorite pursuits of sleeping around and snorting coke."

Gerry's support of Linden was unexpected, but Alex stayed silent as the other man walked onto the patio with a tray of coffee mugs.

"Those guys don't have a brain between them," Gerry continued, setting down the tray, "and wouldn't have a job if Daddy didn't own the company."

"At least they don't live off their wives," Melanie shot back.

"Only because they can't find a trust fund baby dumb enough to marry them," Gerry retorted with equal fury.

The couple glared at each other until Alex reached for a mug of coffee. As he added some sugar Melanie looked at him.

"In case you missed the point, Mr. Blair, my husband doesn't approve of my friends. And all Linden cares about is her stupid designs. Twenty-eight years old and already stuck in her ways."

"For God's sake, stop making her sound like an old maid," Gerry said. "That isn't her at all. She's fun, great sense of humor."

"You should know," Melanie snapped. "After all, you had plenty of time to learn everything about her."

"Jesus, Mel, can't you let that alone," Gerry exploded. "It happened *once*, weeks ago. And how often do I have to tell you? Linden and I met by accident outside the tennis center. If we were hot for each other, do you really think I'd have brought her home?"

"If you thought you could get away with it, of course. Just like Linden expected to get away with this. Bet she's been planning it for months. I wouldn't put anything past her."

A woman walked out of the great room, and catching sight of her, some of the tension left Melanie's body.

"Hi, Liz. I wondered where you were."

Immaculate hair and a designer dress proved the younger Mrs. Lambert took her position as a rich man's wife very seriously. She was also a woman who knew how to make the best of herself, but even expertly-applied cosmetics couldn't disguise her thin lips or hide the coldness in her eyes.

"I'm Elizabeth Lambert," she informed Alex, hostility and haughtiness divided into equal parts. "Has Melanie convinced you that the little bitch ran off with the Judas Hoard?"

Although her venomous tone surprised Alex, his face remained expressionless.

"No. All we can say with any certainty is that Ms. Travers

has disappeared. We don't even know if it's the result of foul play."

"Fat chance," Elizabeth scoffed. "This stunt was in the works for months, ever since she learned my father-in-law rewrote his will. Her Little Miss Sweetness and Light act never fooled me for a second. She was only after the money. Imagine how she felt to find that her inheritance was reduced to a lousy half million dollars."

"A hell of a lot better than to learn it was nothing," Alex said.

"Which is *exactly* what she deserved," Elizabeth retorted. "Just because she was treated like a daughter by the family, it didn't mean she was entitled to an equal share of its fortune. She's had more than her share of good luck."

"I wouldn't call being orphaned at seven years old good luck." Alex observed.

"What else do you call being adopted by the Lamberts?" asked Elizabeth. "From then on she lived a charmed life, entitled to everything her cousins had. Acted like she owned this place, too."

"It has been her home for over twenty years," Alex pointed out. "What's your husband's opinion of Ms. Travers?"

"Same as mine," Melanie interrupted. "My brother and I both considered her to be one of life's ultimate survivors. All she cared about was pleasing our parents, and she was real good at that. They gave her everything she wanted, including her college tuition—and four years at the Rhode Island School of Design isn't cheap."

Elizabeth's eyes gleamed with malicious pleasure.

"Well, the good times are now over. That's why she needed to find another source of income. The Judas Hoard was the perfect solution."

"And the minute she got her hands on it, she was off," Melanie added. "Didn't waste a second."

From experience, Alex knew that much of the attack on Linden was probably untrue, but he was making mental notes of the family dynamics.

"It's too soon to accuse her of anything."

"Then why isn't she around to defend herself?" Elizabeth demanded.

"It isn't unusual for an adult to be out of touch for a few days," Alex reminded everyone. "She may still turn up."

"Can't see why," Gerry said. "Especially if she's seen the chatter on social media. Some of the sites even call her a murderer. Which, as everyone here knows, is a crock. George was terminally ill."

"George's illness is *not* the issue," Elizabeth flared. "Linden abandoned us at our moment of greatest need."

"She can't be allowed to get away with this," Melanie choked, her eyes brimming with tears. "I want her to suffer for all the pain she's caused."

As she broke into body-shaking sobs, Gerry rushed to comfort her. With an arm around his distraught wife, he urged her into the house while Elizabeth watched, expression compassionate.

"Poor Melanie," she sighed. "She adored her father. It wouldn't surprise me in the slightest to discover that little bitch hastened his end."

"Mr. Lambert was a very sick man. Even before the virus attacked his heart, he was suffering from congestive heart failure."

"But he still wasn't expected to die so soon," Elizabeth argued. "Roger and I have been married three years and George was never sick a day until a month ago. Don't you think it's more than a coincidence that he died the very night Linden took off with the coins?"

Alex didn't have to share his thoughts on the case with anyone except Helena Lambert.

"I think it's too soon to reach any conclusions or make any accusations. A whole lot more work still needs to be done."

"What about all the grief and anguish she's brought on us? She sure is guilty of that. Which is why she must be found, and the sooner the better." Elizabeth's face twisted with hatred. "I want her punished to the full extent of the law."

* * *

Inventing another appointment, Alex left the Lambert home as eagerly as a prisoner being granted early parole. Twenty minutes later he was in Charlton. The quaint little town dated back to 1767, but the red brick house where Thomas R. Blair & Associates conducted business was neither small nor rustic. Furnished with Federal antiques, its mahogany-paneled rooms exuded an aura of luxury and privilege.

After parking his car, Alex decided to see if his uncle was available. While informative, the meeting with Linden's relatives had also raised many questions about George Lambert's will. Alex hoped the answers lay in the company's files. His uncle was out at a client's, which resulted in Alex having to review the documents under the watchful eye of Tom's partner. Seated in Peter Sinclair's spacious office, Alex browsed through the stack of papers.

"This will's a little strange," Alex observed. "Since Linden was considered a member of the family, it seems only natural that she'd be a major beneficiary."

Peter twirled a pencil through his fingers.

"Apparently he considered the honor of disposing of the Judas Hoard to be sufficient reward."

"Why have Linden handle the sale? Couldn't Lambert just donate it outright?"

"Because both he and Linden shared a love of those coins. It was almost an obsession with them. Over the years many collectors had approached him but he wanted the Hoard to go to a museum. He felt only Linden could be trusted to carry out his wishes."

"For which she'd receive a $500,000 commission," Alex noted.

"From the buyer, not the estate," Peter emphasized.

"Where did the figure come from?"

"It was an arbitrary amount. Over the years George had received offers as high as nine million dollars, which helped establish a value."

Alex scanned a thick file labeled *Collectors*.

"Why bother with the commission?" he mused. "Look at all these fat cats ready to pay millions to get the Judas Hoard for themselves. Even though nothing's been released to the media about the theft or Linden's involvement, it's only a matter of time before word gets out."

"Bringing out every bottom feeder and sleaze ball," Peter said. "And putting Linden in a lot of danger."

"If she's innocent," Alex stressed. "Lambert must have discussed this bequest with her and warned about unscrupulous collectors. Since she knew their names, she may have been the initiator and contacted one of them to set this up."

Peter swiveled his chair around to face Charlton's main street. For a few minutes he stared at the passing traffic.

"Perhaps, but it will be quite a while before she receives that commission payment. Much quicker to go straight for the multimillion-dollar payoff—tax free."

"What's your feeling?" Alex asked. "Do you think she stole the coins?"

"If you're asking did she have the brains? Absolutely," Peter replied without hesitation. "Emotionally? That's a tough one. She always seemed such a caring person."

"How well did you know her?"

"Well enough. We dated a few times but the chemistry wasn't there. On her part," Peter ended ruefully. "Too bad, she's cute. You've seen photos of her."

"She's not in the same league as her cousin, though."

"Melanie's extraordinary, but you know how the saying goes, Linden has personality."

"The Jekyll and Hyde type, from what I hear," Alex laughed. "The family thinks she's the spawn of the devil, but to Mr. and Mrs. Brunnings she was an angel. They seem very fond of her."

"Everyone likes Linden. She has a knack for making friends."

Face thoughtful, Alex tapped a knuckle against his lips while mentally reviewing the latest information.

"Could she and Brunnings be in it together? No better combination for a crime than a disgruntled employee and a disinherited relative."

"Right. The butler did it." Derision edged Peter's voice. "That's so trite it's laughable, and you're totally off the mark. Brunnings and his wife not only have very cushy jobs up at the Lambert mansion, George also set them up with an annuity to see them through their golden years."

"Maybe Brunnings wasn't too impressed with the annuity and decided to do better for himself," Alex speculated. "Then it's conceivable that he and Linden planned this whole thing together."

Peter gazed out of the window again.

"Sounds plausible," he finally answered, "but I just don't buy Brunnings involving himself in something so risky. He'd never do anything to jeopardize his pension. In addition, George helped them buy a house for their retirement. He was very generous to his employees."

"Yet he practically cut off his own niece," Alex pointed out. "Her anger could have been building for months, just waiting to erupt, and no one would know. Her cousins are convinced that's what happened."

"You can't really blame them for thinking that way."

"Very diplomatic, but then you know which side your bread's buttered."

Alex decided to test the man sitting across the desk. Flaxen hair and an aquiline nose gave Peter the look of an Austrian aristocrat, but it was his air of confidence that rubbed Alex the wrong way. Peter was a man used to success.

"You're an excellent lawyer, yet you left a highly respected company to work here. Don't you miss being with the major leaguers?"

"Been checking up on me?" Peter's pale blue eyes turned glacial. "Not that it's any of your business, I resigned for the simple reason I didn't like being a little cog in a big wheel. Too many rules and procedures. There was no sense of autonomy. Here, I work *with* your uncle, and my efforts are amply rewarded."

"Even so, Charlton's a far cry from New York." Noting the other man's well-tailored suit, Alex added, "You don't look like a country boy."

"I'm not, but I *am* a golf addict. Working in New York, I could spend either half my day commuting or half my weekend travelling to golf courses. I decided to put golf first." Peter leaned back in his chair. "Now I belong to two country clubs. They're both just a short drive away so I can even play during the week. Great for networking. I've already brought in a few new clients."

"And dated their daughters."

Peter's lips tightened. "You have been doing your homework. I just believe in making the most of opportunities. Why date poor girls if you have access to rich ones? It didn't do Gerry Hammond any harm. For a tennis coach, he really hit the jackpot."

"Or not," Alex said, recalling the scene earlier. "I think Melanie's money comes with quite a price tag."

# Chapter

# 5

Linden knew that the best place to hide was in a crowd, which made Denny's Den the perfect choice to meet Julia. When she walked in at six o'clock on Wednesday evening, the midtown bar was already mobbed, but she managed to snag a minuscule table and order two glasses of wine. Arriving a few minutes later, Julia didn't recognize her friend at first, and under any other circumstance her double take would have been comical. Without a word, she dropped into her chair and picked up her glass. After swallowing a mouthful of wine, she indicated Linden's wig.

"Great disguise."

Linden fingered a strand of brunette hair. "I don't look like me?"

"Absolutely not. Short and curly suits you." Head cocked to one side Julia studied the other woman. "And those rectangular glasses really add to the camouflage."

Pushing the brown plastic frames further up her nose, Linden said, "They're reading glasses, and even though they're the weakest, everything's a bit blurry."

"Just so long as they work—which they do. What's happening?"

"I still haven't contacted my family because I don't want to be bombarded with questions that I can't answer. All I know is that I've been set up."

"Any names?"

"Not a one. That's why I want to stay under the radar until I figure out who's responsible. I know I've ticked off some people, but this is beyond overkill."

"I agree. We're looking at major payback time."

"And vague references to a multimillion-dollar theft don't help." Linden sounded dejected. "Could be anything, even Uncle George's coin collection. Do you remember it?"

"Sure. I got such a thrill out of holding coins from the time of Jesus. It was an amazing feeling."

"But no one would be dumb enough to steal the Judas Hoard! It's unsalable—unless it was for some nutty collector who didn't care it was stolen."

"Some collectors get their kicks from owning something that's illegal," Julia pointed out.

"True," Linden conceded. "And now it's being reported that there's a bunch of evidence to connect me to the crime scene."

"Of course they'd find evidence at the crime scene." Julia quivered with indignation. "It's your home! But that's how law enforcement works, by trying to force you into making mistakes."

Sipping her wine, Linden said, "On a positive note, I haven't heard from The Voice since yesterday, so I must be doing something right. All thanks to you."

"Anytime," Julia smiled.

Linden's eyes filled with tears. "Although it may seem very soon, Uncle George's funeral is tomorrow. He knew he wasn't going to recover so he and Aunt Heni planned it together. I think it brought them a measure of comfort."

"It still doesn't make it any easier," Julia sympathized.

"Nothing does, but I still want to be there."

Julia stared at Linden in disbelief. "Are you out of your mind? The church will be crawling with police and FBI agents. They always attend funerals."

"I don't care," Linden retorted. "I still want to go."

"You can't," Julia shot back. "You may have fooled me for a few minutes, but law enforcement uses face recognition technology nowadays. They'll pick you up almost immediately."

Linden was as stubborn as her friend.

"It's worth the risk. The worst they can do is take me in for questioning."

An uneasy silence fell over the two women, broken eventually by Julia.

"Okay. Since it's so important, I'll help you. Where's the funeral?"

"Long Island. Radford." Linden twirled her wine glass in embarrassment. "I have another favor to ask. You never think about money when you can hit up an ATM machine at any time, but it's very easy to blow through cash. My wig cost $40, and I had to buy a dress for tomorrow. It's from Kmart."

"As I keep telling you, money's no problem."

"Thanks, but it still won't get me a rental car. My driver's license and credit cards are in my purse—wherever that is."

"I use car service all the time. I'll arrange for a driver to take you." Julia gave Linden a stern look. "But only to the cemetery. You won't be as conspicuous there, and just going to one place might lessen your chance of getting caught."

"Thank you." Linden clasped Julia's hand. "Any way you can come, too? I'll stand out like a sore thumb by myself."

Julia shook her head. "Tomorrow's a full day . . ." She

was silent for a few moments, as if considering several options, then said, "I have a friend who may be free. Don's an IT consultant and used to rearranging his schedule on a moment's notice."

"I hope he won't ask too many questions about why I'm going."

"All he needs to know is that you're a friend of George's daughter." Julia took out her phone. "Let me give him a call."

* * *

Light rain was falling when Linden walked out of the Sheraton Hotel the next morning. As she hurried across the slick sidewalk to her waiting limousine, she could see that Don was already seated in the back. Sliding into the seat next to him, she felt him studying her curiously.

"You're very kind to attend the funeral of someone you don't know," he said.

"It's the least I can do for my friend," Linden replied. "I hope you don't mind, but I'm really not up to talking."

He shrugged. "Julia asked me to respect your privacy. Don't worry, no more conversation."

Despite the increasingly heavy rain, the limo driver pulled up in front of Radford Cemetery shortly before noon. Holding an umbrella over Linden and Don as they left the car, the driver assured them that he'd stay right by the gates. Inside the cemetery, a somber-looking man in a dark suit directed them to the Lambert burial site.

Huddled under Don's umbrella, they walked through the manicured grounds to George Lambert's open grave, the earth looking as raw as a fresh wound. They were among the first to arrive, and Linden headed for a nearby elm tree whose leaves sagged under the weight of saturated leaves. While waiting for the committal service to start, Linden prayed no one would see through her disguise.

Within minutes several cars turned up, and Linden watched her relatives gather around the casket. Helena was accompanied by Tom Blair, her ramrod-straight back a sign of iron control. Roger stood on her other side, his face as impassive as his mother's except for a slight twitch in his jaw. In contrast, Elizabeth patted away her tears with a lace handkerchief before they could ruin her makeup. Melanie's lack of emotion surprised Linden, and she attributed her cousin's blank expression to Xanax. Gerry's arm encircled his wife's waist, but more at home on a tennis court, he looked out of place even in his custom-made suit.

Linden was too far away to hear the minister speak, and her gaze drifted over the people who had come to mourn her uncle. She recognized many of them, but the strangers concerned her. They, she suspected, were the police and FBI agents that Julia had warned would be present.

Suddenly she found herself staring into a pair of gun metal gray eyes. They held her amber ones with unsettling intensity, as if the other person was running through a mental catalogue of faces. Breaking eye contact, she looked back at her family before glancing sideways at the man. Tall, lean, and with neatly-cut dark hair, he continued to study her, and she hoped that her wig and reading glasses were sufficient camouflage.

Most people had bowed their heads, and anxious to escape the man's scrutiny, Linden bowed hers. When everyone raised theirs a few moments later, Linden followed their example in time to see Helena throw a white rose into the grave. A sob escaped her as she realized her uncle was irrevocably gone.

"Do you want to leave?" whispered Don.

Uncaring of the tears streaming down her face, Linden nodded. "Staying here won't bring him back."

With an arm around her shoulders, Don guided her toward the exit.

"I thought you were just a friend of his daughter."

"I am, but I knew him, too. He was a good man." Her voice broke. "A very good man."

As promised, the driver was waiting at the exit. Once settled in her seat, Linden leaned her head back.

"I hate funerals," she said vehemently.

"I don't think anyone finds them fun," Don responded. "I hope you think this was worth it."

Linden nodded. "Every second."

She said little on the tedious journey back to Manhattan, which was made even longer by the periodic cloudbursts that cascaded over the car with the force of a giant waterfall. At the Sheraton Hotel, Linden thanked Don for his support and darted inside. Surrounded by groups of tourists huddled over maps, she felt almost invisible as she fought her way to the elevator bank.

Up in room 1012, Linden ripped off her wig, put on a tee-shirt and blue jeans, and slipped on the sneakers purchased from KMart the previous day. Taking out her phone, she called the person she trusted the most. The number was one of the few burned into her memory.

"Lambert residence. This is Brunnings. May I help you?"

Even when answering a call from an unknown number, the butler was always polite.

"Try not to act surprised and don't say my name. It's me."

After a moment's shocked silence, Brunnings breathed, "Thank God you're safe. You *are* safe?"

"I'm okay. Just keeping a low profile."

"Where are you? I'll come and get you."

"You're better off not knowing. Any help you give me will make you an accessory to whatever crime I'm accused of. I just want to know how . . . Mrs. Lambert is."

41

"Holding up. Many people came back to the house for lunch. Her son and daughter are a great comfort but it would give her peace of mind to hear from her niece." He paused. "Or have someone pass along a message."

Linden's eyes filled with tears. "Soon. I promise. But until then not a word."

"You know I'll do anything to help you."

Brunnings again paused before speaking.

"We were all asked to give statements about Monday night. I said that Ms. Travers left around eleven o'clock and I watched her drive away, alone. My memory isn't what it was, however, and other people might recall the night differently."

"That's good to know," she said. "I'll be in touch again."

Disconnecting the call, Linden thought about Brunnings' coded words. If her memory of Monday night's visit to Radford ever returned, would it match the butler's statement? And what had happened to her car?

A trawl through her memory bank eventually came up with the number of the garage where she had a permanent parking space. Calling it, she tapped her foot impatiently until one of the attendants answered.

"Hi, Carlos. This is Linden Travers. Can you have my car ready for me in half an hour?"

"Miss Travers!" Carlos sounded shocked. "Your car isn't here. The police came around yesterday asking to see it."

"What did you tell them?"

"That you drove off on Monday at five o'clock and your car's still out. Everything's recorded in the daily log so I couldn't say anything else."

"It's okay. I know you didn't have a choice."

"I was sorry to hear about your loss. Whatever they're saying about you, I don't believe it."

"Thanks, Carlos. That means a lot to me."

As she hung up, Linden's eyes misted over. At least one other person was on her side—or was he just protecting his Christmas bonus?

Mind racing, she looked down at the patchwork of umbrellas bobbing along the rain-soaked sidewalk like a parade of multicolored mushrooms. After leaving Laurel Court, had she headed for the nearest bar to drown her sorrows and been picked up? But she'd never go to a bar alone, especially when driving.

A wave of sadness engulfed her. She needed to get some air. Rain or not, a walk up to Central Park would clear her head and relieve some tension. Pulling on her baseball hat, she debated whether to wear sunglasses, but decided regular glasses were a better choice. With her key card and a ten-dollar bill in her pocket, she strode down the corridor to the elevator.

No one seemed to notice her as she crossed the lobby and walked out on Seventh Avenue where she melted into the crowd. Although intending to go to the park, she let herself be carried along by the throng of people until forced to stop for a red light. It was only then that she looked at the street signs and discovered she was on Madison Avenue and Sixty-first Street. Her subconscious, she realized, was taking her home. Five minutes later she was there.

After the traumas of the last few days she found it hard to believe that her apartment building looked so normal. Equally unchanged was the quiet, tree-lined block, each tree encircled by impatiens that drooped forlornly under the onslaught of rain.

Her eyes drifted up to the building's ninth floor and the vase of wilted peonies in her living room window. Frustration surged through her. If only she could get up there, back to the life that she'd taken for granted. Inside she could retrieve

43

phone numbers and files and try to figure out who hated her enough to set her up.

But she knew her apartment would be under surveillance. And even if she had a key there was no chance of her sneaking in undetected: security in her building was tighter than the Federal Reserve Bank. After all, that's what she and the other residents paid for.

Suddenly lightheaded, she slumped against the nearest building. For the first time all day she was hungry, but she was in no mood to deal with coffee shops and people. The Fifty-sixth Street Atrium on Madison Avenue, she remembered, had a concession stand where she could pick up a snack.

It took her less than ten minutes to walk to the glass-enclosed structure. Inside, she found the soaring space to be almost empty. Most people, she guessed, were only too eager to head home. Taking her coffee and muffin to a table in a deserted corner, she blotted her rain-soaked body with a handful of paper napkins. Even though her sodden hat squeezed her head like a medieval instrument of torture, she kept it on.

Finding a copy of the *Daily News* on a nearby table, she skimmed the front page while cutting her muffin into quarters. The mundane action soothed her; so the screech of a metal chair being dragged over the marble floor was an unwelcome intrusion. Then her table lurched as someone sat down next to her.

"Tell me," a male voice demanded harshly, "how much longer do you expect to stay out of sight?"

# Chapter
# 6

After spending more than a decade searching for people who preferred to remain hidden, Alex had learned to trust his gut. And his gut told him that Linden Travers would be at her uncle's funeral, especially since everyone had emphasized the special bond that existed between her and her uncle. Figuring that parking would be difficult at both the church and the cemetery, he asked his new assistant to drive.

Wednesday morning's rain made a car more of a headache than a help, and Alex was pleased to have left the driving to Joe. It would be the younger man's job to find a convenient place to wait without getting stuck in a parking lot.

During the funeral service, Alex prowled the church's outer aisles, checking faces. Despite having spent hours looking at photos and videos of Linden, no one matched the images stored in his memory bank. But he remained convinced that she was around.

At the cemetery he stood beneath a maple tree and studied the crowd of mourners, the large size proving that few people had skipped out after the church service. His attention was suddenly drawn to a very pretty brunette whose short hair curled around her head. Although just one face among many, she still stood out. Her air of sorrow was almost palpable, making him wonder why she was so upset. As she turned her head toward the minister, all he could see was her profile, but it was enough to send his brain into high alert. The profile was familiar. He'd seen it before—and recently.

Scanning the crowd, he noticed Helena Lambert, and his suspicions were confirmed. The way Linden's aunt held her head, the small straight nose; each feature was an almost duplicate of the brunette's. Looking back at her, he found himself staring into a pair of amber-colored eyes. Even though Linden was blonde and her eyes were described as tawny, this color was sufficiently similar. She turned slightly, giving him another view of her profile. His gaze swung back to Helena. The resemblance was uncanny and, brunette or not, the younger woman needed to be followed.

About to move in her direction, he realized she'd disappeared. He looked around frantically until spotting her near the exit, half hidden by an umbrella. She was accompanied by a tall man whose left arm was wrapped around her shoulders. Pulling out his phone, Alex called Joe who answered on the first ring.

"What's up?" he asked.

"The service just ended," Alex replied, racing after Linden. "Meet me outside the cemetery. Now."

He reached the exit as the Linden look-alike climbed into a black Lincoln Town Car. He had just enough time to memorize the license plate before the car sped away. When a gray Buick squealed to a halt beside him, Alex was in the passenger seat in seconds.

Pointing ahead, he said, "A Town Car left a couple of minutes ago. We need to follow it. And fast."

"Who's inside?" Joe asked, his voice edged with excitement.

"I'd bet the Lambert fee it's Linden Travers. Very well disguised."

"Your gut worked?"

"Yep."

Focused on his phone, Alex was searching for his computer guru's contact information. Once found, he sent her a text with the limo's plate number and requested an answer ASAP.

Joe soon caught up with the other car and within minutes the two vehicles were on the Long Island Expressway, heading west to New York City. When Alex's phone pinged a few seconds later, he shared Syd's response with Joe.

"Julia van Oppen rented the car from Luxury Limos. Told the company she was attending a funeral on Long Island. First pick-up was Don Ferguson at 300 Second Avenue and then over to the Sheraton Hotel on Seventh Avenue to pick up Julia van Oppen. Syd checked with the Sheraton, which confirmed that Julia van Oppen is indeed registered."

"Who the hell's Julia van Oppen?" Joe demanded.

"No idea," Alex snapped, busy texting Syd.

Joe waited until Alex hit the send button. "Any chance you made a mistake about Linden?"

"There's always the chance," Alex admitted. "But her facial profile matched Helena Lambert's. And our woman of mystery looked way too young and far too upset to be just a friend of George Lambert."

Joe indicated the Lincoln, three car lengths ahead.

"Want me to get closer so you can have a better look at her?"

"No. If it is Linden, we can't afford to spook her and have her disappear again."

Several miles passed in silence before Alex's phone chirped again. After scanning the new text, Alex read it to Joe.

"Julia van Oppen is twenty-eight years old and owns a

2,000 square foot loft in SoHo. She was born in Manhattan, educated at Brearley, and has a BA from the Rhode Island School of Design. After graduation, she spent six months in Paris followed by another six months in Milan. She was then hired by Anderson & Wood, which, according to Syd, is the celebs' go-to interior design company."

"Fascinating," Joe observed, "but what's her connection with Linden?"

Alex stared out of the window for a moment then started to text.

"Linden went to the Rhode Island School of Design. Let's see what Syd digs up from that."

An unexpected turn by the limo driver forced Joe into a dangerous lane change which put them on a direct route to Manhattan. Shrouded in rain, the skyline was little more than a pewter-colored blur, but Alex wasn't interested in the sights. Gnawing on a knuckle, he tried to figure out Linden's motives for dropping out of sight and out of touch.

They were almost on the FDR Drive when Alex's phone rang, and this time Syd wanted to talk.

"Connected the dots," she announced jubilantly. "Linden and Julia were at RISD together for four years. Belonged to the same sorority, shared an apartment, then went their separate ways. Next, I called Anderson & Wood, and guess what? Julia was in her office. So unless she's learned how to be in two places at once, that's not Julia van Oppen in the limo."

"Syd, you're a true genius," Alex said. "Another favor. Photoshop Linden's photo to make her a brunette with short curly hair and also check to see if there's a shot of Helena Lambert's profile. We're almost in Manhattan and we're probably going straight to the Sheraton Hotel. Email the photos to Joe and me ASAP."

As Alex predicted, they were at the Sheraton Hotel within

ten minutes, just one of several anonymous sedans that hovered near the entrance. A few car lengths in front, the Town Car glided to a halt and the Linden twin darted out. Hand already on the door, Alex turned to Joe as he stopped their car.

"Go park and meet me in the lobby," he instructed. "If you can't find me, call my phone."

Inside the Sheraton's vast lobby, Alex glimpsed a tangle of brunette curls near the elevator bank. Staking out a spot with a clear view of the doors, he leaned against the wall to wait for the woman's next move. It took him less than a minute to feel as obvious as a Secret Service agent. Although he lacked the earphone and shades, his was the only dark suit among the crowd of casually-dressed tourists.

Slipping off his jacket and tie, he opened the top two buttons of his white shirt and hoped he blended in. Five minutes later Joe was beside him, equally out of place in his suit. While the younger man kept an eye on the elevators, Alex opened Syd's email and studied the photos of Linden.

"These are a help," he said, showing them to Joe, "but there's no guarantee that she'll look like either of them."

Slouched against the wall in an attempt to get comfortable, Joe said, "They're better than nothing. Gives us *something* to work with."

For thirty minutes the elevators disgorged a constant parade of tourists laden with plastic ponchos and backpacks, but there was no sign of the woman. Then Alex stiffened. Another mass of passengers had emerged from the elevator and was drifting toward the lobby like a huge amoeba. Although she was huddled in the center and wore a baseball hat, he had spotted a woman who reminded him of Linden.

Nudging Joe, he said, "The one in the Yankee hat. I think it's Linden."

Joe's eyes went from the photo to the person. "Could be."

"I'm going to follow her. You stay here and keep watch, just in case I'm wrong. Let me know if you see anyone else who resembles her."

Stepping away from the wall, Alex sauntered along with the crowd, his eyes never leaving Linden. Outside, she seemed oblivious to the torrential rain, even though her jeans and navy tee-shirt were soon soaked through. He bought an umbrella from a street vendor, not only to keep him dry but also to conceal his face, and trailed her at a discreet distance as she headed uptown.

At Sixty-seventh Street she came to an abrupt halt. Ducking under the nearest canopy, he pretended to check his umbrella while watching her. Rock still, she stared at her apartment building as if it led to the gates of paradise. Instead of going inside as he expected, she surprised him by wheeling around and heading in his direction. He let her walk by, then followed at a safe distance until she entered the Fifty-sixth Street Atrium. Peering through the rain-splattered window, he watched her purchase a snack from the concession stand, which she carried over to an empty table. She was, he noticed, sitting as far from other people as possible.

And that suited him just fine. Strolling inside, he bought a cup of coffee and called Joe, who said he hadn't seen anyone resembling Linden. Proof positive, Alex decided, that the woman was Linden. Walking up to her table, he dragged over a chair and sat down.

"Tell me," he demanded harshly, "how much longer do you expect to stay out of sight?"

# Chapter

## 7

Although the words sent shock waves coursing through Linden, she willed herself to stay calm. Looking at the speaker, she hoped to see a stranger—but instead she recognized him. It was the man she'd noticed at the cemetery, the one who'd seemed to take more than a passing interest in her.

Gripping her knife more tightly, she said, "Go away or I'll call security."

"And risk having them find out who you are?"

"I don't know what you're talking about."

"Then why not call them over?"

"Why don't you get lost?" she answered, sounding far more controlled than she felt.

"Because we need to talk. You're Linden Travers."

"Prove it," she snapped.

Reaching into his pocket, Alex withdrew the photo used by all the news outlets. Linden's face paled, emphasizing the dark circles under her eyes.

"And you are . . . ?

"Alex Blair. I'm a private investigator." He pulled out his

wallet to show a laminated license. "Your aunt hired me to find you."

"And now you have, what are you going to do?"

"Find out what you did with it."

"It?"

"Yes. It," Alex repeated. "The Judas Hoard. Your uncle's pride and joy. Take your pick."

An incredulous expression crossed Linden's face. "Are you saying the *Judas Hoard* was stolen?"

"As if you didn't know," he scoffed.

Recovering, she retorted, "Obviously, I didn't. And I hate to burst your bubble, but I don't have it."

"Then why run away? Drop out of sight?"

"That's not what happened," she said.

Alex raised a skeptical eyebrow. "What part did I get wrong?"

"If I'd dropped out of sight, you wouldn't have tracked me down so fast."

"It wasn't that hard. I was sure you'd be at your uncle's funeral. You might have fooled everyone else, but I recognized you and followed you. By the time you'd reached the Sheraton Hotel I'd made two discoveries. Someone called Julia van Oppen rented the limo you were in, and she was registered as a guest at the hotel. Know what was really interesting?"

"I can't wait for you to tell me."

"At that precise moment Julia van Oppen was in her office at Anderson & Wood on Fifth Avenue, taking phone calls."

"That's all it took to convince you that you'd found your man—or in this case, your woman?"

"It was worth a try, so I hung around the Sheraton's lobby, figuring you'd go out at some point. Sure enough, you came down within the hour and I followed you again."

Alex glanced around the glass atrium.

"Thanks for picking such a great spot for me to introduce myself. This isn't some place you want to make a scene. So, again, why haven't you contacted your family? The police?"

"I don't know."

"You don't *know*?" Anger edged Alex's voice.

"Believe it or not, I woke up Tuesday morning in a strange house with no memory of the previous night."

"Oh, come on! You expect me to buy *that*?"

Linden shrugged. "Suit yourself. It's the truth."

"Unfortunately, your version of the truth bears no resemblance to the facts."

"And those facts are enough to have me hounded like a criminal?"

"Why not? They're enough to make some people decide you're a murderer, but most just think you're a thief."

Reaching for her coffee, Linden gulped down a mouthful. "And you agree with them. I can hear it in your voice. You're convinced of my guilt."

The words were out before she could stop them, and watching Alex's face tighten, she knew she'd made a mistake. She needed him on her side, which meant that sharing information with him would benefit her—for the moment.

Taking a deep breath, she said, "Sorry I lost it just then. As you can imagine, this has been an extremely traumatic experience. Since you seem to have some answers, I'd be very grateful if you'd start at the beginning and explain how, as far as you know, I happen to be in this position."

Her apology seemed to appease Alex. "You were the last person to leave the Lambert house on Monday night. Your uncle died a few hours later and by mid-morning your fingerprints were found plastered all over the safe in his study."

"Of course you'd find them there," Linden exploded, good intentions forgotten. "I've opened that safe a million times."

"What was found isn't important. It's what was missing."

"If you mean the Judas Hoard, I don't believe you. It was locked in the safe and that safe was burglarproof."

"Not for someone who knows the codes and has access to the house."

Linden tried to stay calm. "I hope you don't consider me to be that someone. It was my job to protect the Judas Hoard, not steal it."

Leaning forward, Alex's expression reflected his cynicism. "To a lot of people, the Judas Hoard is just a bunch of old coins, but *you* know they're worth a fortune. I'm also willing to bet that you're aware there's a South American collector who's willing to pay nine million dollars for them."

"They're not for sale." Linden's tone left no room for argument. "Of the original thirty pieces of silver paid to Judas Iscariot for betraying Jesus Christ, these six are all that remain."

"So I've been told," Alex said. "But even if the story were true, it's hard to believe any of these coins exist."

"The story's true all right. The bible's backed up by plenty of documented evidence from contemporary records."

"Still doesn't prove these are the real McCoy."

Linden spoke with exaggerated patience. "Nowadays, we live in a very high tech world with such innovations as carbon dating."

"All that shows is the age. These could just be six random coins . . ."

"They're not random," Linden interrupted. "And they've always been stored in a linen bag with a distinctive weave. Not only do analyses date it back to the time of Christ, but to the Jerusalem area as well. In addition, the coins all share such characteristics as similar dirt, friction marks and patina, evidence they've been together in one place for a very long time. Around two thousand years in fact."

"That *is* a long time," Alex conceded.

Still annoyed, Linden said, "I still don't understand why I'm your prime suspect. My uncle and I agreed the coins would never be sold. They're to be on permanent exhibit at a museum with me as curator."

"Not anymore." He shot her a speculative look. "Unless you know more than you're admitting. So I'll ask one last time. Where are they?"

"Beats me," she answered.

"Bull. *You* stole them and *I* intend to find what you've done with them."

Linden barely managed to control her fury. "Are you always this pigheaded? How many different ways can I say this? I don't *have* them."

"Then I'll repeat the basic facts." His anger matched hers. "*Again.* Your uncle died early Tuesday morning, by which time both you and the coins had vanished. I've been honest with you and now it's your turn. Just what happened Monday night?"

Linden ate a piece of muffin, even though it tasted like dust, while deciding how much to reveal. As she took a sip of her coffee, Alex's gray eyes darkened to charcoal.

"Sorry to disappoint you, but there's not a lot to tell," she finally said. "Although this probably reinforces your negative opinion of me, I have no memory of Monday night. And I mean nothing. Zip, zilch, nada. Every time I try to remember, all I come up with is blackness."

Alex stared at Linden in disbelief. "You remember *nothing?*"

"Not after three o'clock Monday afternoon."

"Shit," Alex observed.

"It doesn't help me much either," Linden pointed out. "Someone set me up, and I've spent most of the last two days trying to figure out who and why."

"Not too successfully, from what I've seen," Alex said. "Let's go back to what you do know. You said you woke up in a strange house. How did you find out where you were?"

"I watched the Weather Channel and learned I was on Long Island."

As she described making her way back to New York City, Linden felt like the events belonged to a previous lifetime. By giving only minimal details, her explanation took less than ten minutes, but Alex's lack of questions told her that it was enough to get him off her back.

After reviewing the notes he'd scrawled on his napkin, Alex commented, "Very resourceful. What's your next step?"

"Contact my family. I want to give them my side of the story before they hear your warped version."

"Here's a news flash—they're not too thrilled with you at the moment."

"I'll deal with it." Linden stood up. "Well, thanks for the help. Now I've been found, I guess I can go home."

"Not so fast." Grabbing her wrist, Alex jerked her back into her chair. "Know what you're going to say to the police? They'll be all over you like an army of fire ants the minute you open your door. Your apartment's under twenty-four-hour surveillance."

Eyes glinting angrily, Linden fumed, "I haven't done anything."

"You need to convince them of that. You're a person of interest."

"Just what sort of evidence do the police have to make me a person of interest?"

"The Judas Hoard disappears. You drop off the face of the earth. Don't you think they'd be interested in you?"

"And that's the reason I've been made into the star of a breaking news story?" Linden demanded.

"It worked. You wouldn't believe the tips that came in. You've been spotted everywhere—except New York."

"So what do I do?"

"Get yourself a lawyer and go talk to the police."

"I guess I'll call Tom Blair." She speared him with a hard look. "Alex Blair. Any relation?"

"My uncle. Saved your aunt from having to check too many references."

"He's still my best choice at the moment. I'll call him from my hotel. I guess another night there won't kill me."

"Don't plan on going too far. I'll be watching you."

# Chapter 8

Linden checked out of the Sheraton Hotel on Friday morning with a profound sense of relief. Even though the hotel had been a haven of security, there was no place like home. And that's where she planned to be by lunchtime.

Most of the previous evening had been spent on a three-way phone call with Tom Blair and Peter Sinclair. After hearing her account of the last three days, the lawyers arranged for her to meet with the Radford police the next morning. Since she couldn't rent a car without a driver's license or credit card, Alex was the designated driver. Tom Blair had also asked Alex to keep tabs on Linden by staking out the Sheraton's lobby overnight.

Thursday's rain was no more than a memory when Linden walked outside into brilliant sunshine, the sidewalk sparkling as if sprinkled with fairy dust. Her spirits soared until she spotted Alex standing beside his rented Ford Taurus. His presence made her feel like a prisoner being taken to jail.

"For someone who spent the night spying on me, you look very bright eyed and bushy tailed," she told him as she fastened her seat belt.

"I had some help," he said, starting the car.

"More than a one-person office?"

"Other resources are available when necessary," he replied, easing into Seventh Avenue traffic. "Do anything of interest after last night's marathon phone session?"

"Ordered dinner from room service and called my friend Julia to bring her up to date."

"Ah, yes. Julia van Oppen. Good choice. Completely off the map. Who is she?"

"A friend from college. We hadn't spoken since graduation."

"You were lucky she was willing to help." Alex sounded surprised.

"You have a strange definition of luck," Linden retorted. "I'm accused of a crime I didn't commit. My family won't talk to me. Yeah, I'm real lucky."

As scheduled, Tom and Peter were waiting in front of the Radford Police Station. No reporters were in sight, convincing Linden that she was yesterday's news. The interview with the police turned out to be little more than a formality. Guided by the lawyers, she stuck to her basic story, and filed a report about her missing purse. The lead detective, Frank Gorton, then let her leave along with the warning that she might be called in for further questioning.

Feeling slightly more relaxed, she walked outside into an explosion of cameras. Instinctively, she ducked her head as microphones were thrust at her.

Looking around, Tom said, "Alex is across the street. Ignore them."

"No comment," Peter growled, barreling through the mob.

Fighting their way to Alex's car, Tom and Linden dived in the rear while Peter flung himself into the front seat. Reporters circled the car like sharks in a feeding frenzy, but Alex inched forward, forcing them to scatter. Once clear of the crowd, he stepped on the gas.

"No one seems to be following us," he said. "Tom, Peter, be ready to get out. I'm taking Linden back to New York."

When Alex stopped the car a few blocks later, the two lawyers were out of their seats in seconds. Linden immediately moved to the front, and Alex hit the gas before she had a chance to fasten her seat belt.

"Thank you," Linden forced herself to say.

"You're welcome," he scowled. "I'm assuming only the four of us knew about today. Or did you tell someone?"

"Julia," Linden admitted. "But she didn't notify the media. What did she have to gain? What did anyone have to gain?"

"You'd be surprised," Alex replied. "But it was probably some low level worker at the police station. Even though reporters aren't supposed to pay for tips, you better believe it happens."

"I hope they're not at my apartment."

"We'll find out soon enough."

The rest of the journey passed in silence. Alex seemed to be lost in thought while Linden seethed over the latest invasion of her privacy, which she blamed entirely on him. Until his unwelcome entry into her life, she'd had no problem staying under the radar.

When they reached Manhattan, the scene outside Linden's apartment building surpassed her worst fears. TV trucks lined the street while a throng of reporters milled around on the sidewalk. Without a word, Alex headed for the nearest garage. Delving into her tote bag for her wig, baseball hat and sunglasses, Linden quickly had her disguise in place. Leaving the garage attendant to park the car, they walked the few blocks to her building.

None of the reporters blocking the entrance recognized her, and the long-time doorman looked at her long and hard before he figured out her identity. After dispatching one of the maintenance workers for her keys, he gave a nod of approval.

"Welcome home, Ms. Travers," he smiled. "We'll keep these guys away from you."

Minutes later, she was outside her ninth-floor apartment. Muscling her out of the way, Alex unlocked the door and peered inside. Silence was his only welcome, and ordering her to stay in the corridor, he investigated each room. Satisfied the apartment held no uninvited guests, he beckoned Linden inside.

"This is not good," he warned. "Be prepared for a shock."

The sight of the trashed living room turned Linden's elation into shock.

"Oh. My. God."

Cushions from the sofa and love seat were strewn across the floor like giant stepping stones, the beige leather almost hidden beneath CDs and photographs. Although the wall unit remained intact, books lay in untidy heaps on the shelves or flung carelessly on the floor. Racing from room to room, Linden found the same scene throughout the rest of the apartment. Every closet, cabinet and drawer had been emptied, items tossed onto the nearest flat surface.

The guest bedroom, which also served as her office, was the worst. The contents of her desk had been dumped onto the open sofa bed and floor. Her home, the familiar space she always considered to be her sanctuary, looked as if hit by a cyclone.

Rushing inside, she rummaged through the wreckage and retrieved a green folder.

"My passport," she announced with relief, scanning its contents. "And here's the list of all my credit card numbers along with a copy of my driver's license. At least I can prove who I am and start getting my life back together."

As Linden's gaze traveled from the folder to the epic-sized mess, her euphoria faded. Intuition told her it was the result of a frenzied search. For a moment tears were perilously close until a surge of anger cut through her self-pity. Throwing the folder back on the pile, she stormed from the room.

"Let's see what's missing."

Although Alex said nothing, she sensed his sympathy as he helped her clean up. They started in the living room, moved onto the bedroom, and ended in her office. After stowing the last few files, she finally turned her attention to the phone, which was on the floor under her desk. The answering machine had recorded twenty messages, with the first seven from Roger and Tom, both men equally agitated. Assorted friends accounted for the next ten. Assuring her they didn't believe a word of the charges, all offered their unconditional support and begged her to call.

The eighteenth message made her blood run cold.

"You little bitch," the digitally-altered voice hissed. "I suppose you think you're very clever to have escaped from the house. But you can't escape *me*. You may feel safe now, but you better be looking over your shoulder all the time. I'm going to get you, and when I do, you'll pay for what you've done."

After a brief delay, the message recorder intoned, "Thursday. Ten fifteen a.m."

The final two calls were from friends who had seen Internet coverage of the near-riot outside the police station. They had both left previous messages and just wanted to express their relief that she was safe.

Alex waited barely five seconds before giving full vent to his rage.

"What the hell's going on? Don't you realize the only reason you're not in jail right now is because you have two very smart, very respected lawyers? Think lying to them—to me—is the best way to clear your name?"

"I didn't lie," Linden flared. "I just left out a couple of details."

"*Details!*" Alex bellowed. "Some nut leaves a threatening message on your answering machine and you dismiss it as a *detail*! What part am I not getting here?"

"I . . . underestimated The Voice."

"Who the hell's The Voice?"

"Actually, he—I think it's a he—called the house in Ashton and told me to switch on the TV, which is how I learned I was breaking news. I also discovered every door and window was locked. Naturally, the key was nowhere to be found and I was, in effect, a prisoner."

"A prisoner," Alex spluttered. "This just keeps getting better and better. Any more *details* you want to share?"

Anger radiated from him as Linden described her escape, but he remained silent until she reached her reunion with Julia. Pulling out his phone, he scrolled through the address book.

"I'm going to have someone check out that house. Give me the address again."

"Twelve Mulberry Lane. The name on the mail box was Lawton. But as I said, that house backed onto the one I was in."

"Anything to identify your prison?" Alex asked.

"I never saw it from the front . . . or at least I don't remember," Linden corrected herself.

Closing her eyes, she tried to recall the view.

"When I looked out of the attic window, the house across the street had baskets of brightly-colored flowers hanging on the porch. I think they were fuchsias."

"Maybe it will help," Alex said, hitting Syd's phone number. "Hi. Turns out Linden wasn't entirely truthful. She was locked inside the house and has an almost address to it."

"Great. Another challenge. Just what I need," Syd laughed.

After updating her, Alex hung up and looked at Linden.

"Let's get out of here," he said. "We haven't had any lunch and I'm hungry."

From the look on Alex's face, Linden knew that it would be pointless to argue. Putting on the hated disguise, she grabbed her key and followed him from the apartment. As the elevator whisked them down to the first floor, Alex steamed like an overheated engine but his anger had little effect on her. Although she appeared indifferent, she was well aware of his lean body and the muscles outlined beneath the sleeves of his white shirt.

None of the reporters milling around the entrance gave her a second look when they left her building, and she steered Alex to a coffee shop on the next block. Most people had already eaten and they sat at a booth in the almost-empty rear. Before they had a chance to open their menus, a waiter stalked over.

"What's it to be?" he demanded. "There's a ten-dollar minimum in a booth."

"A plain hamburger, rare, and a diet Coke," Alex ordered.

"Chef's salad," Linden said. "And iced tea."

As the waiter flounced off, Alex drilled Linden with a ferocious glare. "I swear to God; I could very happily tear you apart limb by limb. Why did you lie?"

"How was I to know if you were really a private investigator?" she countered. "Anyone can get a badge these days. When a total stranger walks up to you in a public place, you don't take anything on faith."

Alex smiled, a killer smile that took Linden completely by surprise. "Okay. I guess I could have handled it better."

"After today's scene at the police station, it was clear you're one of the good guys."

"Thank you."

Alex fell silent as the waiter banged down their drinks. Taking a long swallow of Coke, he waited until the other man was out of earshot. "And at some point you'd have told me about The Voice, right?"

"Yes," she snapped.

"Glad to hear it." Alex sounded anything but pleased. "But we've lost three days where we might have discovered something."

"I'm sorry." Linden's tone matched his. "Maybe you forgot that I'm accused of robbing my dying uncle. Can you blame me for not being too quick to cooperate?" After a brief pause, she added, "I also think my home was ransacked on purpose."

Alex steepled his fingers. "I agree. Whoever did that was searching for something specific."

"Yet nothing seems to have been stolen," Linden pointed out.

"Did you notice that The Voice's last call came in less than ten minutes after you left the police station?"

Expression speculative, Linden said, "Meaning his source may not be the Internet or TV."

"Correct. Which begs the question, is there a snitch at the police station, or is it someone we know?"

"You think Julia's that someone," Linden bristled. "I keep telling you. Up until Tuesday, we hadn't spoken in more than six years. And what does she have to gain?"

"People can change a lot in six years," Alex stated.

Instead of defending her friend, Linden remained silent. The waiter was approaching with their food, which he plunked down on the table. He deliberately avoided making eye contact with them before hurrying back to the cash register.

Grabbing the ketchup, Alex doused his French fries with a thick layer. "You need to see the police again. Amend your statement."

"I'm sure Tom can fix it for me."

"And you've been totally honest with me? You still have no memory of Monday night?"

"None. But Tuesday, after I took a shower, my arm ached. Know the feeling after a flu shot?"

Alex chewed a mouthful of hamburger. "Now that might mean something. You have no recollection of leaving your home; you wake up the next morning, a prisoner in an unknown house; and you have no idea how you got there."

"Plus the mother of all hangovers," Linden reminded him.

Alex pointed a red-tipped French fry at her. "Sounds like roofies."

Linden furrowed her forehead. "The date rape drug?"

"Right." He paused. "Were you . . . ?"

Shaking her head, she said, "Seems like that was the only thing that didn't happen. After my shower, I took a blood sample using the freebie sewing kit in my hotel room. It's in my purse, if you want it."

A faint smile escaped him. "Very inventive, but it probably won't prove anything. However, traces of the drug have remained in hair for up to a month. Can you spare a couple of strands?"

"As many as you need." For the first time, Linden felt a glimmer of hope that Alex was taking her seriously. "You're very up on this."

"Got to be up on everything in my line of work."

"And what is your line of work?"

"Finding people who don't want to be found, including but not limited to runaway adolescents, kids taken by noncustodial parents, and scumbags with monetary judgments against them who then disappear without paying one cent."

Linden eyed him shrewdly. "Sounds like finding people in the last group is your particular favorite."

Alex's face tightened. "Those people are the worst. They scheme to earn trust and then exploit it for personal gain. It could also explain the Judas Hoard's disappearance."

"I hope you don't have me in that category!" Linden exploded. "I would never hurt my family."

Alex shrugged. "It's been done . . . and often."

His phone rang, and seeing the caller's name, he said, "Hi, Syd. What do you have?"

Linden couldn't hear anything, but the length of Alex's silence told her that Syd had a lot to report. Still fuming, she stabbed at her salad, taking out her anger a slice of tomato. With a quick word of thanks, Alex finally hung up and looked at Linden.

"Syd found your house. I'm going to call Detective Gorton. He needs to check it out."

A combination of relief and apprehension surged through Linden.

"I want to see it. That was my prison—no matter how briefly. It's my right to be there."

"Figured you'd say that," said Alex, signaling for the waiter. "Let's go."

# Chapter
## 9

Guided by Alex's GPS, they drove to Ashton where they were directed to a residential area of half-acre lots and manicured lawns. After a final turn into Hickory Street, Alex stopped in front of number eleven. Unlike the neighboring houses, four cars were parked in the driveway, two emblazoned with the Nassau County Police logo.

As Linden's eyes trailed over the colonial-style house, she experienced only disappointment. Nothing was familiar until she stepped out of the car and glanced at the house opposite. She remembered seeing the hanging baskets along the verandah.

The door to number eleven opened and a man in his early forties emerged, his tanned face an almost-match to the color of his wrinkled lightweight suit. Striding down the driveway, the lead detective on the Lambert Case indicated Linden and Alex should stay by their car.

"Hello, Detective Gorton." A hint of guilt tinged Linden's greeting.

"Ms. Travers," he acknowledged. "Didn't expect to see you again so soon. The ink's barely dry on your statement."

"Things were still a bit fuzzy this morning so some stuff slipped my mind."

"Won't be the first time," he said, his rueful smile disappearing when he spoke to Alex. "Thanks for the tip about the house, Mr. Blair."

"Always glad to work with local law enforcement," Alex replied.

"Happy to hear that." Gorton's tone proved he wasn't. "The Lambert name carries a lot of weight in this state and the governor's become personally involved. He suggested that we keep you in the loop."

Expression sardonic, Alex said, "Appreciate it."

Arms folded, Gorton leaned against one of the squad cars. "So now another player's entered the picture."

Linden nodded. "The Voice, but I've no idea who he is. What have you learned?"

"The house's owner isn't our guy. He's in Paris for a year."

"Can he prove it?" Linden asked.

"Absolutely. He works for a major accounting firm and the HR department confirmed everything."

Alex gazed at the house. "He rented out his home?"

"Yep. It took a while, so he was happy to get someone for six months," Gorton said. "Lease runs from April through September. The renter is one Angelo Morella, and everything's quite normal except for one thing. He paid the entire cost in advance, in cash."

"That had to be quite a hunk of change," Linden observed.

"Morella's a consultant and sometimes gets assignments on a moment's notice. He wanted to pay the full amount up front so the owner wouldn't worry about being stuck with a broken lease."

Linden's eyes hardened. "How thoughtful."

"My guys are digging deeper. Turns out Mr. Morella's a

real man of mystery. None of the neighbors have ever seen him or even noticed any activity here. A yard man and housekeeper come in once a month, but they're both holdovers from the original owner."

"What about Monday night?" Linden demanded. "Someone must have seen something."

"Not according to the neighbors."

"But I didn't just materialize through the wall. I was brought here by someone, dumped in the den, then locked inside."

"So you say, but when we entered we found nothing to show anybody had been inside . . . apart from this."

Digging into his jacket pocket, Gorton withdrew a small suede pouch. From the way the blood drained from Linden's face, it was obvious she recognized it.

Reaching for the pouch, she took comfort in the familiar softness. She and her uncle had opened it many times and marveled at its contents.

"This is the outer case for the Judas Hoard. Where did you find it?"

"In the den. Tucked down in the back of the sofa."

"Were there any really, really old coins?"

"Just $1.73 in pennies, dimes and quarters," Gorton replied, taking back the bag. "We need this for evidence. Any idea when you last saw it?"

"Yes. About three weeks ago." Linden's eyes took on a faraway look as she remembered. "On May 23."

\* \* \*

Spring had been in full bloom that morning. Fluffy white clouds sailed across the blue sky like stately galleons and the trees were heavy with blossoms. Seated by the window in her uncle's sickroom, Linden's gaze lingered on a grove of crab apple trees that looked to be topped with pink frosting.

"It's perfect walking weather," she remarked.

"Go out if you want," said her uncle. "Don't stay in on my account."

"This won't be the last nice spring day. There'll be plenty of others. I'll wait for when we can go out together."

George looked at her sadly. "I'm afraid we won't be sharing any more walks, my dear. There are still plenty of other things I'd like to do, too, but I shouldn't complain. I've had a good life, and you've brought me a lot of pleasure. You were always so much more giving than Melanie."

"It was the only way to show how much I appreciated all you did for me," Linden smiled. "Melanie simply took everything for granted. Why shouldn't she?"

"Melanie didn't have to accept reality the way you did. I'm not sure she'll ever make a mature decision. You'd think being married to Tony Wentworth would have taught her a lesson."

Linden's eyes danced. "Poor Mel. It never occurred to her that she'd be replaced by Trophy Wife Number Five."

"Didn't mean she should rush straight into the arms of Gerry Hammond," George grumbled. "He was obviously a fortune hunter, yet what could I do?"

"Nothing. She's over eighteen and considered to be responsible."

George gave a wry smile. "Too bad there isn't a test to prove it. New York's full of suitable young men, why couldn't she wait to meet one of them? Look at you; you're in no hurry to get married."

"I have my work. Melanie doesn't." Linden had always defended her cousin. "Be happy, Uncle George. Compared to what's out there, Gerry's a treasure. And my life's just fine the way it is, plus I have you and Aunt Heni."

"You won't have me much longer; I wish you'd accept that. So little time and so many loose ends," he fretted. "Like Tom Blair's decision to retire and turn my affairs over to Peter Sinclair. Helena's very impressed with him, but I still have reservations."

"Why?"

"Probably for the same reason you only dated him a few times," her uncle observed. "He likes you a lot."

"I know, but something about him bothers me. I get the sense that underneath Peter's charming and handsome exterior he's totally ruthless." Linden laughed. "I've nothing to prove it, but I swear his veins are filled with ice water."

"To be honest, I agree with you," George chuckled.

Crossing the room, Linden sat on the bed.

"Peter isn't my type. I'm waiting for another you to turn up. You make me feel special, important. No one else has come anywhere close."

Her uncle reached for her hand. "So long as you've been happy."

"Very," she smiled, returning the pressure of his fingers.

"I wanted to marry your mother, you know, but she passed me over for your father," he reminisced, eyes tender. "Melanie's just like her in that respect, follows her heart not her head. You take after Helena, more concerned about others."

"Sometimes I wish I could be more carefree like Melanie."

"Frivolous is a better description," George grumbled. "You're fine just the way you are."

He stared out of the window for a moment, then gave a sigh.

"I'm sorry I can't leave you the Judas Hoard," he said. "You're the only one who really appreciates it. Letting you handle its sale is the best solution, even though the commission will be far less than you deserve."

"We've been through this time and again," Linden said. "You and Aunt Heni have been more than generous over the years. I don't want any of your estate."

"Not to mention the fact that Roger and Melanie might contest your share." He sighed. "How could I have produced such selfish children? They'll both have more than enough money, although Melanie can't spend the capital too freely. That's the point of her trust fund."

"While still allowing her to maintain her current life style—which is all she's concerned about," Linden couldn't help adding.

After a moment's silence, her uncle's next words took Linden by surprise. "I made a mistake having the Judas Hoard brought here."

"Want me to take it back to the bank?"

"No. I'm glad it's a home with me. With all our security, no one can steal it."

"And it couldn't be sold, anyway," Linden pointed out. "No reputable dealer would touch it."

George's eyes sparkled with traces of his old humor. "The Judas Hoard doesn't need a dealer, reputable or otherwise. It sells itself. I'm going to give it a new home. Would you get it? Just bring the coins," he ended, unclasping the gold chain around his neck.

Along with the combination number, the tiny key that dangled from the chain was also needed to open the safe. As he handed it to her, Linden's first reaction was to argue until she sensed how important it was to him. Reluctantly she took the key and headed for his study.

Like the rest of the house, the room was deserted, but the French window was ajar and Linden could hear her aunt and the gardener discussing the best way to prune roses. Unlocking the safe, she opened the box that held the Judas Hoard and removed the suede pouch. Five minutes later she was back in George's bedroom.

"Only Aunt Heni and Martin were around, but they didn't see me," she told him, as he slipped the key back onto the chain. "As usual they were criticizing each other's gardening techniques."

"I'm glad no one saw you," George said, opening the suede pouch. "I want this to be our secret."

Perched on the edge of his bed, Linden watched him take out the ancient linen bag, the fabric as fragile as gossamer. Carefully, he eased the coins into his palm, and for a moment they both stared at the six small circles of silver. Their luster had long since faded, and several were so smooth that Hercules' head was barely visible, but as a piece of history the Judas Hoard was unsurpassed.

"If they were able to speak, what stories they could tell," George said. "The family, too, but no one's left. Communist Russia wasn't kind to the last owners, and by the time they reached Israel the past finally caught up with them."

Linden knew the story by heart. "It's so unfair that they didn't get the chance to enjoy their new lives. But at least they briefly tasted freedom."

"And loved every second. I'll never forget the old couple's joy at finally being in Israel, their misplaced conviction that I was solely responsible. They insisted on giving me a gift and wouldn't take no for an answer, although it was weeks before I had time to open the package."

The years fell away from George's face as he relived the long-ago memory.

"I was overwhelmed when I first saw the Hoard and read their note, but it was far too valuable for me to keep. By the time I tracked them down, it was too late. They'd already died and there were no other relatives."

"They knew you were a special person, that's why they gave you the Judas Hoard." Linden touched the nearest coin. "These coins are true survivors. It's only right that they end up on public display."

"And the safest place." George gripped her hand. "My will stipulates that you're to be the Hoard's sole trustee. There will be no power sharing and only you can name a successor. If the buyer won't allow it, the deal's off."

"You're giving me quite a responsibility," Linden said.

George relaxed a little. "No one is better suited—or more capable, but we need to take extra care until things become settled. I want you to hide the coins and I have the perfect hiding place."

Linden's response was immediate.

"Uncle George, I think that's a really bad plan. They belong in the safe. Let me put them back."

"Maybe you're right," George sighed, gently sliding the coins back into the linen bag.

* * *

The image faded and Linden found herself staring at a dogwood tree, the branches covered with lush green leaves. Looking around, she saw Alex and Gorton watching her, their expressions a mixture of interest and compassion.

"Can you prove you put them back in the safe?" Alex asked.

"You want me to be guilty, don't you?" Linden erupted. "Of course I put them back. And contrary to what people say, there was activity in that house on Monday night. I know because I was inside. The foyer has green striped wallpaper and there's ratty coconut matting up in the attic."

"True," Gorton conceded.

All fired up, Linden continued, "Even though I never saw The Voice and I can't remember anything, my fingerprints and DNA have to be all over the place. I assume you've taken samples. And unless The Voice wrapped himself in plastic, his DNA has to be there, too."

A network of fine lines appeared around Gorton's green eyes, and he seemed more amused than annoyed to have Linden telling him how to do his job.

"We have plenty of samples, but they're not much use if we don't know who The Voice is."

Leaning against his car, Alex remarked, "You needed a warrant to enter the house. What did it say?"

"That Ms. Travers had been kidnapped and imprisoned. She needs to amend her statement so it fits her new story."

"I'll talk to Tom Blair again," Linden said. "I want to look around. Maybe being inside will jog a memory."

"Sure. We've finished collecting evidence, such as it was."

At the front door, a chill crept over Linden. It was her unconscious, she decided, stirring up memories best left buried.

About to follow Alex and Gorton into the den, she couldn't move her feet. It was as if they were glued to the floor. *Nothing*, she swore, would get her to enter that room again. Just to look inside took a supreme effort of will.

Closing her eyes, she tried to remember the missing hours but whatever had happened remained locked away in her brain.

"I'm out of here," she said. "I've had enough."

# Chapter 10

Following the GPS's reverse directions, Alex said nothing until they were back on the Long Island Expressway. With the car on cruise control, he looked over at Linden.

"Okay. Time to sort out what we know."

"Not much," she snapped, still resentful that he remained convinced of her guilt.

"Are you always this negative?" he exploded. "We know for a fact you were locked up in a house. The house was rented by someone who spent at least a month planning this. And someone—you or he—walked off with the Judas Hoard."

"Thanks for giving me the benefit of the doubt," she said sarcastically.

"I'm trying to help here." Alex was barely holding onto his own temper. "If you'd stop playing the martyr, we might get somewhere."

Instead of fighting back, Linden took a moment to think about his comment and decided it was time to test him.

"George's study was just down the hall from his sickroom. Even though he was very ill, he could have walked there if he felt it important enough. It's quite possible he hid the coins himself."

"Where?"

Frustration edged Linden's voice. "Your guess is as good as mine."

"How did he end up with the coins?" Alex asked. "All I know is he had them for years."

"As a young man, he was an adventurer and wanted to see the world before settling down." Linden's face glowed at the chance to talk about her two favorite subjects. "His travels included six months in Israel where he helped process immigrants. One couple was so grateful that they give him the Judas Hoard as a gift. He tried to return it, but by the time he tracked them down, they were dead."

"So he knew it was worth a lot of money," Alex commented.

Linden nodded. "He was always interested in rare coins and immediately realized it was something extraordinary. The previous owners also left him a letter summarizing the Hoard's history. Even that letter was more than a hundred years old."

"I saw it, and agree that the letter and carbon dating prove the coins are genuinely old but there's nothing to support the story behind them."

"Do you know anything about the betrayal of Christ?"

"Only that Judas was paid thirty pieces of silver by the priests and committed suicide shortly after receiving his money."

"Very good," Linden said. "Except it didn't happen quite that fast. Back then, the chief priests ran the temples. They taught people about the laws and rituals, and even made sacrifices. It was the chief priests who arranged for the Romans to arrest Jesus as soon as Judas identified him. Even though Judas was directly responsible for the arrest, he was overcome with remorse and tried to return the money to the priests.

Their refusal to take back the money only added to Judas's guilt so he decided to kill himself. After buying a plot of land for his grave, he left instructions that his body was to be buried there. The Bible refers to it as the Field of Blood."

"And the connection between this story and the Judas Hoard is . . . ?"

"The change," she answered.

"The change?" he repeated in puzzlement.

"According to scholars of the period, such a plot of land would have cost around twenty shekels, the coins probably used to bribe Judas. His death caused quite a stir, and afterwards his family kept a number of his possessions, including all the money lying around—six shekels. Everything was handed down from generation to generation, including a written record someone had made for posterity, but that's long gone. Although rumors flew from the start, the family kept silent which only fueled the speculation. Over the centuries, the coins became known as the Judas Hoard."

"A rumor is still very far removed from reality," Alex observed. "Nobody would have the foresight to save anything from that period."

Linden smiled. "Why not? By the time of his death, Christ had a large number of followers who were determined to keep his name alive, so anything associated with him became important. As a result, the world, especially Italy, is full of Christ-related relics. In fact, there's a fourth-century church in Rome that houses numerous items from the time of the Crucifixion, including the remains of the True Cross itself."

"Are you serious?" Alex asked, voice incredulous.

"It's still there for sceptics and true believers alike," Linden assured him. "Then there's the Scala Sancta in the Church of St. John Lateran. That's the staircase where Pontius Pilate sentenced Christ to death. Another must-see for the faithful."

Alex showed a spark of interest. "How did these things end up in Rome?"

"Through the tireless efforts of St. Helena. She was the mother of Constantine, the first emperor to be baptized—even if it was on his deathbed. She was an early convert and took off for the Holy Land to look for articles of faith that could be shipped back to Rome. As you can see, she was pretty successful. Do you want me to go on? There are plenty of other examples."

"No, you've made your point."

"And that's why the Judas Hoard meant so much to Uncle George. It was his most prized possession, but he always intended for it to go on public display."

"With you in charge."

"Right. Designing the exhibit would have made my rep, which was Uncle George's plan." Depression settled over Linden like an iron weight. "But unless a miracle happens in the very near future, it isn't going to happen."

Arriving in Manhattan around four o'clock, Alex parked at a meter two blocks from Linden's apartment and walked her home. In response to her acid remark that she was quite capable of finding the way, he reminded her that his job included making sure she didn't disappear again. Although reporters still thronged the sidewalk outside her building, her Yankee hat and sunglasses seemed to be enough of a disguise that none of them recognized her.

Alex entered her apartment first. After checking every room to make sure that the intruder hadn't returned, he waved Linden inside. She immediately headed for her answering machine and raced through the fifteen messages which all turned out to be from friends. Although she looked relieved, grief shadowed her eyes. For a moment Alex wanted to take her in his arms and soothe away her sorrow. The urge passed when he remembered that he'd been hired to find the Judas Hoard—not comfort the prime suspect.

"I'm leaving," he said, his voice harsher than he intended. "I have things to do. Hopefully, you can be trusted to stay out of trouble."

Her tone was equally sharp. "Believe me, I didn't ask to be in this situation."

"Maybe not, but it's what we have. Don't let down your guard for a minute. It's not a case of being paranoid. Someone *is* out to get you."

"How can I forget?" she shot back.

Temper simmering, he forced himself to remain civil. "I need samples of your hair for lab tests. See if they turn up anything useful."

Yanking out several strands, she sealed them in a baggie and handed it to him. In return he gave her a card with his cell phone number. Their actions did nothing to relieve the tension and they stared at each other in silence. Realizing he had to leave before they got into another shouting match, Alex headed for the front door.

"I'll be in touch," he said. "Don't do anything dumb."

"As if," she retorted, raking him with a look of total contempt before slamming the door.

* * *

By ten o'clock that night Alex was beyond furious—although the sight of Linden four hours earlier had prompted a surge of pure lust. After leaving her apartment, he'd hung around her building and kept her under surveillance when she headed out to a beauty salon. She had entered it drawn and dejected, only to emerge an hour later transformed into a stunning blonde. Silky hair swirled around her head and she wore a little black dress that enhanced her subtle sexiness.

But that was then, and now he was back to being the hard-boiled investigator with little sympathy for someone who didn't have enough sense to stay out of the spotlight. Despite being stalked by an unknown person, Linden had gone to dinner at one of New York's most popular restaurants. She also remained a prime media target, and the paparazzi had gathered outside Vacuna while she was inside.

It was close to ten o'clock when she left the restaurant and her shocked expression showed that she was completely unprepared for the crush of photographers. Muscling his way through the crowd, Alex clamped an arm around her shoulders.

"This is your idea of not doing anything dumb?" he growled in her ear.

"What are you doing here?" Linden hissed, surprise morphing into hostility.

"I followed you in case something like this happened. Come on. My car's across the street."

Hauling her to a black SUV at the edge of the mob, he shoved her into the rear. As soon as he was in the adjacent seat, the driver stepped on the gas. The vehicle's speed forced the photographers out of the way, but the frenzied photo-taking continued. Ignoring the commotion outside, Alex simultaneously glared at Linden and pointed to the man up front.

"This is my assistant, Joe. Get used to having him around since you seem determined to screw up your life."

"Dinner with my friend is not screwing up my life," she shot back. "Julia's the only person I can talk to at the moment."

"You could have waited. She'll still be around when you're no longer the tabloids' flavor of the week."

"I owe her money and wanted to pay her back."

"Couldn't you just invite her to your apartment and order up pizza?"

"That's not the way to repay someone who stuck her neck out for you," Linden informed him icily. "I also went to a beauty salon first and changed my appearance."

"Did you really think that having your hair styled and a taking a change of clothes would be enough? I recognized you *immediately*," Alex raged. "And I wasn't the only one. The media has spies everywhere and the vultures started to gather about five minutes after you walked into Vacuna. What did you do? Send them an engraved invitation?"

Linden's anger matched his. "Stop treating me like an air head who can't figure out the basics. The only person who knew about Vacuna was Julia, and obviously she had to know so we could arrange a place and time to meet."

"Maybe she told someone."

Taking a deep breath, Linden regained enough self-control to spear him with a cold stare. "Julia's not the weak link, and for a one-man outfit you sure have a lot of backup. First Syd, now Joe."

Alex wasn't surprised by her comment. She was far too sharp to miss something so obvious and he'd been ready for it. "They do it for the experience."

Before she could respond, he pulled out his phone and checked his messages.

Seething, Linden looked out of the window. Dinner with Julia had been the high spot of her day. After reimbursing her friend, Linden had updated her on the day's events and then they'd caught up on the missing years. From the way Julia's face lit up when she described her partner, Ben, it was clear that she'd found the love of her life. By the time dinner was over, they'd filled in most of the blanks and promised never to let anything keep them apart again.

Now, sitting in the back of the SUV, Linden's pleasure in the evening disappeared into a sea of resentment.

Although they reached her street without any major delays, the paparazzi were faster. Seeing them camped out on her doorstep, Alex ordered Joe to stop at the end of the block and dialed a phone number, telling whoever answered to be ready to let them in.

"Pull up in front of the building opposite Linden's," he said to Joe. "We'll both get out and walk over to her entrance."

Face scornful, Linden asked, "That's going to stop them from getting a piece of me?"

"No, but it's the best I can do. Your doorman's ready to open the door, so just keep moving."

At first no one noticed them, but a ripple of recognition spread through the crowd as they neared the entrance. Like predators scenting lunch, the mob circled her, cameras flashing with the brilliance of a July Fourth fireworks display. As instructed, the doorman cracked the door open just enough for them to squeeze through.

"You're safe now, Ms. Travers," Frank greeted her, fighting to close the door against the mob.

"Thanks for being here," she responded with a grateful smile.

"Anytime. Goodnight."

Once in the elevator, Linden dropped any pretense of civility and glared at Alex who scowled back. Their silence lasted until he finished a quick search of her apartment. He returned to her office as she was hanging up the phone.

"Four messages from friends," she told him. "I'll call them back tomorrow. Thanks for the help. Goodnight and goodbye."

"Not so fast. I talked to your aunt earlier. She wants me to watch your back until those coins turn up."

"This isn't the time to discuss it," said Linden, hitting the phone's *Do Not Disturb* button. "I'm tired and I'm going to bed."

Alex's lips tightened into a thin line. "Okay. We'll talk tomorrow and set some ground rules. Goodnight."

# Chapter
# 11

Cocooned in the familiarity of her own bed, Linden slowly emerged from sleep. A memory tugged at her: she was trapped in a stationary car, enveloped by all-consuming darkness. The image faded before she could make sense of it and she dismissed it as the remnants of a dream. A very unpleasant dream.

Opening her eyes, she saw puddles of gold on the ceiling, the sign every sunny morning that it was time to get up. Ignoring the phone's message light, she put on a pot of coffee and headed to the shower. Twenty minutes later, dressed in shorts and a tee-shirt, she took a mug of coffee to her office and played the three new messages. The first two were from friends welcoming her home, but the last one sent a chill down her spine.

"Your uncle's barely cold in his grave," The Voice taunted. "You're accused of stealing the Judas Hoard, and all you care about is having fun at Vacuna. Just like you partied at Moon Lake on Monday night. Don't bet on the police buying your claim of innocence when they learn about that. Want to see how fast you go from being a person of interest to their prime suspect?"

According to the date stamp, the message was five minutes old.

For a second Linden's brain refused to function, then she hit the redial button. *Unknown number* flashed up, followed by the impersonal hum of the dial tone.

Back in the kitchen, she filled a bowl with cereal and ate it mechanically. The taste of slightly sour milk reminded her that she needed to go grocery shopping, although with her life a train wreck, food should be the last thing on her mind. The telephone rang, a welcome diversion, until she saw the name on Caller ID. *Alex Blair.*

Snatching up the phone, she demanded, "What do you want?"

"The police found your car. Be downstairs in ten minutes."

Without bothering to say goodbye, she rushed into the bedroom and exchanged her shorts for a pair of jeans. While pushing her feet into tan Huaraches, she threw the contents of her lizard purse into a more practical leather tote and jammed the hated baseball hat over her hair. Despite reaching the lobby two minutes early, Alex's Ford was already parked out front. To her surprise, only a few cameras whirred when she strode outside to join him.

Once safely in the passenger seat, she said, "Is it my imagination or is the crowd a little smaller?"

"Seen any TV today?"

Linden shook her head. "Haven't listened to the radio either."

Alex flashed his killer smile. "After five days, you've become old and stale. They're onto fresher meat."

"And welcome to it," she snapped, determined not to lower her guard. Struck by a sudden thought, she shot him a hard stare. "You know, you're always on the scene at just the right time. What do you do, live in your car?"

"No, in a suitcase," he laughed. "I live in Boston so home's the nearest hotel at the moment. Check in one day, check out the next."

"I'd hate that," said Linden, taking off her hat and running a comb through her hair. "I like a predictable routine, which is why I can't wait to get my old life back. And finding my car's a good start. Where is it?"

"Ever heard of Three Pines Park?"

A quiver of unease shot through Linden. "Sure. It's less than a mile from Laurel Court."

"The police organized a search and found your car hidden away from the main parking area."

"Did they receive a tip?"

"No. It was good old-fashioned police work. They went out and beat the bushes. Literally." He glanced at her. "Why do you ask?"

Linden shrugged. "Curious, that's all."

"You didn't drive it there?"

Exasperated, she said, "How many times do I have to tell you? I have no recollection of Monday night."

"Just checking. It's a very convenient excuse."

"It's the truth," she corrected him brusquely.

They didn't speak again until Radford when Alex broke the frigid silence by asking for directions. Linden responded with little more than three-word sentences, and her sigh of relief echoed his when they finally arrived at the park. A patrol car blocked the entrance but the driver backed up and waved them over to the narrow road that bordered the lake. Arrow straight, the half-mile stretch of blacktop ended in a parking lot at the base of a hillock. Stiffly erect, three pine trees circled the summit like sentinels guarding against an alien invasion.

Assorted vehicles were parked haphazardly in the unpaved

lot, and leaving the Ford next to a police cruiser, Linden and Alex headed for a gap in a bank of rhododendrons. Inside the shadow-shrouded undergrowth, they followed the sound of voices to a group of people clustered around a navy BMW. As if alerted by a sixth sense, Detective Gorton looked up at their approach and hurried over to them.

"Hi Alex, Linden," he said. "This your car?"

Linden wondered if the use of her name meant Gorton was convinced she was innocent or softening her up for her arrest.

She glanced at the BMW's license plate. "Yes."

"Any idea how it got here?"

"Absolutely none."

"We've just finished checking the exterior for anything suspicious. Seems to be okay and a truck will be here soon to transport it to the forensic lab."

"Did you find my purse?" Linden asked. "It should be in a pouch under the driver's seat."

"Your car's locked but the local BMW dealer sent a guy with a bunch of master keys. Soon as he's opened it, you can check for your purse. The interior's already full of your DNA so a little more won't make much difference."

As they approached the car, the driver's door popped open, releasing a blast of stale air that hovered overhead like a malevolent genie. Sticking her hand under the seat, Linden pulled out her purse, a six-inch circle of black leather barely large enough for the necessities.

Opening it, she exclaimed, "My phone! My wallet with my driver license, thank God. And here's all my credit cards. It's too late for them, though. They've all been canceled."

"Anything missing?"

"No. Even my spare key's here." She jiggled it in her hand. "And I'll tell you one thing, I'd never knowingly leave my purse behind."

Face speculative, Alex said, "Which leads us to the next question. Why did you?"

Gorton reached for her phone. "You can keep your purse, but I want to hear all incoming calls since Monday night. Who has this number?"

"The world. It's on my business card."

Walking around the car, Gorton peered inside the empty trunk. "Maybe forensics will find something. We'll go to my office to listen to these messages. On a nice day like this, there'll be a riot if we don't open the park to the public soon."

\* \* \*

Located just off the parkway, Gorton's office was housed in a modern two-story building with a striking glass and steel exterior. Inside, he ushered them past a warren of cubicles and cramped offices to a windowless conference room where six well-worn chairs surrounded an oval table with several deep scratches. The array of electronic equipment set up on a scuffed credenza was a striking contrast to the room's shabby appearance.

"This is where most of our budget goes," Gorton said, connecting Linden's phone to a laptop computer. "Most of it is beyond me but I've learned how to set up the stuff I use frequently. Saves having to chase after one of the kids each time I need it."

He pressed a button and the printer shot out a piece of paper with several columns of figures. Using two fingers, he typed a command into the computer and the phone's display showed twenty new messages.

"Shouldn't take too long to listen to these," he observed, hitting another key. "Our objective is to connect each number to a name."

Timed at eight-thirty Monday night, the first message was from one of Linden's clients, reminding her of their Tuesday morning breakfast date at the Rockefeller Center Café. Moira was also the next caller.

"Hey, Linden, where are you? It's almost nine o'clock. Did you oversleep? The coffee's getting cold."

She called again thirty minutes later, clearly irritated, and told Linden to call her office ASAP. Six more messages alternated between Roger Lambert and Tom Blair, both demanding to know where she was. Their messages, which started out worried before turning angry, ended after two hours and were followed by an additional eight from friends. None of them believed she was involved in any sort of theft and all offered their complete support.

Linden's face turned ashen during the next call.

"Hope you liked the gift I left." The digitally-altered voice left no clue to the caller's sex or identity. "And this is just the first of many gifts I have for you. You won't escape me again."

Stunned, Linden gasped, "It's The Voice."

Looking down at his list, Gorton read off the phone number. "Is that familiar?"

Linden swallowed heavily. "It's my land line."

"Came in at four a.m. Tuesday morning. Any idea what the gift was?"

"A ransacked apartment," Alex answered. "That's what greeted Linden when we walked in after yesterday's meeting. He must have gone there, hoping to find the Judas Hoard."

"Anything missing?" asked Gorton.

"Not that I could tell. Alex helped me clean up."

"Who has a key to your apartment?"

"My housekeeper," Linden answered. "She's been coming every other Friday for three years; my cousin Melanie; and the building, of course."

"We'll check the two individuals. Cameras constantly monitor your building's service entrance so we'll get a copy of the video for the whole night. The Voice could have arrived at any time."

"And distracted the doorman in dozens of different ways," Alex pointed out. "Those are the hours when they tend to be less vigilant."

Frustrated, Linden said, "There's no point in checking my phone for prints or DNA. I had a cocktail party two weeks ago and made a million calls since. It's mine, for God's sake."

"Okay. Let's get on with the rest of the calls."

Less than a day old, the remaining messages were all from friends, relieved to hear Linden was safely home.

Gorton disconnected the phone. "What about text messaging?"

"I delete them almost immediately."

He still accessed the text function, and scrolling through the few messages, observed, "Nothing helpful. Here's your phone back, but I'll hang onto this list. Thanks for your cooperation."

Promising to keep them in the loop, he escorted them to the entrance and said goodbye. Linden stepped into the sunshine as eagerly as a prisoner granted early release. The hour spent inside the claustrophobic conference room felt like a week in a dungeon.

"What now?" Alex asked.

"A drink," she replied without hesitation. "With alcohol."

"Yeah. Not the best of days. You're the expert on the area. Know any place?"

After a moment's thought, she said, "Dylan's. It should still be serving lunch, even though it's pretty late. Hungry?"

"I thought you'd never ask."

Guided by Linden, Alex drove for ten minutes along a

four-lane highway and then pulled into the restaurant's parking lot whose weather-beaten sign promised great food at great prices. The white-shingled walls needed to be repainted, but Dylan's location at the edge of Long Island Sound promised an excellent water view.

"Don't judge this place by its appearance," Linden warned. "The food really is great. Excellent seafood."

"Want to sit outside?" Alex asked as they walked toward the entrance.

"Yes, I've had enough of being confined indoors recently."

With its paneled walls and hard wood floor, the restaurant's decor resembled a whaling ship. It was also deserted, but a sign by the bar directed them outside to a paved patio. Although only two tables were occupied, Linden headed for a vacant one as far from them as possible. Shaded by a yellow umbrella, she gazed across silver-capped waves at Connecticut's hazy outline. In the nearby marina, a small armada of moored boats bobbed up and down on the Sound's gentle swell.

"I wish I could sail away and leave all my problems behind."

Alex ignored her forlorn expression. "You had your chance on Monday night. Why didn't you take it then when no one was looking for you?"

Linden glared at him. "As I told Julia last night, you're obnoxious, patronizing and do not improve upon acquaintance."

"Bet she can't wait to meet me," he grinned.

A server strolled over, bringing a temporary halt to their sniping, but the multi-pierced teenager immediately picked up on the tension that hung in the air. Eyeing the couple nervously, she dropped her pen which Alex handed back with a smile. The dimple in his left cheek left her even more flustered.

Mystified by the server's reaction, Linden studied Alex covertly. His regular features were marred by a slightly crooked nose that looked like the result of a long-ago break. Given his tall, lean build, she wondered if he played basketball. Overall, she reluctantly concluded, he did possess a certain degree of magnetism that some women might find attractive. Unwilling to credit him with any redeeming features, she turned her attention to a sail boat on the horizon.

Five minutes of venomous silence followed before Alex spoke again.

"Here, maybe this will mellow you."

Ignoring Alex, Linden thanked the server for the glass of white wine. While grateful for the drink, her angry sip did nothing to improve her mood.

After taking a long swallow of his beer, Alex asked, "Know what's interesting about the call from The Voice?"

"That he called my cell phone. He knew I didn't have it with me."

"Probably figured it would turn up sooner or later," Alex observed. "But it's not the call that's important. This is his way of letting you know he's in control."

"Not anymore," Linden interrupted.

"You're missing the point." Alex sounded exasperated. "What's *interesting* is that he knows your cell number, which means he knows you."

"Everyone has that number," she reminded him. "It's on my business card."

"Then he could even be a business associate. I've been thinking about yesterday's media circus at the police precinct. Outside of Tom, Peter and me, who knew you'd be there."

"Julia."

"And yesterday at Vacuna's?"

"Julia." Linden glowered at Alex. "She's the only person who *doesn't* have my cell number. I didn't get my phone back until an hour ago and I haven't had a chance to call her."

"What about mutual friends from college? Do any of them have your cell number?"

"I guess so," she conceded. "But you're headed in the wrong direction. I haven't been totally honest with you. The Voice called this morning about ten minutes before you did."

"*Now* you decide to tell me," Alex thundered. "What did he say?"

"He threatened to tell the police I'd been at Moon Lake early Tuesday morning."

A muscle throbbed in Alex's jaw. "And this is important, why?"

"Do you know where Moon Lake is?"

"Never heard of it," Alex said curtly.

"Then you're not from around here. We were just there." At Alex's puzzled expression, Linden explained, "Moon Lake. AKA Three Pines Park. All the kids around here call it Moon Lake. It's the local make out spot."

Alex's lips twitched. "You know it well."

"I went to high school here. Naturally I was *aware* of it."

"Naturally. In my neighborhood, our make out spot was known as Lock Lips Lane. Not that *I* was ever there."

An unwilling smile escaped Linden. "Yeah. Right. But that means The Voice is local."

"Or knows someone local."

Alex fell silent as the waitress approached with their lobster wraps and waited until she was out of earshot before resuming the conversation.

"Back to The Voice. I'm not surprised he visited your apartment early Tuesday morning. After all, he knew you were safely locked away in Ashton."

"When my uncle became ill three weeks ago, he refused to stay in the hospital." The memory of that life-changing event caught Linden off guard. Blinking back tears, she added, "He wanted to be home, so round-the-clock nurses were hired and they were all nice guys. Even though I can't believe any of them would rob a dying man, have you checked them out?"

"Syd's doing it right now." Alex waved a French fry at Linden. "And never be blinded by someone's apparent niceness. You wouldn't believe the number of nice people I've met who turned out to be total monsters."

Linden poked at her wrap with a complete lack of appetite. "Know what's really scary? This didn't just happen. The Voice put a lot of planning into it. I've been in his cross hairs for months, studied like some lab animal." She shivered. "I feel violated."

"Good. Maybe now you'll start being a little bit more cautious about what you say and who you say it to."

Linden's gaze fell on the narrow strip of beach that skirted the highway between the restaurant and the marina. While the few people seated by the water's edge looked innocuous, Alex had made a valid point. For the first time she felt completely unnerved.

Tipping her head toward the beach, she said, "What if he's one of those people?"

"Might be. He's playing mind games with you. His calls are intended to keep you off balance. He wants you to know he's watching you." Alex took a huge bite of his wrap. "What now?"

"I'd like to see Aunt Heni. I know I'm not her favorite person at the moment but she deserves a firsthand explanation."

"And you deserve to be heard."

Shocked into silence, Linden considered how to handle his first overture of friendship. Since it wouldn't hurt to have his help, it wouldn't kill her to accept it. "Thank you. That's good to know."

# Chapter 12

Thirty minutes later they were in Laurel Court, now returned to its normal level of serenity. The seven-foot high hedges that flanked the secluded cul-de-sac glistened like quicksilver in the brilliant sunshine. As Alex made the turn into the Lambert's driveway, Linden indicated the key pad set into the pillar.

"I hope they haven't changed the code since my last visit."

"Only one way to find out. Give it to me," he said, entering the numbers she recited.

The gates swung open and Alex followed the circular driveway to the front of the house where a Mercedes was already parked. Climbing the steps to the front door, Linden lifted the sphinx-shaped knocker.

"This isn't the time to use my key," she remarked.

Within seconds Brunnings opened the door, his face registering no emotion.

"Hello, Linden. Welcome home. Good afternoon, Mr. Blair. Is Mrs. Lambert expecting you?"

Linden shook her head. "Please see if she'll talk to me."

"Let me check," the butler said.

Brunnings soon returned to the paneled entrance hall.

"Mrs. Lambert is in the library."

Bracing for a barrage of hostile questions, Linden followed him to the sun-drenched room. Lined with shelves of books, the library was designed for relaxation, its chintz-covered furniture chosen for comfort. There was nothing relaxed about Helena Lambert. Dressed in a navy linen suit, her neck encircled by a single strand of pearls, she regarded her niece coldly.

"I can't say I'm glad to see you, Linden," she stated. "For some reason, a misplaced sense of family loyalty perhaps, I do feel obligated to hear your explanation."

"I don't have one. Monday night is a total blank."

Amber eyes, slightly paler than Linden's, remained glacial. "How very convenient."

"I was hoping that once I saw you—the house—everything would come back to me. So far nothing has. I've lost an entire night out of my life and I can't get it back." As the strain of the last few days caught up with her, Linden's face crumpled. "You've no idea how hard I've tried to remember."

Through a mist of tears Linden glimpsed movement by the fireplace and saw Peter Sinclair striding toward her.

Putting an arm around her shoulder, he said, "Come and sit down. Maybe you should pour her a brandy, Alex. Looks like she could use a stiff drink."

Feeling the edge of a sofa brush against her legs, Linden slumped down and used her fingers to wipe away her tears.

Peter pushed a white handkerchief into her hands. "Here, use this."

Angry at her loss of control, she blotted her cheeks and mumbled a thank you.

"Helena, we've checked out much of Linden's story and it seems she's telling the truth," Peter said.

"I still find it hard to believe that she can't remember Monday night," Helena responded, but her voice was less sharp. "According to Alex, Linden was imprisoned in a house not too far from here."

Taking the glass that Alex held out, Linden said, "We visited it yesterday, but it didn't jog any memories."

"Well, let's hope that something does," Helena said. "In spite of everything, Linden, you're still my niece and I promised my sister I'd always look after you. I don't have time for you now; we can talk after dinner. You can stay here tonight."

"I'd like that," Linden said.

Linden's neutral tone hid her elation. Spending the night at the house fit neatly with her just-formulated plan. Since the Judas Hoard had disappeared from her uncle's study, the room deserved further investigation. A late-night visit, when everyone was asleep, was her best bet.

Helena turned her attention to Alex. "You'll stay, too, won't you? I'd like an update from you. Peter and I have almost finished our meeting so I'll be free shortly. Linden, I'll see you at dinner."

At her nod of dismissal, Linden left the room and headed straight for the front door. Half a step behind, Alex caught her wrist.

"Where are you going?"

"Out," she snapped, shaking herself free.

"Out where?" he demanded.

"Just out. I need some fresh air."

Linden's lie hid the fact that she wanted to head back up the driveway. She'd had a sudden memory, an echo of her earlier dream. Once again she'd been trapped in a car surrounded by darkness. Only now she distinctly saw light bouncing off a hedge identical to the one along Laurel Court. She was hoping that a walk along the lane would shake more memories free.

"Well, I'm going to *just out* with you. In case you've

forgotten, I've also been hired to watch your back. At the very least some nut's after you, and so far you've done a spectacular job of proving you're not much good at taking care of yourself. Therefore, where you go, I go."

Posted by the front door, Brunnings appeared oblivious to the disagreement, but a hint of curiosity lurked in his eyes. Uncharacteristically, Linden ignored him and stormed outside, stopping on the bottom step to look back at Alex.

"I'm more than capable of taking care of myself, thank you very much," she seethed.

"Not from what I've seen," he rejoined, but his anger abruptly changed to alarm and he rushed down the steps. "Wait!"

"Will you leave me alone," she yelled, and continued walking until a blurry object caught her eye.

A huge animal was streaking toward her. Suddenly it leaped into the air, reaching her at the same time that Alex grabbed Linden around the waist. His grip helped them both remain upright as the beast, a cross between a bear and a wolf, balanced on its hind legs. Front paws on her shoulders, the dog licked her rapturously while emitting little yaps of delight.

"Garibaldi," she cried, burying her face in his soft fur.

After her aunt's animosity, Linden's emotions were still raw and Garibaldi's lavish welcome sent her struggling for control. He continued to shower her with love, overjoyed to see his favorite walking companion again.

"Melanie and I used to joke that we could have used him as a pony if he'd turned up when we were kids," she recalled with a smile, scratching Garibaldi's head. "He wandered into the grounds one day when we were eighteen and no one could make him leave. Poor Garibaldi, someone had been really mean to you. You were all skin and bone, weren't you?"

Garibaldi beamed at Linden in adoration, bushy tail wagging happily.

Unimpressed with Linden's reminiscences, Alex said, "Okay, once more. Where are you going?"

"The front gate. Garibaldi will protect me," she said.

Without giving Alex a chance to argue, she headed for the end of the driveway. A small door was set into the left gate, and she entered a code into the key pad on the pillar. The gate swung open and she stepped through the opening into Laurel Court.

Unaware that Alex and Garibaldi were following her, she walked down the narrow lane until a sudden image stopped her dead. She was in her BMW, but as she completed her turn from the driveway into Laurel Court a car blocked her way. Before she could slam on the brake, her headlights and engine cut off simultaneously, leaving the lane in all consuming darkness. For a brief moment, she recalled a pinpoint of light bobbing toward her and then it, too, disappeared.

"What's wrong?" Alex demanded. "You look like you're about to faint."

Unsure if it was reality or a dream, she choked, "A flashback."

"Describe it," he ordered.

Eyes closed, she relived every minute, the details so vivid that they could be happening in real time. At the end, she found Alex had curled a comforting arm around her shoulders. Shocked by the unexpected gesture of sympathy, she tensed. Alex stepped away from her like a scalded cat, but their eyes locked for a long moment. Dragging his gaze away he stared at the base of the hedge, studying it with more intensity than necessary. When he broke the silence, he was back in private investigator mode.

"So you think this is where you were incapacitated in some way?"

"Then transferred to another car and taken to Ashton. It's the only explanation I can think of."

Alex frowned. "Could be, except that means there were two of them: The Voice would be the one to drive you to Ashton while his little helper stayed here and moved your car to Moon Lake. My gut, though, says The Voice works alone."

Looking around, Linden said, "Since I can't swear any of this really happened, how's this for a scenario? The Voice drove me and my car to the house in Ashton, gave me another dose of roofies or whatever, and then came back here in my car."

"It's possible," Alex conceded. "He could have zapped your car and temporarily disabled it. The Internet's full of such gadgets."

"After hiding my car at Moon Lake, he drove off in his own vehicle, which he'd already parked nearby." Linden did a quick calculation. "He could do the round trip in under an hour."

"The idea sure has merit," Alex said, "although he'd need an accomplice to drop him here."

Linden indicated the end of Laurel Court. "No. Moon Lake's less than a ten-minute walk away."

"It's a dead end."

"For cars," she corrected him. "The woods are the start of Moon Lake or, if you prefer, Three Pines Park. I'll show you. It's also one of Garibaldi's favorite walks."

Garibaldi was investigating a clump of weeds, but on hearing his name he looked at Linden. Realizing where she was headed, he bounded off, his tail waving like a flag in a high wind.

"Melanie and I used to ride our bikes down here," Linden said. "There are only four houses after ours and everyone knew kids would be around."

Indicating the formidable pair of gates that guarded the neighboring house, Alex said, "Any idea who lives here?"

"The Vandergrafs. They're an older couple and spend winters in Florida and summers in Martha's Vineyard. This is where they spend the bits in between." Pointing to the mansion opposite, she continued, "The Sheridans. They moved in my first year at college so I don't know them too well."

As the eaves of the final two houses peeked into view, Alex asked, "What about these people?"

"On the right are the Forsters. They moved in about three years ago. The Carluccis live at the last house. They're great friends of Uncle . . ." Her voice broke. ". . . Aunt Heni. They have a son, Marco."

"Wasn't he one of the people who kept leaving messages?"

"Yes. He's one of my best friends. We've known each other since grade school and his mother and Aunt Heni hoped we'd get married someday. I didn't have the heart to tell them it wasn't going to happen."

"Not your type?"

"I'm not his," she chuckled. "He's gay. He only came out a few years ago when he met the love of his life. Andrew. They're a great couple."

Her smile faded as they reached the end of Laurel Court and she looked at the tangle of shrubs and trees that marked the boundary of Three Pines Park. There was no fence, but a large No Parking sign was planted in the hard-packed earth. Slightly to the left, a gap in the undergrowth revealed a track formed by generations of human feet.

"This path goes directly to Moon Lake," she said. "It leads to the swimming area where the local kids still hang out. It's about a half-mile away."

"Is the park locked up at night?"

"No, but everyone's supposed to leave by sunset."

"Then you'd come back later to make out."

Linden laughed. "Rite of passage. It was common knowledge that the police wouldn't bother us if we didn't make too much noise or stay too late."

"So someone like The Voice could leave his car for a few hours and not be too worried about it drawing attention."

"Exactly. Especially in the area where we found my car."

"Okay. I've seen enough," said Alex, pulling out his phone. "Gorton has the resources to take this further. I'll ask him to check for another set of tire tracks. This could be the break we need."

# Chapter 13

They were almost at the Lambert house by the time Alex ended the phone call. Hanging up, he told Linden that Gorton was intrigued by the possibility of a second car and had agreed to follow up. As they walked up the Lambert driveway, Linden saw that the only car parked outside the house was Alex's Ford Taurus.

"Peter's left, thank God," she said.

"Bet he'll be back for dinner," Alex responded sourly.

"You're not too crazy about him, are you?"

"Very astute. Evidently, Monday night's experience didn't affect your powers of perception."

Buoyed by his recent kindness, Linden dismissed his sarcasm with a smile. "Perception be damned. You oozed dislike."

"That obvious, huh?"

"Very. What's wrong with Peter? He's considered a major catch around here."

"So I've heard, but he's too damn smooth if you ask me."

Side by side, they mounted the steps to the front door which swung open before Linden could knock. Hand on the door knob, Brunnings inspected them with the keen eyes of a drill sergeant.

"My aunt asked us to stay the night," Linden greeted him.

"Mrs. Lambert has already advised me. She'd also like to see Mr. Blair." His stern gaze skimmed over Alex's polo shirt and jeans. "Perhaps you'd care to freshen up first. You're in the Blue Room."

"I'll take him," said Linden, leading the way upstairs.

More Southern Plantation than Tudor England, the entrance hall was dominated by a sweeping staircase. The afternoon sun poured in through a stained glass window and onto a gallery that led to the six bedrooms. When they reached the top step, Linden pointed to the nearest door.

"That's your room. Aunt Heni's is opposite and mine's down at the end of the corridor."

"When was the last time you slept over?"

"A couple of weeks ago." An unpleasant thought struck her. "What if it's been searched, like my apartment?"

"I doubt, it but I'll check it out with you."

Linden's room proved to be tidy to the point of sterility, and drifting over to the window she gazed out at the canopy of trees. An oak tree towered over all the others, setting off an itch in her brain. A memory hovered at the edge, but whatever she wanted to remember remained elusive.

Turning to face Alex, she said, "The trees over there are part of Three Pines Park. You can't see it from here, but a brick wall runs the length of Laurel Court. Each house has a gate in the wall for people to enter the park that way."

"Is it locked?"

"Yes, we never used it, though. It's easier just to walk to the end of the lane and take the path."

With a glance at his watch, Alex headed for the door. "I need to clean up before meeting with your aunt. I'll see you at dinner."

Linden stopped him before he could step into the hallway.

"Thanks for the company today, all the support you gave me. It helped to have someone on my side."

His killer smile appeared, igniting a wave of heat inside Linden. "You underestimate yourself. All I did was my job, or at least an extension of it. I guarantee we'll start to get some answers soon. See you later."

"Right. Later."

In her haste to get rid of him, she slammed the door shut and collapsed against it. Even if his killer smile could turn her on and he occasionally behaved like a decent human being, that didn't mean she found him attractive. Did it?

Deciding the day's traumas had scrambled her brain, she returned to the window and sank down onto the padded seat. Although the view usually brought her a sense of serenity, today her head teemed with too many questions to allow for peace.

The chimes of a distant clock jolted her back to the present and the approaching dinner hour. After a quick shower, she checked out the clothes in her walk-in closet and chose a peach-colored silk shift. Slipping on a pair of high-heeled sandals, she headed for the ground floor. It appeared deserted until Brunnings materialized out of the shadows and told her that everyone was in the living room.

Entering the room, Linden first noticed her aunt who was sitting on the brocade sofa. Ramrod straight and austere in black crepe, she was listening to Peter. He stood by the fireplace with an arm resting on the marble mantle, exuding charm. Over by the French door, Alex seemed mesmerized by the trees of Three Pines Park, the knifelike creases in his white shirt indicating that it had come straight from the packet.

Catching sight of her, Peter exclaimed, "Linden, you look lovely. Would you like a drink?"

"It's almost seven o'clock and we'll be going in for dinner soon." Helena frowned at her niece in irritation. "Couldn't you have made more of an effort this once?"

"I'm sorry. Time got away from me," she confessed.

"Don't worry," Peter smiled. "It happens to everyone."

Although Alex remained silent, he was watching Linden. For a moment their eyes met and his glowed with an intensity that made Linden's blood race.

The room's tension ended only when Brunnings announced that dinner was ready.

Inside the dining room, four place settings had been arranged around the mahogany table, and as soon as she was seated Linden took a large sip of wine from her glass. Porcelain bowls on the mahogany buffet contained vichyssoise, cold chicken with dill, and fruit salad. In addition to serving each course, Brunnings also kept topping up everyone's wine glass with an excellent Chablis.

As if by prior agreement, Helena and Peter confined the conversation to the weather and a request by Walmart to open a superstore a few miles away. Alex contributed the occasional comment, but spent most of his time looking out of the French window at the swimming pool beyond. Positive that her aunt was ignoring her, Linden couldn't wait for the meal to be over.

Once dessert was finished, Helena asked Brunnings to serve coffee in the living room. Everyone followed her into the room where she took a seat in the center of the sofa as regal as a queen on a throne. Linden sat on the love seat opposite while Alex and Peter chose an armchair as far away from each other as possible. After pouring the coffee and handing out the cups, Brunnings silently left the room.

"Alex told me the police found your car today," Helena began.

Peter looked at Linden in surprise. "The police found your car? Where?"

"Up at Moon Lake."

"You mean it was parked there in plain sight for almost a week?" Peter's voice was incredulous.

"Quite the opposite," Alex corrected him. "It was well hidden."

"Did the police receive a tip?"

"No, but since they didn't find anything in the Ashton area and Linden was last seen leaving Laurel Court, they decided this area was worth a second, more thorough search. Her car is now at the police lab and it will be interesting to see what the forensic people discover."

Peter shrugged. "Probably nothing. I can't see whoever was responsible leaving any clues."

"No matter how careful people are, something's always left behind," Alex pointed out.

"Linden also thinks she was abducted right in front of the house." Helena sounded far from convinced.

Alex put his cup back on its saucer. "It's too bad she can't be more definite."

Infuriated by his attitude, Linden bristled, "I'm doing my best."

"Whatever happened, we have to put it behind us and move on. No matter how difficult." For a moment Helena's self-control faltered. "Melanie and Roger have been wonderful but they have their own lives to live. Just as you do, Linden."

"Not until the Judas Hoard is found," Linden countered.

"You mustn't let it become an obsession," Helena warned. "That's what Alex is here for."

"I can manage quite well by myself."

"Don't be too quick to dismiss his help," Helena said.

Derision edged Linden's tone. "So far Alex hasn't done anything especially helpful."

"He hasn't really had much of a chance. It's less than a week since . . ." Helena struggled to her feet. "This has been an exhausting day. Peter, a final word with you. Goodnight Alex, Linden."

Escorted by Peter, she left the room, the low rumble of their voices faintly audible in the tense silence that descended over Linden and Alex. Face inscrutable, Alex leaned against the mantelpiece, his eyes fixed on Linden as she collected the coffee cups.

"I'm going to bed," he remarked after a couple of minutes.

"And leave me unguarded?" Linden taunted. "Aren't you scared I'll take off?"

Producing his car keys, he dangled them in front of her. "How? These will be tucked safely under my pillow, and I don't think you want to get that close to me."

"Yours isn't the only car."

"I'm a very light sleeper and I'd hear an engine start immediately. Of course, you could always hitchhike," Alex said, half-serious, "but it's getting rather late for that."

Linden hung on to her temper with difficulty. "I don't run away from my problems. I'll see you at breakfast."

Intent on putting as much space as possible between them, Linden marched through the French door. *Jerk*, she fumed. *It will serve him right if I don't show up tomorrow.* The sexual attraction that seemed to flare between them was the product of her overactive imagination.

Out on the marble terrace, she headed for the rose garden which was shrouded in darkness. Calmed by the flower's fragrance, she strolled among the bushes almost at peace until the sound of footsteps broke the silence. When a tall figure loomed out of the shadows, she was prepared for another battle with Alex but it was Peter who spoke.

"Escaping the confinement of the house?" he asked.

While not in the mood for company, she forced herself to be pleasant. "Yes, I've developed an aversion to being inside for long periods."

"Finding yourself locked up inside a strange place must have been a nightmare experience."

"I was more angry than scared, and being accused of stealing the Judas Hoard made me even angrier."

"I can imagine. People were very quick to make assumptions."

"As if I'd deliberately cause my aunt pain." Outraged, Linden continued, "So help me, I'd bargain with the devil if he promised to help."

"Isn't that a little extreme?"

"Maybe," she allowed. "I'm sure there's easier ways."

Peter drew her close. "What a time you've had. Lack of memory isn't much of a defense."

His lips descended on hers, gently at first, but growing rougher when she remained unresponsive. Peter had never turned her on and she had no desire to kiss him now, although the rose garden was a very romantic setting. Did he think she was so weak she needed a man to help her? Was he confident that after just one kiss she'd beg for his advice? Incensed, she wrenched free of his embrace.

Peter stared at her, a concerned expression on his face. "What's wrong? Did you remember something?"

"No. I'm just not ready for this. Life's been a roller coaster these last few days."

"Probably feels more like going to hell and back." Peter's voice grew husky. "I'm sorry about the kiss but I've been waiting weeks to do it again."

"Maybe another time when I'm not so frazzled," she lied.

Caressing her cheek, Peter said, "Frazzled or not, you're still beautiful."

"Thank you," she said, stepping away from him. "If you'll excuse me, I'd like to go in. It's been quite a day."

"I can imagine. How fortunate that Alex was on hand to offer words of comfort."

"Yeah, he was a real lifesaver," she replied acidly.

"I had the feeling you didn't like him," Peter observed.

"I loathe him," she spat. "He loves to needle me, probably because he thinks I'll slip up and expose myself as a fraud."

"Poor Linden," Peter smiled, tucking a strand of hair behind her ear. "But you know that *I'm* always here for you twenty-four/seven. Should you remember something, come to me."

"Of course," she replied.

"Tell *me* first," he urged. "You can trust me to do what's best for you. Alex is just out for himself. Recovering the coins will establish his reputation and let him write his own ticket. He cares only how *he* can benefit."

Although Linden didn't argue, she wasn't in total agreement with Peter. Despite Alex's many faults, she felt that he was more interested in the challenge of solving the impossible rather than covering himself in glory.

"I'm so glad you turned up safely." Peter brushed the top of her head with his lips. "Goodnight, sleep well."

She accompanied him to the front door, then closed it behind him with a profound sense of relief. The last thing she wanted was a relationship with anyone. Her sole focus was on finding answers.

She trudged upstairs to her bedroom where Mrs. Brunnings was fussing with the bed's comforter. Looking up, the housekeeper held out her arms. Linden rushed over to her and received a bone-crushing hug.

"Oh, Mrs. B," Linden whispered against the plump shoulder. "I've had such a rotten time."

Mrs. Brunnings rubbed Linden's spine. "Well, you're home now and that's all that matters. I know this hasn't been the best of homecomings but I'm happy to have you back. Very happy indeed. We've both been so worried."

"I didn't feel right involving you."

"You know we'd have helped, no questions asked."

"I'm not sure what you could have done," Linden said. "But I didn't do any of the things I'm accused of."

"We never believed you were guilty of anything, and don't hesitate to ask us for any kind of help. We'd do anything for you, honey. We're equally anxious for the coins to turn up."

Linden's eyes shimmered with unshed tears. "You're the only people who *do* believe in me."

"And we always will," said Mrs. Brunnings. "Goodnight my love, sleep tight. I'm so glad you're home."

Hanging up her dress, Linden mulled over the evening. Although she no longer felt alone, only she could unlock the secrets trapped in her mind.

More anxious than ever to do some snooping, she pulled on jeans and a tee-shirt. Switching off the light, she stretched out on the window seat and listened to the house settle down for the night.

# Chapter 14

The clock on Linden's night table registered twelve-thirty before she judged it safe to leave. By then no sounds had disturbed the silence for almost an hour. Easing open her door, she cautiously headed for the first floor where she received her first shock of the night. A sliver of light, laser bright in the darkness, shone beneath the door to her uncle's study.

Noticing a flashing light on the wall outside the room, she reset the alarm and opened the door. Prepared to excuse her presence with insomnia, she was surprised to find an empty room. For a moment she wondered why the lamp was on; then she remembered. Her uncle had been a night owl, often working until midnight. A vision of him at his desk, poring over papers while she sketched on the sofa, flashed into her mind. The room, she realized, was awaiting his return.

A sense of disloyalty swept over her. Snooping around her uncle's study in the middle of the night made her feel like she was invading his privacy. The thought unleashed a memory that sent a chill up her spine. This wasn't the first time that she'd sneaked into his study when everybody was asleep. Except she hadn't been alone the last time. And the room had been almost dark, lit only by a shaft of light which spilled in through the open doorway. Barely visible, the person beside her had seemed as insubstantial as a ghost—or an evil spirit.

*"Go to the safe."* The metallic voice had demanded total submission.

Like an automaton, she walked to the painting and pulled it away from the wall.

*"Now open it,"* the phantom figure commanded. *"You know the combination. You've done it many times."*

The metal door glittered coldly in the dim light as her fingers reached out and twirled the dial. 14 . . . 26 . . . At the last moment she snatched her hand away. The safe's silent alarm had to be disarmed first; otherwise it sounded at the local precinct, summoning the police instantly.

That night, though, the alarm had been off, and Linden had removed the Judas Hoard's box from the safe. In vivid detail she saw herself carry the scuffed leather box across the room to where The Voice waited. Little more than a shadowy outline, he emanated an aura of demonic glee as he ripped open the top.

But the coins were already missing. Despite the thick fog that still obscured most of Monday night, she recalled The Voice's rage at finding only the suede pouch and the letter. When he ordered her to return the box to the safe, she had complied instantly. Now, remembering her unhesitating obedience, she was surprised that she'd stuck the suede pouch in the pocket of her slacks.

She shivered, as if someone had walked over her grave, and found herself staring at the safe. Guilt enveloped her like a lead cloak, but she knew one thing with absolute certainty. She wasn't the thief: which could only mean that her uncle had removed the coins. No matter how sick he was, there were plenty of hiding places nearby.

Pushing the painting back into position, she lifted the ceramic tile set into the side of the fireplace. It concealed the alarm's control box and was impossible to find by chance. The alarm could only be unlocked by one key—which George kept with him at all times.

How, then, had the key been in The Voice's possession that night?

Frustrated, she flopped into the leather chair behind the desk. Here was another crack in the steel wall surrounding that night, yet she still had no recollection of being at the house or saying her final farewell to her uncle.

Blinking back tears, she moodily contemplated the photographs on the wooden mantel. Who had let The Voice into the house? Through a family insider—or had she? And was she really drugged at the time? Although Linden couldn't deny being in the study, she wasn't about to admit to being a willing participant. The Voice had been firmly in charge, issuing orders that she passively obeyed.

With a body-shaking sigh, she turned her attention to the desk. The top two drawers contained mostly letters of condolence but her luck changed with the last drawer. Clipped together were financial statements for The Lambert Trust that showed each family members' monthly allowance. Gerry Hammond, Linden discovered, stood to lose thousands of dollars by alienating Melanie, which explained why he put up with so much from his wife. But maybe he'd had enough, she mused. Could he be The Voice? The idea made her sit bolt upright. As Melanie's husband, he would know everything as it happened. And from her vague impression of The Voice, he and Gerry shared a similar build.

Slouched in her chair, she spun numerous scenarios until a flutter of movement behind the left drape caught her eye. As the heavy fabric billowed into the room, she frantically tried to account for her presence. Walking around was one thing, sitting at her uncle's desk with a stack of financial statements was quite another.

But a human figure never appeared. It was Garibaldi who eventually trotted into view, checking the room as part of his regular guard dog duties. Seeing Linden, he let out a joyous yelp and threw himself at her, licking her face deliriously.

"That's it, Garibaldi," she told him after a minute. "You've made your point. I know you're glad to see me but enough is enough."

As her words penetrated, his behavior changed dramatically. Biting the hem of her jeans, he tugged the fabric.

Linden gave his muzzle a gentle tap. "I don't know where you learned that but stop it." When he continued to pull, she let out an exasperated, "*No.*"

Obeying instantly, he padded over to the window and then returned to Linden's side with a plaintive whine. As if encouraged by her puzzled expression, he crossed back to the window, gazing at her expectantly.

Comprehension dawned. "You want me to go outside, don't you? Oh no, Garibaldi. You're all grown up now and big enough to stay out all night by yourself."

His next whine completely aroused Linden's curiosity. "Okay, you found something interesting. Let's take a look."

Slipping the statements back into the drawer, she rummaged around for a flashlight and followed him outside. Beneath the star-studded sky, the lawn stretched before her as smooth as black glass. Garibaldi took off like a bullet toward the wood and was pacing up and down in front of the inky barrier by the time Linden strolled over.

Voice firm, she said, "This, my friend, is as far as I go. If you have something to show me, you can bring it out. I'm not going in there under any circumstances whatsoever."

Ignoring her tone, he advanced a few feet then gave her a look of entreaty. She ignored it and they continued to stare at each other until he finally emitted a heartbreaking whine.

"Okay, Gari old buddy, I'll go with you; but no further than the first bend," she warned.

Grinning happily, he charged deeper into the wood and, guided by the thin beam of her flashlight, she followed. The darkness was absolute, all traces of sky hidden by the canopy of leaves, but the sounds of night creatures filled the air. With her limited vision, Linden could do little more than shuffle along the rough path, acutely aware of rustles in the undergrowth. She came upon Garibaldi the hard way, tripping over him as he lay across the path.

Automatically, she extended her arms but instead of crashing into hard earth she found herself entangled with something soft. It also created a curious sound, almost like a human groan.

"This better be good," Linden grumbled.

Picking up her flashlight, she played its beam along the black mound to find Garibaldi had given her something much better than good. It was Alex. Sprawled on his stomach, he appeared to be out cold. Exploring his head with gentle fingers, she encountered a large bump above his left ear.

"Must you be so brutal?" Although weak, Alex's voice dripped sarcasm.

"I was trying to help," she snapped.

"It was more like torture."

"Then maybe you prefer to be left here," she retorted.

"No, don't do that," he said quickly. "I'm sorry. I'm not in the best of moods at the moment."

Slightly mollified, Linden asked, "Can you make it back to the house?"

"If I have all night," he said, struggling to his feet.

Even with his arm draped over Linden's shoulder, he still swayed alarmingly and she clutched his waist more tightly.

"Maybe I should get Brunnings," she said.

"Not necessary. I'll be all right in a minute," he said, his voice tight with pain. "Okay, time to move on. I'm feeling better now."

They stumbled along the narrow path, their progress hampered by unexpected turns and low branches until eventually the trees ended. The house seemed an impossible distance away, and midway across the lawn Alex leaned more and more heavily on Linden. She encouraged him on with a combination of threats and promises, but when they reached the terrace he sagged against the wall outside George's study.

"Rest, please," he panted. "I can't make it any further."

"You can rest later. We're nearly there." Looking at the dog, she said, "Okay, Gari. You did very well but this is where we part company."

With a look of reproach at Linden, Garibaldi slunk toward the end of the terrace and melted into the shadows. Restored by his brief rest, Alex made it across the study and into the entrance hall where Linden reached for the light switch.

With a speed that startled her, he grabbed her hand and whispered, "No lights. We don't want to wake Helena."

"I'm sure she wouldn't mind," Linden groused as they shuffled toward the staircase.

The darkness made everything twice as difficult, and Linden had to haul Alex the last few yards to his room. While she eased the door closed, he collapsed against the wall. The lamp on the night table revealed bedcovers turned invitingly back, but when Linden urged him over to the bed he shook off her arm.

Breathing heavily, he said, "I need a few minutes to recover."

Suddenly Linden noticed rivulets of blood on his left hand. An ugly stain on the sleeve of his navy shirt told the story.

"What happened?" she gasped.

"Someone shot me," he answered wearily.

She reached for the doorknob. "I'm going to call the doctor. It must be looked at."

Belying his exhausted appearance Alex clamped fingers of steel over her wrist.

"I don't want anyone coming here and I don't want to go to the hospital. The last thing we need to do is wake people up."

Who, Linden reasoned, would then want to know why they were up so late in the first place.

While agreeing with his logic, she didn't want to seem too eager. Pretending reluctance, she said, "If you say so."

"We'd also be opening up a can of worms. Gunshot wounds have to be reported. There's a doctor in New York I can trust to say nothing. I'll see him tomorrow."

"Something needs to be done now," she said, unbuttoning his shirt. "Let me look."

His body tensed as her fingers grazed his skin. "You're very good at this, do you make a habit of undressing men?"

"If that's your attitude, do it yourself," she snapped, and stalked toward the bathroom.

Like her room, it was separated from the bedroom by a walk-in closet. Alex had hung up his white shirt along with slacks, jeans and two polo shirts, but most hangers were empty and rattled noisily on the rail.

Rinsing a washcloth in hot water, Linden returned to the bedroom to find Alex slumped on the edge of the bed, shirtless and shoeless. Although determined not to show him any sympathy, Linden's hands were gentle as she dabbed at the area around the damaged flesh. A crust of congealed blood hid the bullet wound, and after a few minutes she held up the washcloth.

"I have to rinse this through again. You might feel better if you lie down."

Alex responded with an indifferent shrug, but when she returned a few minutes later he was stretched out on the bed.

Sitting beside him, she placed a dry towel under his arm and stared at his injury for a second. "I'll be very careful but I'm afraid this will hurt."

Alex stiffened and Linden took a couple of deep breaths before swabbing the wound. Despite a few grimaces, he withstood her ministrations stoically.

"Even though there's a lot of blood, the bullet just grazed your arm," she observed, studying the torn skin with little enthusiasm. "There's some alcohol in my room. I'm going to get it. Don't go away."

"Very funny." His clenched teeth muffled the words.

"You should probably get under the covers now. Try to keep the washcloth in place."

A few minutes later she was back with the alcohol, a vial of codeine pills dated February, and a first aid kit.

"What are you, some sort of hypochondriac?" Alex asked.

"It never hurts to be prepared."

From beneath the sheets, Alex regarded her doubtfully. "Do you know what you're doing?"

"Want me to call in a pro?"

Her reward was a ferocious glare. "Point taken. Since I've survived so far, I guess you're doing something right."

"Such gratitude warms my heart. If it weren't for me, you'd still be lost in the woods. You might have *died* by the time someone found you," she ended, opening a package of cotton.

"Highly unlikely in this heat wave. By the way, what were you doing out and about at this time?"

"Thank Garibaldi. I . . . couldn't sleep and was on the terrace when he spotted me. He clearly wanted me to follow him so I decided to be a pal. I hope you're grateful."

"I'm reserving judgment until you're through."

"I suppose you have a good reason for skulking around in the shrubbery?"

He hesitated for a moment before saying, "I was looking at trees."

About to unscrew the bottle of alcohol, she looked at him in surprise. "In the middle of the night!"

"It was my first opportunity to get away. When you first walked into your bedroom, you seemed very interested in the trees, as if the sight of them jolted your memory."

"That's strange. I don't remember seeing anything unusual. Sorry you had to suffer unnecessarily," she ended, placing the wad of cotton on his wound.

Alex gasped at the bite of alcohol. "That hurts like hell."

"Got to get it clean," Linden commented. "Since talking will take your mind off the pain, why don't you tell me how you ended up like this?"

"Your bedside manner could use some improvement," he grumbled. "Where was I? Oh, right, creeping around the woods. I was trying to figure out what had caught your attention when I realized I wasn't alone. Except the other person wasn't as quiet as me, and he wasn't trying to hide, either."

"Did you see him?"

"No, but he had a strong flashlight and he was lucky enough to get me in a beam of light. That's how I learned the guy had a gun."

"I didn't hear any shots."

"He had a silencer. I dived into the nearest bush and sweated it out while he searched for me."

"What makes you so certain he was male?"

"Good question." Alex frowned in concentration. "I guess it was from all the noise he made. It sounded like there was a lot of meat walking around. Thank God he couldn't find me and finally left. When I was sure he was gone, I had to find my way back to the house. At some point, I tripped over a root in the darkness and used my good hand to protect my arm so my head took the impact."

Linden diverted her attention away from the wound long enough to study his other injury. "Looks all right, no skin broken."

"You enjoy seeing me suffer like this," he complained bitterly. "Since you say conversation's a distraction, how about giving me an account of your evening. What was it like being kissed by Mister Smoothie?"

"If you mean Peter, very pleasant," she lied, smearing antibiotic cream on a piece of gauze.

"Damn it Linden, you hurt me on purpose that time," Alex exploded, as she pressed the gauze against the wound.

"Sorry," she apologized, sounding far from it. "I thought that would make you feel better. Maybe the memory of the pain will teach you not to spy on other people's intimate moments."

"I was not spying, I was working," he corrected her in an indignant voice. "And the quickest way to the wood was through the rose garden. How was I to know Sinclair was about to put the moves on you?"

"All he did was kiss me."

"Oh, yeah," Alex jeered. "From my vantage point it looked to be much more than that. He also seemed to have quite a line of b.s."

"Well, you're wrong on both counts. If you really want to know, he was telling me what he thought of you."

"The guy's crazy. I wouldn't have wasted my breath on talking at a time like that. And what was his opinion of me?"

"Positively underwhelming," Linden answered, wrapping a length of bandage around Alex's arm. "I thought I showed tremendous self-control by not agreeing with him."

Alex smiled. "But I guarantee your silence spoke volumes."

Linden ignored his comment by retreating to the bathroom where she filled a glass with water. Marching back to the bedroom, she handed him the glass and two codeine tablets.

"Here take these. The label says they're for headaches. Very appropriate."

Wincing, Alex swallowed the tablets with some water and collapsed against the pillow. Automatically, Linden fluffed it up and neatened the blankets around him.

"Do I get a goodnight kiss, too?" he grinned.

"Don't be fresh," she retorted, turning out the lamp. "I hope you can sleep. The codeine should take effect soon. Goodnight. I'll see you in the morning."

Alex said nothing until she reached the door. "Never ask me to recommend you for a nursing position, but you did an excellent job just now. Thanks, Linden, I'm really glad you were around."

"You're welcome," she answered lightly, and slipped into the dark corridor without another word.

Safely back in her own room she put on a nightdress and turned out the light. Too wired to sleep, she wandered over to the window, her thoughts on Alex. Although his attitude toward her ranged from outright condemnation to pure dislike, his human side had occasionally shone through. And once or twice he had even been unexpectedly pleasant.

Quite an enigma, she decided. But very attractive.

# Chapter 15

Bright sunshine catapulted Linden awake. Even with her eyes closed, she knew she was in her childhood bedroom.

"I want to talk to you." Helena Lambert's voice jolted Linden into a sitting position. "Alone."

Rubbing her eyes, Linden tried to clear away the last vestiges of sleep. Her aunt, immaculately dressed in a linen shirtwaist the color of her eyes, made Linden feel at a distinct disadvantage.

Helena stared at her niece coldly. "I'm here to ask some questions. I was shocked to learn that you were a thief, but to find out that you ran off the night George died was beyond comprehension. And then to be so cruel as to miss his funeral!" Helena's control dissolved into anger. "How could you not be there, after all he did for you?"

"I was at the cemetery but I wore a disguise. It didn't work too well, though. Alex still recognized me."

"Why on earth did you feel it necessary to go to such lengths?"

"What else was I supposed to do? The media was treating

me like a criminal, and Melanie and Roger certainly didn't make it any easier. I still haven't heard from either of them."

Helena's hostility fizzled into bewilderment. "I can't even pretend to understand your motives, what you're involved in. If you're so desperate for money, all you had to do was ask."

"I don't *have* any money problems and I *didn't* steal the Judas Hoard. Quite the opposite. Uncle George wanted me to be its guardian, like he was, and I was honored to be chosen. It was the only way I could pay him back."

"You have a strange way of showing it."

Even though Helena sounded unforgiving, Linden believed that her aunt still felt a trace of affection for her.

"I just wish there was some way I could make everything up to you."

"I hired Alex for several reasons, but his main job was to track you down." For the first time Helena allowed her pain to show. "I needed to know what made you behave in such a heartless fashion; find out what I'd done to deserve such punishment."

To Linden, it seemed that her aunt was giving her the chance to explain. And she hoped that by being honest, she would regain Helena's love and trust. The first step would be to reveal her experience in the study the night of George's death. Although Linden wasn't happy to admit her participation, she could no longer deny it. Sliding out of bed, she paced the floor.

"I haven't been entirely honest," she began. "I was in Uncle George's study on the night . . . Monday night. I remember being there."

Helena's face paled with shock. "You mean you *did* steal the Judas Hoard?"

Shaking her head, Linden said, "It was already gone. Last night, long after everyone was in bed, I went downstairs. It was like watching a horror movie. I knew something awful was about to happen the second I entered the study. The scary part was hearing someone tell me to take the Judas Hoard out of the safe."

"Who?" Helena interrupted.

"I haven't a clue, but I'm almost positive it was a man. He's phoned me several times so I call him The Voice."

"Does Alex know about this man?" Helena demanded. "Do the police? Or is this Voice person just a figment of your imagination?"

"He's very real," Linden answered. "In addition to calling, he even searched my apartment. Alex and the police know all about him."

"What did this *Voice* do when you took the coins out of the safe?"

"Nothing. The box they were stored in was empty."

"Why should I believe you?" Helena demanded. "Just a few hours ago you said you couldn't remember anything about Monday."

"I'm starting to have flashbacks. Although they're disjointed and don't last long, I *do* remember how livid the Voice was when he opened the box and found the coins were missing."

Visibly overwhelmed, Helena sank onto the window seat. "This is just too much. Why pick on you?"

"That's what I need to find out," Linden answered, "and to do that I have to go back to New York."

Helena's grief was almost tangible, but when she spoke her words were obviously meant to comfort Linden. "I should have realized there was a reason for your callousness, but when I didn't hear from you, what was I supposed to think?"

Linden touched her aunt's arm. "At least you know the truth now."

After a couple of deep breaths, Helena squeezed Linden's

hand and forced a smile that only emphasized her sadness. "I need to talk to Alex. Get his input. Now that I think of it, I haven't seen him all morning."

Linden glanced at the clock on her night table. "I don't believe how late it is! It's almost lunchtime."

About to leave the room, Helena turned to face Linden. "If you ever need help, go to Alex. No one else, just him. He's far enough removed from all of us to be objective. I trust him implicitly. You can, too."

"What makes him so special?"

Surprised, Helena replied, "He's Tom Blair's nephew. Didn't you know?"

Linden shrugged. "I just find it very convenient."

"I wanted someone immediately and he came highly recommended. The media was hounding us and showing no respect for our privacy. Not only was Alex qualified, he could start right away." Helena's eyes softened. "I realize you met under difficult conditions, but there's no need to be concerned, he's entirely dependable."

Linden stared at the closed door thoughtfully. Her aunt's faith in Alex was reassuring and his respect for Helena was obvious. Linden could understand why Alex believed she stole the Judas Hoard—even if the evidence was entirely circumstantial. Having reached that conclusion, some of Linden's antipathy faded, making her resolve to be nicer in the future.

Her conscience pounced on the moment of weakness, demanding that she check up on him. Although she suspected he was fine, she quickly pulled on jeans and a tee-shirt and headed down the deserted hallway. When her tap on his door went unanswered, she entered the room anyway to find Alex lying on his back. He was fast asleep, the covers pushed down to his waist to reveal his well-muscled arms and washboard abs. Admiring them, Linden wished his personality matched his great body.

Annoyed by the direction of her thoughts, she poked his good arm. "Wake up."

Instantly alert, he jerked upright but fell back against the pillow at the sight of her.

"If it isn't my little tormentor of last night." His grin was reassuringly normal. "Come to hurt me some more?"

"I think you've suffered enough," she teased. "I just saw Aunt Heni and she mentioned that she hadn't seen you. Since lunch is less than an hour away, I decided to check up on you. If she learns you've been shot, she'll call the doctor no matter what you say. How's the arm?"

He grimaced. "I know it's there, but fortunately I'm right-handed so getting dressed shouldn't be too difficult."

"I was going to offer to shave you."

"My dear Linden, I wouldn't allow you anywhere near me with a loaded razor," he responded genially.

"Considering your condition earlier, you've made a remarkable recovery. I guess you slept well."

"Like a rock. The tablets were incredible." His eyes hinted at respect. "Thanks for all your help."

"Anytime, but I'd prefer that you stay out of trouble. See you at lunch," she said and hurried back to her room.

The cloudless sky promised another hot day, and after a rapid shower she inspected her closet. Several sun dresses took up space near the end of the rail, and selecting one in lavender cotton, she slipped into it.

Despite his injury, Alex beat her downstairs. When she walked into the library, she found him in deep conversation with her aunt, a white shirt concealing his bandage. At a sign from Helena, he stopped speaking.

After a brief silence Helena produced a bright smile. "Just

in time for lunch. It's such a lovely day I thought we'd eat out on the terrace. Alex and I were just saying how warm it's been lately."

"A typical early heat wave," Linden agreed, knowing full well that the weather was the last thing on their minds.

Helena seemed determined to be cheerful as she led the way outside. Encouraged by Alex's friendly manner, Linden was less defensive and the three of them chatted about a variety of mundane matters over lunch. For the first time in days, she felt almost hopeful.

Eager to return to New York, Linden suggested leaving shortly after lunch to which Alex readily agreed. Helena walked them out to his car where she startled Linden with a quick hug and urged them to come back soon. Settling into the passenger seat, Linden reflected that the trip had one positive aspect: her relationship with Helena seemed to be on the mend.

As they approached the expressway, Alex pulled into a gas station.

"We need gas," he announced

While he filled the tank, Linden left her seat and hurried to the driver's side of the car. When she slid behind the steering wheel, Alex looked at her in obvious annoyance.

"You can't drive with that bullet wound," she told him. "In an hour you'll be in agony."

For a second he looked ready to argue but then he gave a rueful smile. "You're right. Just wanted to prove how macho I am by driving."

Watching him cradle his left arm with his right hand as he gingerly sat in the passenger seat, Linden observed, "Looks like you're already having a problem."

"Yeah, it's kind of painful," he admitted. "I called my doctor friend earlier. Even though it's Sunday, he'll meet us in his office."

"Surely you're big enough to go alone. You don't need me to hold your hand."

"It's not for me, you're the one I'm worried about," Alex retorted. "I want to be there when you open that door. What if The Voice is waiting for you? Feel like handling him by yourself?"

Linden's expression hardened. "Absolutely. He won't know what hit him." After a brief pause, she said, "I'm sorry. Maybe you have a point. Thanks for the offer."

"You're welcome," Alex smiled, and stared out of the window. "Helena told me about your little chat earlier. She said you remember being in the study on Monday night."

Linden sighed. "Just when I thought things were starting to get better."

"Like to repeat the conversation?" he asked. "Don't fight me, Linden. By helping me, you help your aunt, too."

"I've already reached that conclusion." She was silent for a moment, organizing her thoughts. "I kind of skirted the truth last night. I was searching my uncle's study, not out for a walk when Garibaldi found me. He almost gave me a heart attack, coming through the curtains the way he did. And I was still in shock from finding myself about to open the wall safe. As I told Aunt Heni, it was like watching a movie—a zombie movie—where I was just mindlessly following orders. There's no way to prove it, but if it's a true memory, someone was telling me what to do."

Alex tapped his thumb against his teeth. "It sort of ties in with everything you've said all along. What about the alarm?"

"Already off."

"Which means either you or The Voice took the key," Alex surmised.

"It had to be The Voice, but how? Uncle George never let that key out of his sight. He was obsessed with the Hoard's safety."

"Why were the coins at the house and not in the bank?"

Linden's eyes filled with tears. "He knew he didn't have much time left and he'd insisted on having them brought home. He wanted the coins nearby so he could see them whenever he wished." Blinking rapidly, her grip tightened on the wheel. "And I know I'd never take the key from him, even under duress."

"I agree with you." Alex's tone left no room for doubt. "I've been very wrong about you. You're smart, compassionate and caring. You loved your uncle, everyone said so, which is why your disappearance came as such a shock. It was totally out of character."

"Then how could people be so quick to brand me as a thief?"

"Unfortunately it's human nature." Alex gazed out of the window again. "I only had time to call a few of your friends before the funeral. Even though every single one refused to believe you were guilty, your family was less charitable."

Flashing him an angry look, Linden snapped, "So you went with them."

Alex gave a self-deprecating laugh. "I should have known better. You spent far more time in Radford than Melanie or Roger."

"It didn't stop you from all but accusing me of stealing the Judas Hoard," Linden retorted.

"My pool of suspects was—and still is—very limited. I made a mistake, okay? I'm sorry." After a moment's hesitation, he added, "Sometimes it's difficult to remain detached. Years ago, my mother's brother went into partnership with a friend in Ft. Lauderdale. They bought a yacht that tourists could charter for trips to the Florida Keys and the Bahamas. Nothing fancy, but it was a profitable little business. One day my uncle woke up to find his partner had taken off with the yacht, cleaned out the business checking account, and left him with a ton of debts."

"Did your uncle take the guy to court?"

"Sure, and got a judgment against him. But by then both he and the money were on an island where no one could touch either him or his offshore bank account. My uncle finally paid off the debts and now works for a company doing what he used to do for himself."

Face thoughtful, Linden said, "You saw me as ripping off my family, just as that guy ripped of your uncle."

"I saw similarities and let them affect my objectivity. Now I know better."

Linden drove in silence for a minute while she mulled over Alex's admission. It certainly explained his hostility, made him seem more human.

"Your uncle caught a bad break."

"And the fallout didn't stop with his family. My mother was devastated." Alex's voice turned harsh. "No one should get away with pulling shit like that."

"You're right," said Linden softly. "Thanks for sharing."

With the thickening traffic demanding Linden's total attention, Alex switched on the radio, scanning the stations until he found a baseball game. By the time they reached their destination, it was almost five o'clock and Boston had a four-run lead over the Yankees. Linden stopped the car to let Alex get out and drove off in search of a parking spot.

Ten fruitless minutes later, she pulled into a garage and hurried over to the doctor's Park Avenue office. As she walked into the waiting room, Alex entered through another door accompanied by a scarecrow of a man whose unruly dark hair brushed the collar of his polo shirt.

Alex greeted her with a smile. "Hi, Linden, meet Vic Greene. We were roommates in college. Back then, all he could cure were hangovers."

"They're still my specialty," laughed Vic, his brown eyes

twinkling behind thick glasses. "You did a good job on my buddy."

"She hurt me," Alex complained.

Vic displayed little sympathy. "She also stopped any infection. I gave him a tetanus shot and some antibiotics."

"There won't be any permanent damage?" Linden asked.

"Nah. It's only a flesh wound, but keep the dressing on for a few days, Alex. You'll know if it's not healing properly, and let's hope the shooter doesn't try again. Next time you may not be so lucky."

Since Linden's apartment building was less than ten blocks away, they strolled over, stopping at a supermarket for some sorely-needed staples. To her relief, photographers no longer crowded the sidewalk in front of her building and the doorman welcomed them cheerfully.

Once outside her apartment, Alex seized her keyring and unlocked the door. Nothing unusual awaited them, and Linden followed him as he strode through the various rooms. The few signs of untidiness were hers and even the answering machine was blank.

As they left her office, Alex asked, "Notice anything unusual?"

"Nothing. No one's been here."

"In that case I'll leave you," he said, heading for the front door. "Thanks for looking after me so well, and for getting me back to the city safely."

"You're welcome. I was concerned about my own neck, too," she joked, although his warm tone ignited the now-familiar glow around her middle.

Alex's gaze dropped to her lips, and for a moment the air between them sizzled before he stumbled backwards as if pushed by an invisible hand.

Grabbing the doorknob, he said, "Call if you need me, no matter how trivial. I'll check in first thing tomorrow."

Linden could only look at him in stunned silence. The man was impossible. In the blink of an eye he could turn from a regular guy into robo man. Well, she had enough problems without having to add therapist to the mix.

"If anything happens, I'll be just fine by myself," she informed him icily and slammed the door.

# Chapter
# 16

Carrying a generous glass of Chardonnay to her bedroom, Linden flopped into the armchair by the window and switched on the TV. A news program came on, but too tired to concentrate, she dozed off until a loud buzz jerked her awake. As she shook her head to clear the cobwebs, she noticed her nap had lasted barely five minutes. When she answered the intercom, the doorman told her that she had a delivery of flowers.

"The order slip says they're from Mrs. Helena Lambert," he continued. "Okay for the messenger to come up?"

Linden smiled with pleasure. "Sure. Thanks, Frank."

Rummaging through her purse for a tip, she opened the front door. The messenger was halfway down the hallway, his head and upper body almost hidden behind a huge bouquet of flowers. Absently, she registered the canvas satchel slung over one of his oversized shoulders.

"Down here," she called.

Instead of giving her the flowers, he forced his way into the foyer, hooking his foot around the door before she had time to react. His lips curled into a cruel smile as he dropped the flowers onto the floor.

Treading on them, he said, "Best hundred bucks I ever spent."

Although the digitally-altered voice was instantly familiar, Linden didn't recognize the person, especially with oversized sunglasses covering his eyes. A Mets baseball hat hid much of his face while a matching Mets jacket clung to his bulky torso.

For a moment, she could only stare at the circular voice changer held against his throat by a narrow leather band. Her brain finally caught up with his words, galvanizing her into action, but she was too late. As she reached for the door knob, The Voice pulled a gun from his jacket and she froze, mesmerized by the glove protecting his hand. Latex gloves were never a good sign.

"Not so fast," he said, dragging her into the living room.

Shoving her onto the sofa, he stuffed the gun back into his jacket and put the satchel on the coffee table. Almost incoherent with rage, Linden sprang to her feet.

"Who the hell *are* you? What have I ever done to you?"

The Voice yanked her back onto the sofa.

"It's not what you've done. It's what you have," he answered. "I know you have the Judas Hoard and you're going to tell me where it is."

"I don't have it," Linden yelled.

"Don't give me that crap. You and your uncle were in this together. You know exactly where the coins are."

Although she couldn't see his eyes, Linden knew he was watching her as he reached into his satchel. Taking out a syringe and a vial of clear liquid, he put them on the coffee table.

"And this time you're getting double dose of sodium pentothal."

Intent on ripping off the syringe's plastic wrapper, The Voice appeared not to notice that Linden stood up. She chanced taking a stealthy step backward. She had remembered that her front door was unlocked and she was hoping to reach it before he could retrieve his gun. Once outside, she figured he wouldn't risk shooting her in the public hallway. It wasn't much of a plan, but it was all she had.

With her eyes fixed on The Voice, Linden waited until both his hands were occupied. The moment came when he started to fill the syringe with the pentothal, and Linden didn't waste a second. Sprinting to the foyer, she grabbed the knob but The Voice was beside her before she could open the door.

"Seems like you forgot something," he snarled, jabbing his gun into her side.

Ignoring the pain, Linden tried to struggle free. "Pumping me full of drugs again is useless. It didn't work then and it won't work now. This is my home and there are people around to help me."

The Voice ground his gun deeper into her ribs. "Not when they see this."

A loud buzz ended the taut silence but Linden made no move to answer the intercom. Heart pounding with fear, she stared at the gun until the buzzer sounded again, longer and more insistent.

Mouth painfully dry, she said, "I have to answer it. Frank knows I'm home. He probably noticed you haven't left yet."

"Find out what he wants," The Voice raged.

When she spoke into the intercom, she sounded almost normal. "Yes?"

"Hi, Mr. Blair's on his way up," the doorman announced.

The Voice quivered with fury. "What the hell's going on?"

"I've no idea."

Hauling Linden into the living room, The Voice rammed everything into his satchel. "When Blair gets here, let him in."

"What are you going to do?"

"Make sure he remembers my visit," he snapped.

Dragging Linden back to the foyer, The Voice stood behind the door while pressing his gun into Linden's side. Opening the door, she forced a smile as Alex barreled down the hallway with the air of someone ready to fight.

"You never told me where you parked the car," he barked. "And you didn't give me my car keys."

Hoping to appear nonchalant even with her brain working in overdrive, she said, "It's in a garage just a few blocks from here."

At her lack of anger, some of Alex's belligerence disappeared. "I need the ticket so I can take it out. There's plenty of street parking now."

"That's a good idea in case an emergency comes up."

"Hopefully there won't be any, now that you're back." Alex sounded almost friendly.

"Emergencies happen when you least expect them."

"Yeah, don't I know it," he said, shooting her a quizzical look. "You okay?"

The gun ground against her ribs. "Fine. After all I've been through, I guess I'm just hung up on emergencies at the moment."

Expression suddenly wary, Alex walked into the foyer and turned his head directly into the path of The Voice's raised gun. Although he reached for it, he was a second too slow, and the butt slammed into his skull with a sickening thud. Linden automatically tried to catch him, but she was off balance and they both crashed to the floor.

Winded, she lay pinned beneath Alex, dimly aware that The Voice was escaping. Pushing Alex off her, she struggled to her feet only to find a deserted hallway and the door to the nearby stairwell wide open. Rushing toward it, she heard The Voice bolting down the cement stairs, his footsteps growing fainter by the second.

Her immediate impulse was to call the doorman until she remembered the gun. Nor was there any guarantee that The Voice would still be in messenger gear when he reached the lobby. Frustrated, she returned to her apartment just as the door opposite opened. Dressed in a classic Chanel suit, a frail old woman peered out, but her eyes sparkled as brightly as the huge diamonds dangling from her ears.

"I heard a lot of noise. Are you all right, Linden?"

"No problem, two of my boyfriends turned up at the same time," Linden lied glibly. "There were some hard feelings."

A smile lit her neighbor's too-smooth face as she stared at Alex sprawled on the floor. "Looks like he came off worse."

"Nothing serious," Linden assured her with a conviction she was far from feeling.

"Hope he thinks it's worth it," the older woman continued. "And he's your favorite."

Linden tugged Alex's feet out of the way of the door. "Yes, he is. Thanks for your concern."

Slamming the door shut, Linden raced to the kitchen and jammed a handful of ice cubes into a dish towel. Back at Alex's side, she pressed the ice against the swiftly-growing bump on his head and tried to remain calm. Several long minutes passed before his eyelids fluttered open.

"This is getting to be a habit," he said with a feeble smile.

Linden let out a sigh of relief. "How do you feel?"

"Like I was run over by a Mack truck. What happened?"

"You met The Voice. He conned the doorman into thinking he was a messenger."

Alex struggled to sit up. "Let's see if I can make it to the living room."

Clutching Linden for support, he staggered across the room and collapsed onto the sofa. Perched on the arm, Linden inspected his wound before applying the compress again.

"You're not bleeding but maybe I should call Vic."

"Don't bother. I've had worse and it doesn't feel like concussion. No double vision, dizziness or nausea," he recited, moving the ice pack around. "I just feel like my head's about to fall off."

"I'll check my supply of painkillers," Linden said.

Although she only had aspirin, she took him the bottle and a glass of water. Shaking out three tablets, she said, "This is the best I can offer. You can probably take more than the suggested dose without risking permanent damage."

Carefully she raised his shoulders and held the glass while he swallowed the tablets. With a grimace, he fell back on the sofa, pressing the ice pack to his head. Linden pressed gentle fingers against his cheek, finding the skin above his light stubble surprisingly soft.

"Poor Alex, you've really taken some hits lately."

"All in a day's work," he replied with a glimmer of humor.

"I hope I can make it up to you some day."

For a second heat replaced the pain in his eyes. "I'm sure we'll find a way."

Desire shot through Linden like an electrical charge and she whipped her hand away from his face. This wasn't supposed to happen. Finding the Judas Hoard was her only goal. She didn't want to be involved with anyone—especially Alex, with his Jekyll and Hyde personality. But she remained by his side until he fell asleep. For a second, Linden's eyes lingered on the coffee table while she tried to remember if The Voice had touched it. Not that it would matter. He'd been wearing latex gloves.

Going to the foyer, she picked up the flowers and viciously shoved them in the garbage where the petals scattered like slivers of dried paint. Twenty minutes later, over salad and microwaved lasagna, she wrote down every detail about The Voice's visit. Even though she had now met him, he remained as unfamiliar as ever.

# Chapter
# 17

An intruder was inside her apartment.

Alerted by her subconscious, Linden shot upright, her heart almost pounding out of her chest. Several moments passed before she recalled the previous night. As the aroma of coffee drifted into the bedroom, she realized Alex had made another of his miraculous recoveries.

After a quick shower she threw on shorts and a tee-shirt and headed for the kitchen. Alex was seated at the counter, munching on a slice of toast. Despite looking rumpled and in need of a shave, his broad smile dispelled any worries about permanent injury.

"I see you've made yourself at home," she chuckled. "How are you feeling?"

"Much better. I just took another two aspirins, which should get me back to normal in a few minutes."

Coffee mug in hand, Linden sat on the adjacent stool. "I'm so sorry about last night. The word emergency was supposed to clue you in."

"My fault for being too dumb to pick it up," he joked. "What happened?"

"Frank buzzed me to ask if it was okay for a messenger to bring up flowers from Mrs. Helena Lambert. Turned out the delivery guy was none other than The Voice. He'd bought a huge bouquet and was inside my apartment with the door closed before I realized who he was."

Taking a sip of coffee, Alex observed, "That might be the oldest trick in the book but it still works. What did he want?"

"The Judas Hoard."

"Figures. Would you recognize him again?"

Linden stared into her coffee, trying to conjure up the man's face. "Probably not. He wore sunglasses and a baseball hat, and looked like a linebacker. When he had me trapped near the door, though, his jacket felt squishy."

"As if padded?"

"That's right! Now I think about it, his shoulders seemed too outsized."

"Height?"

Face thoughtful, Linden said, "Taller than you, but that could have been an illusion as well. He was wearing cowboy boots with a heel."

"And his voice?"

"He had a synthesizer around his neck." Linden let out a frustrated sigh. "I know this isn't very helpful but it all happened so quickly. He also had a gun."

"Always remember one of life's golden rules," smiled Alex. "Never argue with someone who has a gun."

"I still shouldn't have let him get away," she groused.

Alex patted her hand. "What were you supposed to do, tackle him? Even without artificial aids, he sounds like a big guy. Could have turned very ugly if Frank had tried to stop him, especially since he was armed. Don't worry, we haven't seen the last of him."

"What makes you so certain?"

"After all he's been through, he isn't going to give up so easily."

"He implied my uncle and I were in cahoots."

"More like he's convinced of it," replied Alex. "And in case you do know the Hoard's location, he won't want to be too far away."

"I hate to be morbid but why didn't he just shoot you?" asked Linden.

"Even if no one heard shots, dead bodies don't remain undiscovered in luxury apartments for long. The last thing he wants to do is attract attention."

"My neighbor across the hall heard enough as it was. She also saw you lying on my foyer floor, out cold. Thinks you did it for love." Linden couldn't believe what she'd just said and abruptly changed the subject. "Do you have any plans for today?"

"Once I've finished my coffee, I'm off to the garage to get my trusty overnight bag from my car, then it's straight back here for a shower and a shave. That will do more for me than all your aspirins. What about you?"

"Start getting my life back in order. My number one priority is to have new locks installed, guaranteed pick proof. I don't want The Voice in here again, poking around when I'm away—or coming inside when I'm here. Next is a call to Moira, last Tuesday's breakfast date. Hopefully, she still wants to see my sketches for her office space."

Alex's face lost its humor. "While I'm gone, you're not to let anyone in here. It doesn't matter who's outside or what the story is. No one comes through that door unless it's me. Promise."

Although tempted to argue, Linden's common sense conceded he had a point. "Okay. I promise."

"Good," he said, an easy smile crinkling the corners of his eyes.

Watching him cross the kitchen to put his plate and mug in the sink, Linden kept a firm hold on her emotions. For all his apparent friendliness, she knew how quickly he could switch into hired assassin mode. Which was too bad, she thought, because life was much simpler with him on her side.

Alex was back in less than fifteen minutes, returning in time to catch her on the phone with the locksmith. Hanging up, she told him the man promised to be over within the hour and led the way to the guest bathroom.

As she straightened perfectly-aligned towels, he followed her inside, fumbling with his shirt buttons. Instinctively she tried to help him, but the sight of a mat of silky hair sent the blood racing through her veins. Looking up into Alex's face, his expression showed that he was equally affected. The air crackled with sexual tension and he moved a step closer.

"With all my injuries, I'm going to need help in the shower," he said in a husky voice.

Self-control hanging by a thread, Linden dropped her hands, her fists curling into tight balls. "I'm sure you can manage by yourself."

"Your fault if I get hurt," Alex grinned, as he shrugged off his shirt.

Backing out of the bathroom, she escaped to her office, but her imagination continued to taunt her with visions of Alex in the shower, rivulets of water flashing like mercury as they rolled down his muscled chest. Stomping over to the door, she slammed it shut to muffle the sound of his presence. This wasn't the time to be distracted by a man. Even one as attractive as Alex.

Half an hour later he came into her office. The edge of a bandage peeked from beneath the sleeve of his polo shirt, but it was the snug fit of his blue jeans that held Linden's attention. The urge to mold herself against his lean body almost overwhelmed her until the insistent buzz of the intercom sent her reeling back to reality. Watching her rush to answer it, Alex quirked an eyebrow as if aware of her thoughts.

The locksmith, she discovered, was on his way up. Leaving Alex to handle him, she again sought refuge in her office. The Voice had left her desk looking like a war zone, and she set about tidying it up with far more concentration than necessary.

By the time the new pick proof locks were installed, Linden's desk was back to its customary neatness and she had scheduled a three o'clock meeting with Moira. Alex not only insisted on accompanying her to Moira's downtown office, but waited patiently in the reception area for two hours.

Back home again, Linden retreated to her office where she spent an hour making business calls and updating her computer files. Feeling more in control of her life, she went in search of Alex who was in the living room hunched over his laptop.

"Don't know about you, but I'm calling it a day," she announced.

Logging off his computer, he stretched luxuriously. "Great idea. I've been reviewing my notes but no smoking gun so far. I could use a break to clear my head. Let's grab some dinner. My treat."

"I really should call Julia or Marco or other friends," she said with little enthusiasm. "The conversation will revolve around my stint as America's Most Wanted, though, and I'm really not in the mood for it tonight."

"As least you won't have to do that with me."

She was also enjoying his company more and more. Dinner with him would be no great hardship.

"Okay. Give me ten minutes to freshen up."

At Linden's suggestion, they went to a nearby restaurant where the owner greeted her as an old friend. He seated them at a corner table in the still-quiet dining room and they studied the menu while waiting for their bottle of Chardonnay to be brought over. The waiter quickly appeared with the wine and as soon as their glasses were filled, they gave their orders.

After an appreciative swallow, Alex asked, "Get much accomplished today?"

"Yes. Moira helped. I really didn't want to lose her as a client. She gives me great assignments and I'm not in any position to turn work down."

"You call yourself a space designer. Sounds like you're with NASA."

"Not quite," Linden laughed. "My clients hire me to figure out the best use of commercial and exhibition space."

"And that's where your involvement with the Judas Hoard fits in?"

"Exactly. The Hoard needs a visual display to tell its story. There are so many parts to it: Judas becoming a disciple; his betrayal of Christ in the Garden of Gethsemane; and the full circle of the coins' journey from biblical Palestine to twentieth-century Israel. The last part would explain how Uncle George came to own the Hoard. We thought we had all the time in the world, but then he fell ill and it became our Number One priority."

"Is that why you were spending so much time in Radford?" Alex asked.

Linden nodded. "I remember . . ." She paused, her face suddenly fearful as a suppressed memory struggled free.

\* \* \*

So clear it could be happening in real time, she saw herself in her uncle's sickroom. Both George and Matt, the night nurse, appeared to be asleep. But she knew that couldn't be right. Matt would never doze off while on duty.

Pain shot through Linden's body as someone shoved her against the wall. Even though she just wanted to curl up in a ball and sleep, she seemed to be locked in an upright position. Through slitted eyes, she watched a shadowy figure walk over to the bed where her uncle lolled against a pile of pillows. For an instant the light from the floor lamp revealed the man clearly, but shaggy hair and heavy-framed glasses concealed much of his face. The man pulled the gold key chain back over George's head and roughly repositioned the cannulas and tubing under his nose. Despite her dulled senses, Linden suddenly understood the reason for the callous treatment. Her uncle no longer struggled to breathe.

"He's dead, isn't he?" Her head pounded from the effort of talking. "You murdered my uncle."

In three quick strides, the man crossed the room and hissed, "Everyone knows he was about to go any minute. He went just after I got here."

With his arm tightly around Linden's shoulders, the man pushed her from the room and to the front door. Although she could barely function, she managed to reset the house's alarm system. He then dragged her down the driveway, seething with impatience while she tried to enter the code to disarm the small gate. When she finally succeeded, the man yanked her into Laurel Court where her BMW was parked on the grass verge. Opening the passenger door, he forced her inside.

Grateful to sit down, she slumped into the seat but alarm bells shrilled when he loomed over her. Although she struggled to escape, he pinned her down while aiming an aerosol can at her face.

With an effort, she whispered, "Get away from me."

Instead, he pressed the top of the can.

"That will keep you quiet," he said, as she inhaled the fine mist. "The other dose will wear off soon and I don't need any more problems."

Sliding behind the wheel, the man eased the car off the grass and headed for the highway. For Linden, trapped on the edge of sleep, the journey was little more than a blur of lights that flickered like fireflies. When the car finally stopped, she forced herself to concentrate but her surroundings were as fuzzy as an out-of-focus photograph. It took less than a minute for the man to open the passenger door and haul Linden from the passenger seat.

"This is where we get out," he said.

"Where are we?" she mumbled, even though forming words made her skull feel like it was about to explode.

"Never mind. Just walk."

A paved path took them to a two-story house with a white front door. Unlocking it, the man steered her through the darkness to a room in the rear. Her legs brushed against a piece of furniture, and collapsing onto it, she identified its softness as a sofa. Dim light from a floor lamp abruptly lit up the room, laser bright to her drug-addled brain,

After checking that the drapes were tightly closed, the man turned his attention to the leather attaché case on the coffee table. Strapped to the inside stood a neat row of vials, and selecting one, he put it on the table. Next, he took out a hypodermic needle and ripped off the plastic wrapper.

"First, you're going to tell me where the coins are," he said, "then I'll take care of tonight's memory. Can't have you telling the world what happened here."

Icy fingers of fear slithered up Linden's spine as she watched him fill the needle, but she was unable to move, a captive of the substance already in her system. With ruthless efficiency, the man plunged the needle into her arm. A wave of heat surged up to her shoulder like wild fire.

"Hurts," she groaned.

"Effective," he responded.

Waves of darkness enveloped Linden, a mind-numbing paralysis that made coherent thought impossible.

"Tell me what you did with the coins," the man coaxed, his tone now gentle. "Where's the Judas Hoard?"

Despite her efforts to fight the whirling blackness, she felt herself sucked ever deeper into the abyss, aware only of the whispery voice that oozed into her mind like primeval slime.

"Where's the Hoard? The Judas Hoard?"

\* \* \*

"Linden, come back," a different voice ordered.

Forcing her eyes open, Linden crashed back into the present.

Eyes concerned, Alex remained silent as she grabbed her wine glass and took a long swallow. White-knuckled, she said, "Well, that has to help my case for being abducted."

"Remember anything about the man?"

Linden's gaze dropped to the table where Alex's elbows formed dents in the white cloth. "His hair was dark but the ones on his arms were light."

"Sounds like he was wearing a wig. What else?"

"He had a thin scar on the inside of his left arm. It was about two inches long and started just above his wrist."

"Very good," smiled Alex, topping up their glasses. "All we have to do is ask every guy with blond or brown hair to show us his left arm."

After another sip of wine, Linden said, "Matt was so conscientious, I can't imagine him falling asleep voluntarily."

"Probably drugged with whatever The Voice used on

you. Sounds like ketamine or something similar, which leaves victims with no idea of how long they've been out."

"Matt could have been asleep for several hours and not realized it," Linden observed.

Alex stared into his wine glass as if it were a crystal ball. "I think you were targeted the minute you entered Laurel Court and The Voice had you unconscious almost immediately. Once you were safely out, he restarted your car and drove you to a secluded place to wait until Brunnings and his wife were asleep. Then he returned to Laurel Court and took you into the house."

"Even barely awake, I was still able to work the codes," Linden added.

"Yet despite all that planning, he still doesn't have the Judas Hoard," Alex said grimly, "which is going to make him even more determined to get it."

"And all the more dangerous."

# Chapter 18

Although the day's freneticism had subsided when they left the restaurant, the heat lingered as oppressive as a rain forest. About to say goodbye to Alex, Linden felt a distinct pang of regret. While she valued his input, she enjoyed being with him even more.

"Thanks for dinner," she said with false cheerfulness. "I guess I'll see you tomorrow."

"Whoa. Don't expect to get rid of me so fast. Your aunt hired me as your bodyguard, remember? I'm moving in with you."

Linden hid her pleasure behind tough words. "Good. Now if The Voice decides to try for a repeat performance, you can watch while I settle a few scores."

They strolled back to Linden's apartment, chatting easily as twilight deepened into night. The office sofa was quickly transformed into a bed, and leaving Alex to sort out the sheets and pillows, she retreated to her bedroom.

Even though she was exhausted, Linden couldn't sleep. Lying in her canopied bed, she stared into the darkness, haunted by the hours-long gap in her life. No matter how hard she tried to remember Monday's visit to Laurel Court, the final goodbye to her uncle, all she could recall was her afternoon run in Central Park. Despite the flashbacks, too much still remained buried in her mind.

Around one o'clock, she gave up trying to sleep. Taking a glass of water into the living room, she stood by the window and stared out. The occasional flicker from a TV or the headlights from a passing cab proved she wasn't the only person up. With few sounds to disturb the silence, the whisper of footsteps made her spin around in alarm.

"It's me."

Alex's disembodied voice floated across the darkened room.

"You can't you sleep either?"

"Too wired," he said, joining her by the window. "A lot's happened recently."

Resting her glass on the windowsill, she pushed it in aimless circles.

"I let The Voice kill my uncle," she eventually said.

"You were too drugged to realize what was happening."

Linden shook her head. "It's no excuse. Uncle George was like a father to me, always there when I needed him. He loved me like a daughter. And I repaid him by deserting him when it counted. Never got to say goodbye."

"Stop being so hard on yourself," Alex said. "At the time, you were as helpless as he was."

"I should have made more of an effort. It's as if he meant nothing to me. How will I ever forgive myself?"

As the full impact of her uncle's death sank in, great sobs racked her body and she wept for her loss. Alex pulled her to him and she cried out her pain against his chest. Soothed by his closeness, she dried her face on his tee-shirt, slowly becoming aware of his hands on her gossamer-thin nightdress.

Although his feather light touch was meant to comfort, the erotic overtones were impossible to ignore. Almost of their own volition, her arms snaked around his neck. Alex sought her lips, but as much as she welcomed the feel of his body against hers she forced herself to pull away. It was too soon. Too fast. Her customary caution wouldn't let her give into what her body craved.

"Sorry about that," she said, voice overly loud. "I'm much better. Thanks for being so understanding."

Alex took a deep breath. "Anytime."

"I'm sure I won't have any problems sleeping now," she added briskly, backing away from him.

They walked in silence to her bedroom door where Alex said, "Sleep well. If you need me for anything, just call out."

Automatically, she turned to thank him, but the words stayed unspoken when she saw his face. The fire in his eyes reflected her own hunger and she flew into his arms. As they kissed with almost bruising force, all her recent loneliness and heartache receded.

The heat consuming them demanded more, and unlocking their lips for an instant, Linden stripped off her nightdress while Alex tore at his shorts and tee-shirt. When he claimed her mouth again, his naked flesh seared hers, igniting a flame that ended any attempt at self-control. The need to touch each other—be a part of each other—was all that mattered and they fell onto the bed. Unexpectedly, Linden stiffened in Alex's arms.

"I didn't expect this to happen so quickly."

"I didn't expect it to take so long," he said hoarsely.

Reaching for his tee-shirt, he retrieved a small packet from the pocket and pushed her back against the sheets. "I hoped we'd end up this way and came prepared."

Eager to taste and explore every inch of her, his mouth

again descended onto hers and they were consumed by an ocean of fire and pleasure. As their bodies fused into one, everything except the two of them ceased to exist.

\* \* \*

The clock on the bedside table read eleven o'clock when Linden finally opened her eyes. A shaft of sunshine glowed on the pillow next to Alex's head and she snuggled up to him, basking in her good fortune. During their passion-filled night he had both told and shown her how deeply he cared.

"Will I always wake up to find you beside me?" he smiled, his eyes suddenly open.

"Always," she replied.

Pulling her to him, he used hands, lips and tongue to unleash a torrent of desire that inflamed them both. Together, they soared on a cloud of ecstasy while seeking new ways to fulfill the other.

The morning was long over by the time they got up. Eyes fixed on the street below, Linden absently sipped a mug of coffee as Alex came up behind her. Rubbing his freshly-shaved cheek against her porcelain-smooth one, he sent tremors of delight up her spine.

"It's hard to believe that just five short days ago you could hardly stand to have me in the same room," he murmured, nuzzling her ear.

"Now that you mention it, I do recall such thoughts," she smiled, turning to face him. "We've come a long way since Thursday when all you did was glower, criticize, and patronize me."

"You were no Little Mary Sunshine yourself."

"Considering your attitude, do you blame me?"

"I guess I was a little rough on you at times," he chuckled.

"But remember, my investigation had conclusively proved that you were a conniving little thief. Granted, nothing could have been further from the truth, but my first loyalty was to your aunt. After all, she pays the bills."

"What encouraged your change of heart?"

"The way you handled the situation. It was you against the rest of the world and you aroused all my protective instincts." He grinned. "You aroused other feelings, too, even when we were fighting."

"It didn't feel that way to me."

"I didn't want to tip my hand." His face turned serious. "That's when I realized you were no longer just part of my job."

"Thank heaven," she whispered, resting her face on his chest.

Startled by the ringing of the phone, they jerked apart and Linden's eyes fell on the caller ID display. Seeing Gerry Hammond's name, she showed it to Alex before answering with a distinct lack of enthusiasm.

"Hey, Linden. You sure sound like you're having a bad hair day," came the overly-cheerful response.

"What do you want, Gerry?" she responded ungraciously.

"I think we should meet."

"Why?"

"You have something for sale." His voice turned self-important. "And *I* know someone who wants to buy it."

"And that something would be . . . ?"

"You know perfectly well. The Judas Hoard."

"What makes you think I have it?"

"For Chrissake, you told Helena you took it," he retorted.

"No. I told her I took the box from the safe. The coins were already missing."

"We only have your word for it."

"They're gone, Gerry." Impatience edged Linden's voice. "What part don't you understand?"

"Humor him," Alex whispered.

Linden searched for a way. "Did Aunt Heni also tell you I'm having memory problems? Maybe you can help me fill in the blanks. When do you want to meet?"

"Rose's. It's a bar on Second Avenue. I only have one appointment this afternoon so I can be there at three o'clock."

"Fine, see you then." Hanging up, Linden gave Alex a quizzical look. "I hope you have a good reason for this."

"Unless the Judas Hoard turns up, you're guilty until proven innocent—despite what the law says," he said. "But you can use other people's suspicions to work for you. The Voice could be trying to get to you through Gerry."

"Could be. There's no way on earth that Gerry's smart enough to work alone."

"Exactly. But I know he'll do anything for a fast buck. Perhaps The Voice thinks you'd be more inclined to trust family."

"I trust Gerry about as much as a rattlesnake," Linden said. "He made a pass at me shortly after he and Melanie were married."

"No surprise there."

"And you think that Gerry Hammond, a true world-class mental lightweight, can help us?" Linden asked scornfully.

"It's worth a try," Alex responded. "We can't just wait for something to happen."

As usual, his words made sense. "You're right. It's time to take the offensive, and who better to use for bait than me? All I have to do is put on my helpless act."

A roar of laughter escaped Alex. "He'd never buy it, and don't try playing dumb either. Like everyone else, he's aware you're anything but."

"Meaning my only option is to string him along."

"It shouldn't be too hard to make him think you have the

coins. Maybe then he'll lead us to The Voice. But first things first, unless you can convince Gerry you have the coins, we're not going to get anywhere."

Linden dismissed his concern. "That won't be difficult. What if I'm too successful and he tries something this afternoon?"

"Don't worry. Any meeting will be held on our terms, not his, and you'll never be out of my sight. The Voice won't have a chance to try anything, let alone get away with it. If Gerry does try to get cute, he won't know what hit him."

# Chapter 19

Although the pace of the city always slowed during the summer, Rose's was still strangely quiet for a Tuesday afternoon. It was as if people had extended their weekend by yet another day. Pausing in the doorway, Linden let her gaze drift over the six customers seated at the bar. Although they were little more than shadowy outlines in the gloom, she immediately picked out Alex at the far end. Nursing a beer, he appeared engrossed in the baseball game on the large screen TV. Closer to the door, Gerry flirted with a young woman on a nearby stool. Linden found the temptation to embarrass him irresistible, and sauntering over to him, she walked her fingers up his arm.

"Sorry to be late, darling," she cooed. "Looks like you managed to occupy yourself, though. Order me a glass of Chardonnay, please."

Giving him no time to react, she headed for a booth at the rear. Evidently convinced he had another conquest, Gerry swaggered over and sprawled in the seat next to her. With his arm draped along the wooden ledge behind them, he waited until the server had brought their drinks before speaking.

"Figured out where the coins are yet?" he asked as the man walked away.

Linden took a sip of wine. "What's in it for me?"

"Didn't take you long to change your tune," he taunted. "The word money sure worked its magic fast. As I said, I know someone who's interested in the coins."

"He better be rich, because *should* I have the coins, they aren't cheap."

"You mean you'll sell?" Gerry seemed astounded by her sudden cooperation.

"Why not, if the price is right?" she replied. "Hanging onto them won't do me much good."

Gerry's eyes gleamed greedily. "What made you change your mind?"

"Lots of reasons," she shrugged. "Most important, I've realized that it's time to start looking out for Number One. Every day, I'm growing older and life's passing me by. My financial portfolio looks good on paper, but liquidating it won't get me all that much, not enough for real freedom. In short, Gerry, I'm not having any fun. And selling those coins would buy me plenty of fun. I could join the jet set and travel anywhere I wanted, always welcome."

"Money definitely has a way of opening doors," Gerry agreed. "Especially for someone young and beautiful."

"Ah, but time's marching on relentlessly. I don't want to spend my best years tied to the Judas Hoard and fighting for new assignments. I can do that when I'm old and poor. With all that lovely money, I can buy myself a new face, a new identity, and a whole slew of studs to be at my service." A dreamy expression crossed her face. "I can see all sorts of interesting possibilities opening up."

Gerry looked delighted. "Naturally, my uh . . . friend would need to see the Hoard before committing. Nothing personal, you understand," he added hastily. "Just to assure himself that you actually have the coins."

"And what assurances do I have he won't hit me over the head and make off with them?"

"Linden, I'll be with you," he pointed out in a hurt voice.

"I see. Honor amongst thieves and all that," she observed dryly.

His face turned studiously casual. "By the way, where are the coins?"

"In a very safe place."

"My friend's in town and wondered if he could see them," Gerry said.

"No problem—so long as it's between nine a.m. and three p.m., Monday through Friday."

"Banking hours," Gerry stated brightly.

Linden's smile was guileless. "Maybe."

"How about if you just meet him for . . . what do they call them . . . preliminary talks?" he persisted. "Who knows, if he likes what he hears, he might even want to advance you a little money today."

"Sounds real tempting." As if considering the offer, Linden took another sip of wine. "Tell him I'd love to meet him in any public place he cares to name."

"He's very shy."

"And I'm very cautious," Linden told him. "I don't want any surprises, or give him the opportunity to grab me and then work on me to reveal the Hoard's location."

Gerry frowned, insulted. "Linden, trust me. This is a man of honor."

"Bull. An honorable man would contact Tom Blair."

"I hope you won't be such a pain when you meet my friend," he complained.

"Worried I'll scare him off?" Linden inquired tartly. "No

way. I have something he wants, and urgently, too, or we wouldn't be reduced to this secret rendezvous stuff. I'm in the driver's seat here, and it's my terms or not all. There are plenty of other buyers."

"Don't bet on it," Gerry snapped. "But I'll call him and see how far I get."

As he disappeared in the direction of the restrooms, Alex ambled over to the adjacent booth. Opening a copy of *The New York Times*, he leaned against the back of the seat while shielding his face with the newspaper. When Gerry returned a few minutes later, he was too focused on Linden to notice anyone else.

"Reached my friend but he refuses to be seen in public with you," he announced. "The meeting has to be in his hotel suite."

Linden never hesitated. "My terms, Gerry, or forget it."

"Wrong," he shot back. "He sets the terms, and he says it's now."

Throwing some money onto the table, he grabbed her arm but she caught the edge of the table and held tight. As he struggled to drag her from the booth, Alex came up behind Gerry, blocking his exit.

"I thought the lady made her feelings perfectly clear. She doesn't want to go." Alex's voice was dangerously soft.

"Blair, what the hell are you doing here?" Gerry glared at Linden. "I get it. He's wormed his way into your confidence hoping to be the first to recover the coins and claim the nice little bonus Helena's offering. Didn't take him long to figure out the best way to do it."

"At least he doesn't force me to do anything against my will."

"Got it," Gerry snorted. "He's using the gentle treatment on you, all kindness and consideration. Well, I have news for you, sweetheart. That's not his style. He doesn't give a shit about you, but he does know every bit of sleaze. I guarantee he won't hesitate to use what he's learned about you—and the rest of us for that matter—if it will help him find the coins."

Although Alex's eyes turned flinty, his voice remained amiable. "Don't judge everyone else by your own standards. Now, Gerry, old buddy, suppose you tell us exactly who you're working for."

"It's none of your goddamned business. This is between Linden and me. I'm just trying to help her."

"Don't give me that crap," Alex snapped. "You've never done a damn thing for anyone in your life unless you stood to gain by it, usually financially."

"Think you're any different?" Gerry retorted.

Alex shrugged. "At least I'm up front about it and don't deliberately sucker innocent people into compromising situations. Having an affair with a married woman at the husband's request isn't my scene. Of course, Miles Armstrong rewarded you handsomely for providing him with grounds for divorce, didn't he?"

Gerry's face reddened with rage. "That's a lie," he exploded. "Tara Armstrong came onto me and cost me a bundle. Miles was just compensating me for what I spent. God knows who Alex paid for that information, Linden, and I bet it's just a sample of the stuff he has. I'm warning you; he's a ruthless SOB. Finding those coins will set him up for life, and he'll do whatever's necessary to succeed."

"Sounds like you just described yourself," Linden replied coldly.

"There's no comparison," he huffed. "And if you think he's so terrific, why do you still have the coins?"

"She's holding out for the highest bidder," Alex inserted smoothly. "Since she hasn't revealed the Hoard's location so

163

far, all I can do is stick around and watch. Who knows, maybe she'll see the error of her ways and put together an exhibit. If she does, no one will ever know she considered ignoring George's wishes, and of course your part wouldn't be mentioned either."

"Yeah, right," Gerry sneered.

"In return for that favor, though, we'll need a little cooperation. So, again, who are you working for?"

Gerry looked around, but it was obvious no one was about to rescue him. Flopping down in the booth, he reluctantly admitted, "Some guy called Smith."

Alex squeezed next to him. "Very original. And how did Mr. Smith get in touch with you?"

"He called me at the club yesterday. Said he was interested in buying the Judas Hoard, and since I knew Linden, maybe I could persuade her to sell."

"And out of the sheer goodness of your heart, you relayed the message to her," Alex observed cynically.

"Mr. Smith did happen to mention that if she sold to him there'd be something in it for me."

"How much?"

Gerry stared at his glass of Perrier. "Quarter million dollars."

"Not bad for such an easy job," Alex remarked. "I'm surprised you took so long to call Linden."

"I couldn't reach her until lunchtime today," Gerry scowled.

Linden shot him a withering look. "Gee, Gerry, I'm sorry."

"Have you ever met Mr. Smith?" Alex asked.

"A few hours ago. He wanted to give me a little something as a sign of good faith and we met at Grand Central Station."

"Can't get a more public place than that," Alex noted. "How did you recognize each other?"

"He told me to call his cell phone when I got to the concourse and we talked ourselves into the same spot."

"What does he look like?" Linden demanded.

After seeming to give her question a lot of thought, Gerry said, "An accountant. He's a regular guy—about my height, average build, and wears gold-rimmed glasses."

"I think a trip to Mr. Smith's hotel is in order," said Alex. "When we get there, tell him Linden's with you but won't go upstairs. Maybe knowing she's so close, he'll change his mind and come down. But understand this, Gerry. There is absolutely no way that Linden will go up to his room. Don't even think of trying anything."

Gerry was silent for a moment. "Okay, not that I have any choice. You've latched onto a real money maker with Linden, and I can see you getting violent to protect her. You solve this one Blair, and you're set for life."

Alex ignored the jibe but his gray eyes had all the warmth of a gun barrel as he asked, "What's Mr. Smith's phone number and where's he staying?"

Sullenly, Gerry opened his phone and after calling out the number, added, "He's at the Waldorf Astoria."

"Not too shabby," Alex commented drily, entering the information into his notebook. "Maybe he really does have the money to finance the project. Okay, time to leave."

After the bar's overly cool temperature, the air outside felt as hot as dragon's breath. Heat waves shimmered in the brilliant sunshine and the smell of molten tar hung over the almost deserted sidewalk. At the end of the block, drivers waited impatiently for the red light to turn green, twitching like horses at the starting gate.

The sound of gunfire shattered the temporary quiet. About to hail a cab, Gerry instead clutched his abdomen and slowly crumpled to the ground. Transfixed with shock, Linden stared at him but Alex never hesitated. Grabbing her arm, he pushed her behind the nearest parked car.

Second Avenue abruptly erupted into life. Drivers slammed on their brakes and the few pedestrians darted for cover, watched by onlookers from the safety of doorways and windows. In the confusion, Alex pulled Linden down the block, breaking into a run once they reached the corner.

"No, I must stay with Gerry," Linden protested.

"Like hell," came the curt response.

Gripping her wrist, Alex tugged Linden down the street, forcing her to keep up with him. At First Avenue he slowed his pace and signaled a passing cab.

"Sixtieth Street and Third Avenue," he instructed the driver.

Opening the door, he shoved Linden inside where she slumped in her seat, panting heavily. Alex, she noticed, wasn't even breathing hard.

"I need some polo shirts," he remarked calmly.

She stared at him in total disbelief. "Doesn't seeing someone . . ."

"I guess Bloomingdale's has the best selection," he interrupted in a conversational tone.

His callousness shocked her into silence. Gerry's comment about Alex's ruthlessness floated back, along with the vivid reminder that Gerry himself lay sprawled in the gutter, helpless and alone. But, she comforted herself, the police would quickly identify him from his driver's license and contact Melanie.

Dear God, the police!

Linden felt as if someone had poured ice in her veins. Without Alex's quick thinking she'd probably be inside the nearest police precinct. There would be little sympathy for the prime suspect in the sensational Judas Hoard robbery. And even if the police agreed to contact Detective Gorton or Tom Blair—or even Peter Sinclair—it would take time to reach them. She was so busy spinning various scenarios that when the cab drew to a halt Alex had to drag her onto the sidewalk. Thrusting some money at the driver, he curtly told him to keep the change.

Third Avenue's bustle pulled her back to reality and all set to analyze the shooting, she opened her mouth. An angry look from Alex silenced her, and she fumed inwardly as he propelled her into Bloomingdale's where they strolled through the vast store to one of the Lexington Avenue exits. Hailing a cab, Alex asked to be taken to the Asia Society. It was the turbaned-Sikh driver's favorite museum and he spent the short ride up Park Avenue describing its art treasures. Under different circumstances Linden would have been fascinated.

As they left the cab outside the museum, Alex's stiff body language warned her not to speak. As soon as the driver sped off, they hurried toward Linden's apartment building where he tossed a cheerful greeting to Frank. It wasn't until they were inside her apartment that he relaxed, and pouring two glasses of brandy, he handed one to Linden.

"Better?" he asked, watching her swallow a mouthful.

She nodded. "Getting there."

He gave a wry smile. "Forgive me?"

"That had all the makings of a disaster. The last thing I need is more publicity."

"Exactly. At most, the police will get descriptions of us, but they're not much use without names. Even if the first cab driver associates us with the incident, what can he say? All he did was take us to Bloomingdale's, and the second driver will never make the connection."

Still unsettled by Alex's transformation into a cold-eyed stranger, Linden said, "I didn't know what to make of you. It was like an alien had taken over your body."

"That's because I was trying to figure out how to get you away as quickly as possible. Explanations could come later."

"Maybe we should call Detective Gorton," Linden suggested. "He needs to be updated on what happened. Gerry could already be talking to the police."

"I don't think Gerry's in any condition to talk to anyone," Alex responded. "And what do we tell Gorton?"

"That The Voice paid me a visit and then tried to make contact through Gerry," Linden replied.

"How will that help Gorton? These events haven't brought us any closer to identifying The Voice or to discovering the Judas Hoard's hiding place."

"He said he wanted to be kept in the loop," Linden pointed out.

"Okay, I'll call him eventually." Alex pulled her to him. "But always remember that whatever I do is for us. We're in this together."

Although his words should have reassured her, Linden's doubts refused to go away. Banishing them to the back of her mind, she told herself that he wasn't in this to make his reputation, or for the bonus, it was for their future. Gerry was wrong.

Gerry!

With a gasp, she pushed Alex away.

"I must try and find out where Gerry was taken. How he is."

"While you do that, I'll call Syd and give her Mr. Smith's phone number. Even though he probably used a burner phone, you never know what else Syd might find."

The reference to Syd resurrected Linden's unease. "For a one-man office, you sure have a lot of people ready to help."

"Sign of the times," Alex responded easily. "Working for corporate America has lost its appeal. Everyone's a consultant nowadays, and some of the best brains are hiring themselves out by the hour."

"Well, it will be interesting to see what Syd turns up,"

Linden said, somewhat reassured. She, too, was self-employed, with an army of contacts to call on for help when necessary.

Sitting at the dining table, she fired up her computer and brought up a list of local hospitals. Since she wanted to leave an untraceable number, she used her burner phone to call each one. Within thirty minutes she had learned that Gerry was in St. Luke's Hospital, condition unknown.

She was trying to convince Alex that they should go to the hospital when her doorman called. Roger Lambert, he informed her, wanted to come up. Half-expecting it to be The Voice, Alex went to meet the elevator, instructing Linden to dial 911 if she heard him address the visitor as Mr. Lambert.

A faint whirr announced the elevator's arrival, and recognizing her cousin's voice, Linden opened the door. Although casually dressed in a polo shirt and tan slacks, Roger seemed far from comfortable. Giving Linden's cheek a perfunctory kiss, he made straight for the living room and collapsed on the love seat. He looked so beaten down that Linden felt a flash of sympathy.

"Alex and I were about to have some wine," she said. "Want some?"

"Sounds great."

Taking a seat on the sofa, Alex studied the other man with open interest. At first glance Roger appeared unexceptional, an impression reinforced by his mousey colored hair and pale blue eyes. On closer inspection, though, he had an unmistakable air of power, the confidence that came from being groomed to be the future chairman of the Lambert real estate empire. And now was.

Accepting his wine with a grateful smile, Roger took a gulp and said, "I needed that. What started off as an ordinary day has ended up like a scene out of a nightmare. Mel, Liz and I went to Radford to have lunch with Mom."

About to sit next to Alex, Linden asked quickly, "Is she okay?"

"Very good, all things considered. As was everything up until an hour ago when Mel checked her phone. The police had been trying to get in touch with her. Gerry was shot."

"Gerry! Shot!" Linden hoped she wasn't over-reacting. "Where?"

"On Second Avenue. He's in surgery right now."

"That doesn't sound good."

"We won't know how bad until they've finished operating. I left Liz and Mel at the hospital because we need talk."

Linden tried not to look guilty as she reached for her glass. "Why?"

"I want to apologize."

"Apologize!" she spluttered through a mouthful of wine.

"We . . . I . . . haven't been very supportive these last few days. Mom told us what you've been through. I'm sorry. I should have made more of an effort to be in touch."

"It's not been that easy for you either."

"I still can't believe Dad's gone. It was all so sudden. Eight days ago . . ." His voice trailed off and he gulped some more wine. "I also want to apologize for the whole will thing. Liz just couldn't handle you getting anything. Felt everything should go to Mel and me. Especially the Judas Hoard."

"For God's sake," Linden erupted, "your father didn't leave it to me for its monetary value. His will specifically states that it be donated to a museum and put on permanent display. All I can do is choose which institution."

"No matter. Liz is convinced you intend to have your own private auction and sell it to the highest bidder. Refuses to listen to reason."

"Thanks for supporting me, even though it probably caused problems," Linden smiled. "And you know I never wanted any money. Your parents have done more than enough for me."

"Now the Judas Hoard is missing, Liz thinks she was right all along. Can't believe you don't have it."

"I'm doing my best to find out where it is."

"I know. You're that sort of person, which is why Dad left it to you. Knew you'd always go above and beyond to protect it." He pulled a white envelope from the pocket of his slacks. "I also wanted to give you this. Mrs. B was clearing out the room where Dad . . . Dad spent the last few weeks. She found it under the mattress."

Eyes misting at the sight of her laboriously printed name, Linden put the envelope down on the coffee table. "Thank you."

"Aren't you going to open it?" Roger asked.

"Your mother would have a heart attack. She says you don't open a letter until your guest has left."

Roger took another gulp of wine. "Please open it now. Liz won't rest until she knows what's inside. Wanted to steam it open. She's positive it's a check for a million dollars—or the name of a buyer for the Judas Hoard."

"If it will get her off your back, okay," Linden said.

Slitting the envelope, she glanced at the lines of shaky writing scrawled across the single sheet of paper. They were a graphic reminder of George's rapid deterioration. "It's . . . it was our favorite poem," she choked.

As she handed it to Roger to read, his face tightened. "I'm sorry. I know I shouldn't be jealous but he didn't leave Mel or me anything like this. You and he connected on a totally different level, though."

Linden took back the sheet and caressed it lovingly. "He was a wonderful man."

"He was. We were lucky to have him as long as we did."

171

Draining the last of his wine, Roger rose reluctantly to his feet. "I must get back to the hospital."

"Let me know what's happening, and tell Mel I'm here if she needs me. But I'll call her anyway."

"Will do." For all his grief and worry, Roger looked a little less stressed. "Thanks for being so understanding."

"It's a family thing," smiled Linden. "Thick and thin."

He hugged Linden fiercely. "I'll be in touch."

Linden waited by the front door until the elevator swept him away and then returned to the living room. Alex had topped up their wine glasses but, ignoring hers, Linden went straight for the poem. Through a sheen of tears she read aloud,

*"Though my soul will set in darkness, I will rise in perfect light. I have loved the stars too fondly to be fearful of the night."*

"It's obviously very special to you," said Alex. "What's the significance?"

"After my parents were killed, Uncle George and Aunt Heni told me they were in heaven. I was seven, what did I know about heaven? I kept asking when my parents were coming home. One night, about a month later, Uncle George took me outside to look at the sky. I remember it so well. It was March, and there were no clouds, just a gazillion stars. He pointed to the two brightest and said 'Those are your mommy and daddy. Even though you can't touch them, they can see you and they'll always be watching over you. So whenever you want to speak to them, all you have to do is look outside your window'."

"Did it help?"

Linden smiled through her tears. "I still talk to the two brightest stars. Uncle George knew it, and whenever we were out at night we'd look up at the sky and find my parents. Now he's up there with them."

"We'll look for all three the next time we're out at night."
Linden swallowed to clear the tears stuck in her throat.
"Time to get a grip. Move on. Let's eat."

* * *

Banners of crimson and gold streaked the western sky by
the time they had cleaned up after dinner. Although Gerry's
shooting was all they talked about, their list of suspects was
frustratingly short. They were about to take the last of the
wine into the living room when the phone rang. Expecting it
to be Roger with an update on Gerry, Linden almost answered
until she saw the Caller ID display. *Unknown name/Unknown
number.* Alarm bells shrilled inside her head and she regarded
the phone as if it were radioactive.

"I think it's The Voice," she told Alex.

Without a word, he raced into the living room, appearing
seconds later with the other handset. At a nod from Linden,
he pushed the start key just as she pressed her own button.

"What do you want?" she demanded.

"I hope today taught you a lesson, Linden." The synthesized
speech proved she'd guessed correctly.

"You mean Gerry wasn't working for you?"

"I work alone," he said. "I don't like meddlers, and the only
way you'll ever find me is if I want you to. Remember Hammond
the next time you decide to get cute. That was just a warning.
Any more tricks and Blair gets it. Except he won't be as lucky."

Numbly she set the phone back in the cradle. "He's mad."

"He's serious," Alex declared. "And ruthless."

Linden shivered. "I'm going to be in his crosshairs until I
figure out where those coins are."

After a brief silence, Alex said, "I think they're somewhere
in the house."

173

"It's as good a place as any to start looking," Linden agreed. "Except it's a very large house and the Judas Hoard is very small."

"That call also ruled out Gerry's involvement with The Voice," Alex noted. "What about Roger's wife? The way he talked about her, she definitely sounds like a woman obsessed."

"Doesn't shock me. We never hit it off. She's always been jealous of my relationship with Melanie, even though we're not all that close nowadays."

"Your relationship with your uncle didn't seem to thrill her, either," Alex observed.

"Or my relationship with Aunt Heni. But I guarantee one thing. She'd never do anything to jeopardize her position as Mrs. Roger Lambert."

"Which brings us back to our original question. Who the hell is The Voice?"

# Chapter 20

The blackness was without relief, a gaping chasm devoid of sound and movement. Although Linden knew she had to escape before it consumed her entirely, she was a prisoner. Her hands were chained to a tree trunk, the metal handcuffs cutting deeper into her wrists the more she struggled. Abruptly, the darkness coalesced into a person. Grotesquely deformed, he had huge shoulders and bushy hair that writhed like a nest of vipers.

"Why didn't you tell me about the stars?" The metallic burr couldn't disguise The Voice's fury.

Linden refused to be intimidated. "It wasn't important."

"It was important enough for your uncle to send you a message from beyond the grave."

Suddenly, she was on her back, staring at a star-studded sky while hands pinned her to the ground. Frantically she tried to wriggle free, but the grip tightened as a faceless figure loomed over her.

"It's just a poem," she screamed.

"Linden, wake up." Despite its urgency, this voice sounded distinctly human.

Forcing her eyes open, she found herself in bed, her body as cold as if packed in ice. Seated on the edge of the bed, Alex smoothed her hair.

"You were having a nightmare," he said.

She shut her eyes again. "The Voice wanted to know about the stars."

Alex ran gentle fingers across her face. "You're remembering our conversation from earlier but it's all twisted up. Try and let it go."

Switching off the bedside lamp, he joined her under the covers and held her close. As the heat from his body warmed hers, the horrors of the nightmare faded.

*I have loved the stars too fondly . . .*

She was about to drift off to sleep when the phrase stole into her subconscious. Too drowsy to analyze its meaning, she banished it to the deepest recess of her brain where it remained until the next morning. As she soaped off in the shower, images tumbled through her mind like beads of mercury before slowly melding into a fully-formed memory. Senses heightened, her body tingled under the water's spray while the bathroom light took on the brilliance of a supernova. Grabbing a towel, she flew into the bedroom.

"Alex, you'll never believe what's happened."

Undeterred by the empty room, she raced down the hall, calling his name. Skidding to a halt outside the kitchen, she bounced up and down on her toes.

"I know where the coins are."

Looking up from the coffee pot, he exclaimed, "Fantastic! Where?"

"Under the stars," she announced dramatically.

"Under the stars," he repeated dubiously.

"Actually there's only one," she amended. "It's the Christmas tree star and stored in the attic along with all the other decorations. No one looks at them for eleven months, probably never even gives them a thought. Uncle George came up with the perfect hiding place."

Alex continued to look skeptical. "What made you remember now?"

"Dreaming about stars last night. But the connection is Christmas. Even when my parents were alive, we spent it with my aunt and uncle. Every year, on the last Saturday before Christmas, we'd go to their house to help decorate the tree. Uncle George would always say it was his favorite day of the year and because it was his tree, he put on the star."

Impatience flickered across Alex's face. "Get to the point, Linden—if there is one."

"Of course there is," she responded. "Part of the tradition included a trip to the attic to get the decorations. It was the only part I didn't like because Melanie insisted a monster lived up there. As a kid I completely bought the story, and I'm still not nuts about the place. Uncle George probably figured it would be the last place I'd think of, so that's why he left me the poem. Knew I'd get the connection."

"Could also be the reason it took you so long to remember, and why the drugs didn't work either." Alex gave her a resounding kiss. "Linden, you're wonderful."

For the first time she brushed him off. "We need to get to Radford ASAP. I'll give Aunt Heni a call just to make sure it's okay."

Brunnings answered on the second ring, and with his usual courtesy asked Linden to hold while he checked if her aunt was available. Helena was on the line in seconds.

"I was about to call you. It's Gerry. I have some bad news."

"Roger came to see me while Gerry was in surgery. Has he . . . ?"

"No, but he's in serious condition," Helena replied. "I'm just off to visit him."

"Oh." Linden was genuinely dismayed. "I was hoping to come to the house this afternoon. I guess it isn't convenient."

"Really, Linden, you don't need permission," Helena snapped.

Still unsure where she stood with her aunt, Linden said, "I wanted to call first."

"This is your home in spite of everything," Helena retorted. "I expect you to treat it as such."

"Thank you. In that case we'll be over in a couple of hours. Alex will be with me."

"I won't be here but I should be back late afternoon."

"Fine." Linden tried to sound casual. "Roger said Gerry was shot. Have they caught the gunman?"

"Of course not. He was long gone by the time the police arrived and naturally Gerry has no idea why someone would shoot him. Nor does he have any recollection of the incident. The last thing he remembers is being in some bar."

"Well, give him my best and maybe I'll see you later," Linden said.

"What did she say?" Alex demanded as she hung up the phone.

"Gerry's hanging in there and she's off to the hospital. They don't know who shot him, or why, and obviously he's said nothing about us." Linden gave Alex a hopeful look. "Do you think he's forgotten?"

"No way," came the crisp response. "Thank God he had enough presence of mind not to mention it."

Linden poured a cup of coffee. "How will he explain everything away?"

"Easy," Alex assured her. "All he has to say is that after stopping in the bar for a quick drink after work, he then decided it was too hot to walk home. The story contains an element of truth."

"Right," Linden agreed. "Yesterday was sweltering and today doesn't seem any better."

"Maybe not, but you should probably wear something a little more formal than that towel." Desire flared in Alex's eyes as he tugged at it. "I happen to think you're somewhat overdressed at the moment. But I don't think your aunt will see it that way."

\* \* \*

The temperature was on track for a record-breaking high by the time they finally left for Radford. Grand Central Parkway baked under a cloudless sky while the black tarmac shimmered silver in the sun's glare. Stultified by the heat, the trees and grass that flanked the highway looked to be painted in place. Only Garibaldi seemed unaffected. As Alex parked in front of the house, the dog bounded over, emitting yelps of joy.

Leaving the car, Linden hugged him. "Don't you ever rest?"

"It's a good thing he doesn't," said Alex, patting Garibaldi. "Otherwise, Saturday night would have turned out very different."

"You're a good dog and I'll make it up to you later," Linden promised. "Now go and play by yourself."

Casting them a reproachful look, Garibaldi slunk down the driveway, head and tail drooping miserably. Laughing at him, Linden and Alex walked to the front door which Brunnings already had open. With his ramrod stiff posture, the butler cut an imposing figure, the jacket of his dark suit taut across his broad shoulders.

"Good afternoon, Linden, Mr. Blair," he greeted them

formally. "Mrs. Lambert would like you to stay for dinner. Cocktails will be at six o'clock. Can I get you anything now?"

"No thanks, we had lunch on the way," Linden said. "Are today's papers in the library?"

"On the table, in their usual place."

"Fine, that's all we need," she replied. "It's so hot in the city; we just wanted to get away for the afternoon. Go and relax yourself, and for heaven's sake take off your jacket."

Brunnings acknowledged her comment with a brief nod before leading the way across the foyer to the library. Throwing open the doors, he waved them inside as if they were about to enter the presence of royalty.

Laid out neatly on the coffee table were copies of *The New York Times, USA Today* and *Newsday.* Linden and Alex each grabbed a section of the *Times*, and satisfied he was no longer needed, Brunnings quietly shut the door. After a couple of minutes, Linden put the two sections back inside the *Times* and led the way to the attic. An oppressive stillness enveloped the third floor, their footsteps overly loud as they walked to the end of the narrow corridor.

"To think that the evidence proving my innocence was right above our heads all along," Linden smiled.

"It will be interesting to see everyone's reaction when you produce the coins," Alex said.

Indicating the three doors, Linden said, "Aunt Heni's such a neat freak she had the attic divided into separate rooms. This one's an enormous cedar closet for out-of-season clothes. Here's where old furniture goes." Opening the final door with a flourish, she added, "And this is for everything else."

Obscured by shadows, boxes and trunks took up much of the airless room. A single dormer window grudgingly allowed daylight to filter in and Linden stared into the gloom. A foot-high bronze angel stood on a table by the wall, the patina dulled by age except for the toes which gleamed as brightly as a new penny.

Linden automatically touched a toe. "Whenever I come up here, I always rub the angel first. Melanie swore it would protect us from the monster."

Walking across the room, Linden felt herself transported back to childhood. A primal fear of the darkness still lingered, the impression that someone—or something—lurked in the shadows. And as vivid as ever was the sense of menace where each whisper of sound was magnified. But when Alex flipped the light switch, jolting her back to the present, it wasn't some supernatural being that caused Linden's eyes to widen with horror. It was a battered leather trunk stuffed with boxes.

"Dear God," she gasped. "Someone's been here already."

"How can you tell?" Alex asked, looking around. "Maybe this was never the hiding place."

"I know it was, and Uncle George would never leave a mess like this."

Almost in a frenzy, she emptied the trunk, piling the boxes on the floor until she could no longer deny the obvious. "The coins aren't here. Someone beat us to it."

"How were they stored?"

"In the original linen bag, which is extremely fragile, and then kept inside the suede pouch. Everything could fit in the palm of your hand. For extra protection, Uncle George had a leather box custom made, and the bag and pouch were *always* kept in that box."

"Since both the pouch and the leather box were still in the safe when you opened it on Monday night, your uncle must have used something else," Alex said. "Any idea what?"

Throat thick with tears, Linden shook her head and silently began to put back the boxes. After they were all neatly stowed away, she showed Alex a miniature sleigh with a cracked runner.

"This was undamaged last January, and those bulbs weren't smashed either. Aunt Heni's rule is that anything broken is either repaired immediately or thrown out. The star's always on top, too, not jammed down the side the way it was. It's the first thing to go on the tree. That's how I know another person was here."

"You need to leave this room," Alex advised. "It won't give us any answers."

Linden gave one last look around. "God, I hate being up here. Always have, especially after Melanie locked me in this wardrobe when I was thirteen." She opened the massive piece of furniture to reveal a surprisingly cramped interior. "The door stuck and she had to fetch Mr. B to get me out. I was convinced I was going to die inside."

"That was a cruel trick."

"Maybe, but I got my own back the next day by locking her in the cellar." Linden smiled at the memory. "Our punishment was the same—bed at seven o'clock for the next week. By then, though, we were friends again and spent the evenings exchanging girlish confidences. Melanie and I were either very close or bitter enemies. Somehow we survived. I miss those days," she ended sadly.

Downstairs, she walked straight into her aunt's office, the magnolia-colored walls giving it a distinctly feminine look. French doors opened onto a marble terrace that sloped down to a swathe of green lawn as perfectly groomed as a golf course. The grass disappeared into a thicket of old growth trees, branches swaying in the slight breeze. But the room was also where her uncle had spent his final weeks, and the metal hospital bed and reclining chair were stark reminders of its most recent function. As memories cascaded through her mind, Linden forgot about Alex until he spoke.

"How mobile was your uncle?" he asked, pointing to the walker and canes leaning against the wall.

"He could manage alone, if it wasn't too far."

Alex didn't look convinced. "Enough to make it up two flights of stairs?"

"He was very stubborn. See the gazebo at the end of the lawn? He walked there every day. Sometimes he'd have to rest for fifteen minutes before walking back, but he said it was the only thing he could do by himself. If he wanted to walk up two flights of stairs, he'd do it. He didn't have to set any speed records."

"Wasn't someone always with him?"

"Not every minute. There were times when he preferred to be alone." A wave of grief threatened to engulf her but she fought it back with words. "Let's go outside. I feel like the walls are pressing in on me."

Without waiting for a response, Linden led the way to the swimming pool. An awning shaded part of the blue stone patio from the brilliant sunshine, and sinking into an armchair, she stared moodily at the pool's placid surface. Tail wagging with delight, Garibaldi rushed over and flopped down on Linden's feet, panting as if he'd just run a marathon. Over at the well-equipped bar Alex mixed them each a vodka and tonic. Accepting hers with a grim expression, Linden took a long swallow, her gaze fixed on a huge rhododendron whose glossy leaves glittered like emeralds.

"Well?" she demanded, absently fondling Garibaldi's ears.

Alex shrugged. "If those decorations were put away as neatly as you say, then the trunk was definitely searched between your last visit and today."

"Thanks for the vote of confidence," she snapped.

"Hey, I'm on your side, remember," Alex said mildly.

"It was The Voice." Her voice left no room for argument.

Alex's grey eyes turned flinty. "I agree. And the only way he could know about the attic was by hearing you tell me. In other words, he bugged your apartment."

"Which means he's aware of everything we say." The color drained from Linden's face. "And do—even in the bedroom."

The ice cubes rattled against Alex's glass as he swirled his drink angrily. "Especially the bedroom."

"Now he's free to disappear with the coins and I'll always be branded as a thief." Rage surged through her like an inferno. "Producing the Judas Hoard was my only hope."

"He won't drop out of sight so fast," Alex observed. "Anyone disappearing at this point, no matter how unlikely, would automatically become a suspect. He's been this patient. He can afford to wait a little longer."

Linden refused to be comforted. "Patience doesn't seem to be his strong point."

"He can do it," Alex assured her. "Look what he's survived already. It will also take time to make the necessary financial arrangements with his buyer, set up electronic transfers."

"I guess," Linden acknowledged morosely, her gaze drawn to the woods beyond the lawn. The giant oak tree rose above the green canopy like a sentinel and a pensive expression entered her eyes.

Seeing her face soften, Alex asked, "Another trip down memory lane?"

"I was thinking of the time Melanie dared me to climb to the top of that oak tree. When Uncle George found out, he was furious and stopped my allowance for two weeks."

"Considering all the scrapes you and Melanie got into, you were lucky to make it this far," Alex chuckled.

"I was far worse than Melanie, a real tomboy. I loved the woods and had climbed most of the trees by the time I was twelve. It's still one of my favorite places." Noticing the watch on Alex's wrist, she exclaimed, "Look at the time! I must get ready. Aunt Heni won't be happy if I miss cocktails again."

* * *

At precisely six o'clock, Linden entered the living room to find Alex and her aunt deep in conversation. Reluctant to interrupt them, she paused just inside the door, but the slight movement was enough to catch Helena's attention.

"Hello, my dear," the older woman called out. "You certainly look better than before, much less tense."

Although encouraged by her aunt's warm greeting, Linden wished she and Alex were alone. Seeing that the top two buttons of his shirt were open, the urge to kiss the base of his neck was overwhelming. Their eyes met and the desire in his gave a hint of what to expect later. As she crossed the room to join them by the French door, Brunnings appeared with a glass of sherry balanced in the center of a silver tray.

"What's the latest on Gerry?" she asked, accepting her drink with a smile of thanks.

"As the saying goes, the doctors are guardedly optimistic," Helena replied. "One bullet just missed his heart but another did some internal damage. He won't be back to teaching tennis for quite some time."

"How's Melanie taking it?"

"Surprisingly well. You know what she's like, never does anything in moderation and hasn't left his side since yesterday. If she maintains her current level of devotion, this might do them some good. Maybe they'll even find they like each other."

"Do the police have any leads?" Alex inquired

"Nothing very helpful. They've questioned Gerry but he can't remember much. After his last appointment, he decided to have a drink in a nearby bar before going home. Apparently, he's a regular there."

"That probably goes for a lot of other customers," Linden pointed out.

"According to the police, a number of witnesses said he'd been talking to a young woman." Tipping her head to one side, Helena's eyes rested on Linden for a long moment. "Now I think about it, the description fits you."

"I'm hardly unique," Linden said. "And it's no secret that Gerry has a wandering eye."

Footsteps sounded in the entrance hall and Helena glanced toward the doorway. Linden shot Alex an apprehensive look that rapidly turned into dismay when Peter Sinclair walked into the room. His blue eyes glowed with affection as he approached Helena.

"Good evening, Peter. I'm glad you were able to join us," she greeted him. Turning back to Linden, she explained, "Peter has been extremely good to me this last week and has come for dinner several times."

"Great to see you again, Linden," he said, kissing her cheek. He and Alex merely traded cool nods.

"Peter called earlier to say he had some papers for me so I invited him to dinner," remarked Helena, giving him a fond smile. "You didn't need to make two trips today."

Linden rounded on him sharply. "You were here this afternoon?"

"He's my lawyer, Linden," Helena chided. "Many things still need to be settled."

Linden forced a smile. "How nice to have a lawyer who makes house calls."

"It was no problem; I was on my way to play golf anyway. In fact, I didn't even need to leave my car. Brunnings came out for the envelope." The wattage of his smile could have lit a small village. "If you were my client, I'd be available twenty-four hours a day."

"That's good to know, although my estate hardly deserves such dedication," Linden countered, determined to be pleasant, even as she wondered if Peter's altruism was genuine or a smoke screen to hide an ulterior motive. As a freshly-minted widow,

Helena was extremely vulnerable to someone looking to take advantage.

"Alex was telling me you're starting to recall more about your abduction," Helena said.

Peter grew instantly serious. "Anything useful?"

"Not really. They're mainly disconnected flashbacks. A lot's still missing."

"It's hard to believe that someone got inside the house." Helena was outraged. "Our security system is supposed to keep people out. And why didn't Garibaldi stop him from abducting you? He can be quite vicious, when necessary."

"Nothing's ever a hundred percent," Alex cautioned. "The Voice even got by security at Linden's apartment by pretending to be a messenger. Fortunately, he didn't hurt her, but he got away before she could ID him."

"Helena's told me about The Voice." Despite his casual tone, Peter's clenched fist revealed barely controlled anger. "By God, I'd like to find out who he is."

"Can't argue with you there," Alex said.

A discreet cough from Brunnings caught everyone's attention. It was his signal that dinner was ready and Helena started across the room, Peter by her side. But instead of following them, Linden refastened the clasp on her sandal, waiting until the other two were through the door before speaking.

"Don't leave me alone with Peter," she whispered to Alex. "The last thing I want is a repetition of the rose garden scene."

"I've no intention of going anywhere," he replied.

His eyes were on her toned legs but they slowly traveled up her body to the sea-green mini dress that clung to her curves. When he spoke, his voice was slightly hoarse. "Too bad this is the start of the evening and not the end."

"Think pure thoughts," Linden teased. "Works most of the time."

Although dinner was far less strained than Saturday's, Linden was still relieved when the meal ended and they went outside onto the terrace for coffee. While a gentle breeze brought some relief to the sultry evening, the conversation didn't match the pleasant surroundings. All they discussed was The Voice, and after an hour's speculation about his identity Helena stood up.

"Please excuse me, it's been a tiring day," she apologized. "Linden, I hope you and Alex will stay the night. Mrs. B has freshened both your rooms. Peter, I'll see you tomorrow at eleven o'clock as arranged."

Already on his feet, Peter said, "I realize how hard it is for you with everything that's happened. As soon as the paperwork's completed, I can get out of your hair once and for all."

"It's always a pleasure seeing you, even when it is business," Helena smiled. Walking over to Linden, she kissed her niece's cheek lightly. "I've really misjudged you, my dear. This last week has been a nightmare for everyone, but now we must put it behind us and make every effort to clear your name."

"It helps to have Alex on my side," said Linden, touched by her aunt's affection.

Helena's look showed her own gratitude. "He's done extremely well so far. At least we have you back. Hopefully he'll be as lucky with the Judas Hoard."

With a final smile that included everyone, she disappeared into the library. Waiting until Helena was out of earshot, Peter was the first to speak.

"Got to hand it to you, Alex, you sure are adaptable. First Helena hired you to find Linden, a feat you accomplished in record time, and now you're her bodyguard. Duties you're certainly taking very seriously."

Alex shrugged. "The most important part of my job is being able to think on my feet and adjust accordingly."

"Which you're doing admirably. The women here seem to think you can walk on water. Didn't take you long to make yourself indispensable."

"The same could be said about you and Helena," Alex said. "Just what sort of papers were so important that they had to be delivered in person?"

"That's between me and my client," Peter answered smoothly. "My coming here was a professional courtesy."

"Strange it should bring you here so often," Alex mused.

"Helena's had a rough time lately. All I've done is try to make it a little easier."

"Your consideration has not passed unnoticed," Alex observed dryly.

As the two men stared at each other with open hostility, Linden rushed to defuse the tension. Grateful for Peter's kindness to her aunt, she ignored her own dislike and played peacemaker. "Neither Aunt Heni nor I would know what to do without either of you."

Peter gave a short laugh. "Don't mind us, Linden. We got off to a rocky start and never looked back. He drew his own conclusions and made all kinds of insinuations."

"I never said anything that wasn't justified," Alex said.

"And believe me, Linden, Blair knows everything about you," Peter was quick to add.

"I know, but he's revised most of his initial judgments."

"Don't kid yourself. Solving this case won't do him any harm, and the quickest way to success is through you. It isn't going to hurt him to offer you friendship, affection even," Peter ended.

Linden tried to conceal how much his words disturbed her. Gerry had made similar comments the previous day and they continued to fester in her brain like a malignant tumor. She didn't need another person reinforcing her own doubts, especially Peter. Yet even as she sprang to Alex's defense, she wondered who she was trying to convince.

"Being enemies wouldn't accomplish anything," she said.

"I should have known," Peter mocked. "Sympathy and understanding are much more effective. Psych 101. And how convenient that Alex was the only one to recognize you at George's funeral."

"He'd been hired to find me," Linden reminded him sharply.

"Talk about great timing," Peter needled. "There you were—friendless and alone. Not only did he drop into your life like a gift from heaven right after George was buried, but he came with all the answers, too. Incredible!" He paused. "Although how can you be positive he told it exactly right?"

"I know the truth when I hear it." Acid etched her tone.

Peter never missed a beat. "Then there's the way he suddenly materialized in the office saying he'd been hired by your aunt."

"Any time you wish to see a copy of my contract you're more than welcome." For the first time, Alex's voice carried a hint of anger.

"Ah, but who contacted whom?" Peter goaded.

"My uncle called me," Alex shot back.

"Tom never struck me as being capable of such blatant nepotism," Peter stated. "Are you sure it wasn't the other way around? Linden's disappearance was breaking news. A beautiful woman vanishes with a fortune in rare coins—it was better than any reality series the networks could dream up. And the story got to play out in real time."

"Destroying my life in the process," Linden exploded.

"How could any investigator resist such a case?" Peter continued, unruffled by her interruption. "And want to hear the best part? Private investigators don't come with a money-back guarantee of success. It would be quite easy to lie about the outcome of the investigation and pretend that the coins were lost forever, although in reality they'd been recovered."

"Success is much better," Alex said impassively. "It impresses potential clients."

"He's always like this, Linden. Has an answer for everything."

Linden had heard enough. As much as she tried to ignore Peter's reasoning, it was playing to her own doubts. Standing, she said, "It's getting late. I think it's time to call it a night."

"So gracious," Peter jeered. "The way you've risen above your humble origins never ceases to amaze me. You always did play the lady of the manor well, Linden. It's just one of your many endearing qualities. Remember that when you're over your infatuation for Blair."

"It's not an infatuation," she corrected him softly, and led the way inside.

The thick carpet muffled their footsteps as they walked through the house. No one spoke until they reached the front door which Linden quickly opened.

"Goodnight, Peter. Thanks for all you've done for my aunt," she said, sounding far more grateful than she felt.

"My pleasure," said Peter. "And Linden, if you do find the coins, I hope the truth won't be too painful to bear. So long, Alex. I guess you consider it all worthwhile, not that it's any great hardship. I told you that Linden was cute, even when all you wanted to hear were the negatives."

With a satisfied smile, he strode outside and within minutes was racing his Mercedes down the drive. As Linden pushed the button to open the gates, Brunnings hurried toward them. His eyes automatically settled on the monitor by the door to make certain the lawyer drove out into Laurel Court.

"I'm sorry. I didn't realize Mr. Sinclair was leaving," he said.

"Don't worry," Linden replied. "Since he seems to consider himself part of the family, he really doesn't need a formal sendoff. Time he left anyway. It's been a long day for all of us and I'm off to bed."

"Then if you're finished outside, I'll lock up," the butler said.

"Thanks, Mr. B. Goodnight."

Wearily, she trudged across the wide entrance hall and up the stairs. The day's emotional roller coaster had left her totally drained and even Alex's quiet presence failed to comfort her. When they reached the upper floor, he stopped outside his door.

"See you in the morning," he said.

For a moment she looked taken aback. "I forgot. The house rules are different here. It will be strange without you."

Caressing her cheek, he smiled, "Don't give up hope. We haven't finished fighting."

Inside her room she exchanged her dress for a nightgown and drifted over to the window, too unsettled to sleep. Only the oak tree retained any shape in the darkness, its distinctive outline in sharp relief against the other trees. Ablaze with stars, the sky stretched into infinity.

*For I have loved the stars too fondly to be fearful of the night.*

Repeating the words, Linden searched the heavens for the two brightest stars until she heard a tap at the door. Hurrying across the room, she turned the knob to find Alex in the hallway outside. With a grin, he walked inside and caught her in his arms.

"I had no intention of leaving you alone for the night but I didn't want to be too obvious. Brunnings probably wouldn't approve of our sleeping together."

"Or Aunt Heni," she smiled.

"If she ever finds out, I'll say I was concerned for your safety and spent the night in the armchair."

Gently pushing him away, she crossed to the window and stared at the lawn which gleamed silver in the moonlight. Garibaldi appeared at the edge of the wood, prowling through the shadows like a predator hunting for prey.

"Peter sets my nerves on edge. I'm always wondering what he's going to say next."

"How well do you know him?" Alex asked. "He said you dated."

"We only had a couple of dinners. He still seems resentful that I wasn't interested in taking it any further. He's not too thrilled with you either."

"That's an understatement," Alex chuckled. "As he said, we had problems right from the start. I was curious to find out what made him want to practice small-town law. He told me it was because a large company was too regimented and too hung up on proper procedures. Reasonable I guess, but still hard to believe."

Linden looked at Alex lounging against the wall beside the window. He had an air of dependability that fit him as comfortably as the jeans and tee-shirt he'd slipped on. His continued support was a much-needed counterbalance to other people's accusations, and she suddenly felt ashamed of her suspicions, the fleeting speculations as to his sincerity.

Yet her misgivings were not entirely unfounded. Both Gerry and Peter had claimed that the recovery of the Judas Hoard would benefit Alex the most. Stifling a sigh, she wished for a way to ignore their charges, forget each had aired similar thoughts. And as Peter had remarked, she was the logical source for anyone wishing to locate the coins.

She gave a guilty start. Repeating Peter's innuendoes was

the first step toward believing them. How could she do that, when she didn't entirely trust him, either?

"Come back, my love," Alex said in a soft voice. "You've gone to that place where I can't reach you."

Deliberately, she stopped the flow of unpleasant thoughts and forced herself to meet his eyes. He stared back with a combination of tenderness and desire.

"Oh Alex, things aren't happening at all the way they should."

"I'm always here, just remember that."

"And never fail to make me feel better," she smiled, looping her arms around his neck.

"Do you mean by doing this?" he murmured, and as his lips met hers, all her doubts and fears disappeared.

# Chapter 21

Buffeted by the wind, ancient trees creaked and groaned as if in pain. Terrified, Linden ran deeper into the overgrown garden trying to escape the squad of centurions. The rattle of swords grew ever louder, but when she risked a backward glance her only pursuer was a long-haired man dressed in the flowing robe of a disciple. He clutched a linen bag filled with coins and as he pulled back his arm to throw it at her head, vines curled around her body, bands of steel that . . .

"Honey, wake up. Don't be afraid, everything's fine. You're having another nightmare."

Beside her she could feel the warmth of another person, the softness of sheets on her skin. "Alex?"

"Of course," he reassured her. "Who did you expect?"

Heart pounding, Linden gasped, "Thank God you're here. It was such a horrible dream. He nearly caught me."

"Who nearly caught you?"

"I don't know. Some man. He was chasing me but I couldn't see his face."

"I won't let him catch you," Alex soothed, gathering her close.

Safe in his arms, Linden relaxed and her tension slowly dissolved into another emotion, one that Alex also shared. As lips and fingers found favorite spots, their bodies floated in an ocean of pleasure. Gentle swells grew into billowing waves until they climaxed together as weightless as the water that supported them.

The next time Alex woke her, pewter colored light outlined the edges of the drapes. In response to the feather-light kisses that grazed her face, she molded herself against him.

"I must go," he groaned, rolling away. "It's nearly six o'clock. People will be up pretty soon."

Dropping one last kiss on her forehead, he stood up and pulled on his jeans. Drowsily, Linden followed him out of bed, and grabbed his tee-shirt off the floor.

"I wish you could stay," she whispered, smoothing out the creases.

"Me, too," he replied, his eyes tender. "I work for your aunt, though, and I can't afford to upset her."

Cautiously he cracked open the door, and when no sounds disturbed the early morning tranquility he slipped into the corridor. Fully awake, Linden sank down on the window seat. Enveloped by the cool, sweet air, she listened to the birds sing in the morning.

Several hours later, she poured herself a cup of coffee in the deserted morning room and scanned *The New York Times* for any report of Gerry's shooting. Finding nothing, she assumed that the Lambert corporate PR department had squashed the story. She was on her second cup of coffee by the time Alex joined her. Helena's arrival a few minutes later set off a flurry of greetings and small talk, but neither he nor Linden gave any hint of their passion-filled night.

Smiling at her niece, Helena said, "Why don't you stay over for a few days? The city must be unbearable at the moment."

Convinced the house held the clues to the Judas Hoard's disappearance Linden jumped at her aunt's offer. "I'd love to."

"Good. I'll be glad for the company. The house is very empty nowadays."

Helena's comment caused a wave of sadness to wash over Linden. The remark, she knew, was the closest her aunt would ever come to admitting self-pity.

"Will you also be staying, Alex?" Helena added.

"Yes. I want to be near Linden. Although she's safe enough here, I still prefer to be close enough to keep an eye on her personally."

"Your room will be available as long as necessary."

"Thanks. My suitcase is still at my uncle's office so I'll pick it up this morning. Tonight, I'd like to take you and Linden out for dinner."

"You're very kind. I'll look forward to it," Helena said. "Linden dear, I'd appreciate it if you'd sit in on Peter's meeting. While he's very conscientious and discusses my portfolio in great detail, I don't understand half of what he says. Since you've dealt with lawyers and accountants for years, I'm sure you can explain it later in simple terms."

Only too anxious to help, Linden went to the library where a copy of Peter's papers was laid out on the coffee table. It was only a breakdown of May's disbursements but she still studied each item thoroughly, writing down a list of questions on a yellow pad.

The consummate professional in front of her aunt, Peter displayed only pleasure at seeing Linden when he walked into the library for their meeting. His presentation included a detailed review of every expense, and she allowed him to finish before speaking. Her first question was about a transfer of funds in the amount of $700,000.

Pointing to the figure, she asked, "What exactly was this for? Supplementary investments doesn't mean much."

"Convenience," Helena answered quickly, like a pupil anxious to impress a favorite teacher. "Peter suggested maintaining a separate account. Then, if we heard of an attractive investment opportunity, we could take immediate advantage without all this tiresome paperwork."

"Sounds logical," Linden acknowledged. "How much is in the account?"

"Almost ten million dollars, I believe," Helena replied, to which Peter nodded in confirmation.

"You can buy a lot of blue chips with that," Linden joked. "Is there a complete accounting of all the financial transactions made in behalf of the estate over the last three months?"

"In other words, the period since I took over full time from Tom," Peter observed.

Helena gave an embarrassed laugh. "Really, Linden, you sound like you don't trust Peter."

"Don't be silly. I just think you should see how that one account affects overall cash flow. You control everything except for Melanie's trust, right?"

Peter's smile never faltered, but his eyes narrowed slightly. "Not quite. Roger handles his own."

"When can we see the figures?" Linden persisted.

"Monday at the earliest."

"Fine. How about eleven o'clock again?" she responded.

Despite his genial expression, Peter seemed to gather up his papers with more force than necessary. "No problem."

"You know how much I appreciate all your help, but maybe Linden's right," Helena said, as the three of them walked outside to Peter's car. "Even though most of the financials are beyond me, we should see some sort of overall statement."

"Never hesitate to ask if you don't understand something," he told her gently. "But I'll make sure the statements are as simple as possible. See you both next Monday."

Getting into the Mercedes, he switched on the engine and drove sedately toward the front gate. With an affectionate arm around Linden, Helena led the way back inside.

"You've no idea what a relief it is to have your input. Melanie's only interest in money is in spending it, and I hate to bother Roger. He's so busy at the moment. Thank heaven you're up on this financial stuff."

"Uncle George insisted on it. He wanted me to be able to handle my own portfolio, although it's nowhere as complex as yours."

At Helena's request, lunch was being served on the terrace where a canvas awning shaded the glass-topped table. As the two women sat in the wicker armchairs, the ever-attentive Brunnings emerged from the dining room with a pitcher of iced tea. When Alex joined them ten minutes later, Linden told him about the morning's meeting, stopping only when the butler brought out lunch. They discussed more mundane topics over poached salmon and salad, the respite from their problems leaving them content to stay at the table. It was Brunnings who effectively ended the meal, appearing as silently as if his shoes rolled on well-oiled wheels.

"Telephone call for you, Linden. It's Mr. Edgeware."

A flicker of guilt crossed Linden's face. "Poor Ned. I should have called to bring him up to date. I wonder how he knew to reach me here? Thanks, Brunnings. I'll use the phone in the library."

Excusing herself, she headed inside to speak to her godfather. He and his wife had been great friends of her parents, and he deserved to hear about the latest developments first hand. Picking up the phone, she was genuinely contrite.

"I'm sorry you had to call me, Uncle Ned," she said.

It was not her godfather who answered, however, but an unknown woman. In a briskly professional voice she asked

Linden to hold for a moment and then a familiar voice came on the line.

"Hello Linden, I think we should have a little talk."

Her body stiffened with tension. "Why the subterfuge, Peter? Still mad at me from earlier?"

"What? Oh, the third degree. Of course not," he said dismissively. "I intended to give Helena a full accounting in a week or so anyway. I called your aunt's phone because I wanted to reach you quickly and I sure didn't want Alex to know I was calling. This morning showed that you're quite capable of functioning without him."

"The only reason he's around is because Aunt Heni's worried about my safety," Linden lied.

"Good, because I have some theories which you might find of interest. I think we should discuss them. Alone. No matter what Alex says, he doesn't necessarily have your best interests at heart. Only his."

Linden knew she should stop the conversation right then, but it was too late. Peter had touched a nerve, causing all her doubts and questions to resurface. Instead she said, "That could be a problem. I don't have a car."

"How about Moon Lake in half an hour? It's only a short walk for you and we can talk there undisturbed."

"Sure," she replied, spurred by a stubborn streak of curiosity that assured her she wasn't being disloyal.

Hanging up the phone, she returned to the terrace to find all signs of lunch cleared away. Over by the pool, Alex sprawled on a lounger beneath a giant umbrella. He wore only swimming trunks, the bullet wound on his left arm hidden under a large band-aid. The sight of his lean body evoked memories of their most intimate moments, and more than anything else she just wanted to spend the afternoon wrapped in his arms, shielded from all unpleasant thoughts.

"Working hard?" she inquired, sitting on an adjacent chair.

"Extremely," he smiled, opening one eye. "Most of a PI's work is mental gymnastics."

"So why does it bear a strong resemblance to sleeping?"

"I guess cynical people could think that. You'll just have to take my word it isn't. Unfortunately, my job does have a few disadvantages. Staying near clients often means being in unconventional situations."

"And on occasions like this, work could be mistaken for play."

Alex sighed. "The sacrifices we have to make. Suits me fine, though. I really don't like to work hard. Just lying by the pool can produce great results."

"Well, since I might be a distraction, I'll go for a walk."

"In this heat!" Alex exclaimed, sitting up. "You're nuts."

Praying he wouldn't offer to join her, Linden said, "It isn't so bad in the shade."

"It isn't that great either," he laughed, lying back. "But crazy or not, I still love you."

"And I love you," she told him, running a gentle hand over his chest. It didn't mean she had to trust him, too.

With the enthusiasm of someone about to face a firing squad, she trudged through the house to the driveway beyond. There, she found Helena about to leave for New York and wasted a few more minutes while her aunt settled herself in the rear of the Bentley. As she waved at the departing car, Linden's smile hid her growing doubts. She should have refused to meet Peter, stressed that she wasn't interested in speculation, demanded that he provide actual proof.

Garibaldi cured her indecisiveness by bounding over to her, full of excitement at the prospect of a walk. Telling herself that he could set the direction, she followed him to the end of the driveway where he instantly headed for Moon Lake. Ten minutes later, she came across Peter's Mercedes near a sandy section of shore. He was parked by a cluster of Scottish pines and obviously on the lookout for her approach. The passenger door opened as soon as she and Garibaldi ambled into view, the sun-drenched afternoon sapping even the dog's energy.

"Get in," Peter ordered, and at her hesitation, added irritably, "Christ, Linden, I'm not going to abduct you. The air conditioner's on."

Sliding into the seat, she opened the rear door for Garibaldi, who squeezed into the space behind her and rested his head on the back of her seat. Man and beast regarded each other with mutual dislike.

"Why's he here?" asked Peter.

"Garibaldi has feelings, too. He gets very hurt if he's left out of anything." Linden leaned against her door. "Well, what's so fascinating?"

"You, or to be more precise, your connection with Gerry's shooting," Peter replied. "You can't fool me, Linden. The description of the woman in the bar fits you perfectly."

"How do you know about that?"

"Helena tells me everything. Who else does she have? Melanie's far too self-centered, and you sure didn't help your case by dropping out of sight after George's death."

Linden stiffened and transferred her gaze to the far side of the lake. A faint breeze ruffled the water, the ripples glinting like diamonds as they swirled toward the shore.

"I'm aware of that. You don't have to rub it in."

"I didn't mean to upset you. I'm just curious as to why you haven't admitted to being with Gerry on Tuesday or giving a reason for meeting him in the first place." Expression earnest, he added, "I am your aunt's lawyer. That has to count for something."

A minute passed while she thought over Peter's questions.

"You're right," she finally acknowledged. "Gerry called me to say he had someone interested in the coins. Alex figured that Gerry might be talking about The Voice, and if so, then Gerry could lead us to him."

"That was a hell of a gamble."

"We decided it was worth it. Unfortunately, Gerry was shot before we got anywhere." Anger entered Linden's tone. "The Voice called later to brag about being the shooter. He said Gerry wasn't even working for him."

Peter frowned. "So there's yet another mysterious buyer."

"Yes, but Gerry doesn't know his name. He does all his dealings through a man called Smith."

"Interesting. I wonder if the nameless buyer is actually called Alex Blair."

"Don't be ridiculous," she snapped.

"What exactly do you know about Alex?" Peter persisted.

"Not much." The words escaped Linden before she could stop them. "Just that he's a private investigator and Tom Blair's nephew."

Like a prosecutor on the attack, Peter asked, "Has he ever volunteered any information about himself?"

"No, most of our conversations have centered on me," she admitted, suddenly aware that Alex had never discussed his past. Only his likes and dislikes.

"It was very convenient that he was available to take your case," Peter observed. "And free to devote himself to it totally."

"He just started his own business and doesn't have many clients yet."

Her reply was Alex's word-for-word answer when she'd raised the same issues.

"He's also quite a mystery man. I can't find anything about him." Peter gave a deprecating smile. "You can't fault me for being curious. I'm only human. You, too. Considering what you went through last week, it's only natural that you'd respond to sympathy and charm."

Linden's eyes flashed angrily. "I'm not that gullible. Aunt Heni urged me to trust him and I'm glad I did. He's been a big help, especially when I figured out that it was Uncle George himself who hid the coins in the attic."

"What?" Peter looked flabbergasted. "Why didn't you say something sooner?"

Thumping the seat in frustration, she scowled, "Because by the time we got there someone had beaten us to it."

"Well, that explains your reaction to my visit yesterday afternoon," he remarked. "No wonder you were so suspicious last night. Bet you were all set to accuse me until you heard I never left my car."

"What else was I supposed to think?" she asked defensively.

Peter chuckled. "In your circumstances, I'd take any suspect that came along, too. How disappointing to find yourself without any proof." He paused. "How did you get to Laurel Court?"

"Alex drove me."

"Did he leave you at all? Disappear long enough to have called an accomplice?"

"No, never," she answered vehemently, because she had been the one to leave. On the way to Radford they'd stopped for lunch, and after asking Alex to order her a chef's salad, she went to the Ladies Room. He could easily have called someone during her brief absence.

And when they reached the house, the Judas Hoard was missing.

She deliberately changed the subject. "If Alex solves the case, the publicity will bring him a lot of new clients."

"If he finds the coins but doesn't admit it, he'll never have to work again."

Alex's recent comment about not liking to work hard returned with all the subtlety of a sledge hammer. Although she had laughed then, now it no longer seemed funny.

"Don't take it too hard," Peter comforted. "He's conned a lot of other people, too. I'm surprised at how quickly your feelings changed, though. Just a few days ago you detested him."

"We've spent quite a bit of time together since then and I've discovered he's not such a bad guy."

"Because it suited him better. He didn't have a very high opinion of you at first."

"So?"

Although Linden sounded dismissive, Peter's accusations were hitting home. Alex had changed even more dramatically than she had.

"As I said last night, sympathy and understanding are much more effective. It's obvious that he decided to switch tactics." Peter's voice turned somber. "He wants those coins, Linden, and it wouldn't surprise me to learn he's working with The Voice."

Linden's eyes flashed angrily. "Bull."

"Don't be too quick to condemn me. Remember, I'm a lawyer and trained to consider all the evidence. *Fact*: Alex materialized out of nowhere the day after you disappeared. *Fact*: he just happened to trace you to your hotel the day of George's funeral. *Fact*: he miraculously appeared at your apartment just as The Voice was about to drug you. Yet another ploy to get you to trust him. I bet the two of them intended to work on you until you remembered the Hoard's hiding place. And then they'd be off with the coins, never having to worry about money again."

"*No*. Alex would never be involved with something so cruel," Linden half-shouted. "And look at what he's gone through while working on this case. He's been shot and The Voice hit him over the head. Hard."

"The Judas Hoard is worth a fortune." Peter was relentless. "Greed can make people do a lot of things they'd normally find repugnant."

"Not him. He's genuinely concerned about me."

"They say the Boston Strangler was real nice when he wasn't off murdering some innocent victim," Peter said mildly. "Believe me, I don't like having to play devil's advocate but I've a feeling you're in danger. Each time you needed a helping hand, Alex was always on the scene. That guy sure has a knack for lucky guesses."

"You forget, someone took the coins yesterday but Alex is still with me," Linden said, triumphantly offering her final, irrefutable piece of evidence.

"My dear Linden, he wouldn't disappear immediately. That's the quickest way to arouse suspicion," Peter reminded her. "No, he'll wait until you've been lulled into a false sense of security. Then he'll take off, after first giving you a credible reason as to why he won't be around for a few days. By the time you catch on, he and the Judas Hoard will have vanished for good."

"Any way you can support your accusations?" Linden asked acidly.

"This isn't about accusations, it's about trust, and you know you can trust me. Call me if he begins to act suspiciously. Anytime."

Linden had heard enough. His arguments were all too believable, the logic sound. But he'd proved nothing, not even said anything new. She'd already considered every one of his points before burying them deep in her subconscious. Flinging open her door, she escaped the confines of the car and let Garibaldi out.

"Remember, I'm always available, no matter how late," Peter called out as he switched on the car engine.

Numbly she nodded and watched him drive away, his left hand raised in farewell. Emotions in turmoil, she plodded back to the house. Garibaldi never left her side, nudging her hand periodically as if to remind her that she could always depend on him.

Although tempted to hide out in her bedroom, she headed for the swimming pool. Alex was hunched over his laptop, the shade from the sun umbrella making his face look almost sinister. Telling herself to get a grip, she walked across the patio, the faint slap of her sandals enough to alert Alex of her return. A huge smile of welcome lit up his face, and jumping to his feet, he stretched luxuriously.

"Have a good walk?" he asked.

With an effort, she smiled back. "Great."

"Where did you go?"

"Just around," she replied vaguely, pointing toward Radford.

Pulling her to him, he nuzzled her neck. "I don't know where you get your energy. I hope you aren't overdoing it."

For once she didn't want to be alone with him and his concern provided the perfect excuse. "I am a little tired. Maybe I'll take a nap."

His expression turned worried. "We don't have to go out for dinner tonight if you're not up to it."

"No, I'll be fine later. Go back to what you were doing."

Pushing him back into his chair, she dragged herself upstairs and collapsed on the bed. Eyes closed, she willed her mind to go blank. The last thing she wanted was to think.

\* \* \*

A few minutes later she gazed, bleary-eyed, at the clock on the night table and saw that two hours had elapsed. After rapidly showering and dressing, she went downstairs in a much better frame of mind.

Alex and her aunt were in the library, laughing softly, and she paused in the doorway to study Alex. He looked so attractive . . . so civilized in his charcoal gray suit. He certainly didn't look like someone involved in a plot to steal a priceless artifact from a dying man. She decided that her suspicions were foolish. As for Peter's accusations? Peter was a lawyer and he'd admitted that part of his job was to examine the facts and to raise questions. Reassured, she walked into the room.

Helena greeted her with a fond smile. "Do you want to leave or have a drink first?"

"Leave. We'll have drinks at the restaurant."

Parked outside the front door, the Bentley's engine purred softly. As the three of them walked outside, Martin swung open the rear door, a cheerful smile for everyone.

"I know Alex said he was taking us out but we're going to the country club instead," Helena announced, once they were settled in their seats.

Linden's recent treatment by the tabloids had left her with no desire to face Radford's residents.

"Do you think that's a good idea?"

"It's time to stop this silly gossip," Helena said firmly. "And the only way is to show the world that you're still my beloved niece."

Linden covered her aunt's hand. "I wish there was a way to make up for the pain I've caused you."

"You're here now. That's a start."

Apart from an elderly couple sipping brandy in front of the massive fieldstone fireplace, the club's bar was deserted. The restaurant, though, bustled with activity until they appeared in the doorway. As if given a cue all conversation ceased instantly. The silence remained for the space of a heartbeat before the chatter resumed louder than before.

Greeting Helena with his usual deference, the maitre d' led them across the dining room to their table. Conscious of being the center of attention as she followed her aunt, Linden felt like Marie Antoinette on her way to the guillotine. Spine stiffly erect, Helena seemed oblivious to everyone's reaction, but Linden sensed her distress. Yet despite their reception, dinner proved to be enjoyable. Alex opened up with stories of previous cases, his easy manner making even the ordinary seem amusing.

*See, he does have a past*, Linden thought happily. *There's nothing suspicious about him.*

Erasing the last of her doubts, a sense of security enveloped her that ended abruptly when their waiter returned to refill their coffee cups. The back of her neck prickled uncomfortably and she glanced around. Peter was seated at a table in the corner, a beautiful blonde draped over him. His speculative expression resurrected all her questions, this time with a vengeance. Depression descended immediately and she was relieved to hear Helena admit to exhaustion and suggest that it was time to leave.

Once home, they all went directly upstairs and bid each other a polite goodnight before going to their own rooms. Linden had just slipped into her nightgown when a light tap sounded at her door, which she opened with little enthusiasm. Although reluctant to confront Alex, she knew it was finally the time for answers.

"I'll be glad when I don't have to creep down darkened hallways to see you at night," he chuckled, closing the door softly.

Going to the window, Linden kept her back to him. "Alex, how were you able to identify me so quickly at the cemetery?"

"Easy. You were the cutest woman there," he joked.

"Not to mention unbelievable luck," she snapped.

Alex's tone lost its humor. "Luck had nothing to do with it. Your behavior was irrational. Most people are sad at funerals but your grief was so obvious, even though you were trying to hide it. I just felt that you seemed far too upset if George were only a friend."

"You're amazingly perceptive."

"When you've been at this as long as I have, it's something you develop."

"You told me you just started your own company," she accused him.

"I haven't been living in a vacuum," he said in an exasperated voice. "I've worked for other people for years."

While plausible, his explanation didn't entirely satisfy her. Shoulders slumping, Linden tried to sound convincing. "I guess you have a point."

Alex put his arms around her. "Of course I do. What's wrong? You've been down ever since your walk."

Once again, she used his concern as a way to hide her misgivings. "You were right, it was too hot and I should never have gone out. Now I'm really bushed."

Without another word she pulled herself free and slid into bed. Alex watched in baffled silence before shedding his clothes and joining her under the covers. In the warm darkness, he took her in his arms and kissed her forehead.

"Goodnight, my love. Everything will look better in the morning, you'll see."

He soon fell asleep, but more awake than ever, Linden lay beside him, still plagued by questions. As rapidly as she managed to smother one, another popped up.

Leaning on her elbow, she studied Alex's sleeping form. In just a few days, and under the most unlikely circumstances, she'd fallen in love with him. He was the first man to make her feel cherished, and the only one with whom she wanted to share her life. Why then did her doubts continue?

# Chapter 22

Linden awoke the next morning alone in the bed and as confused as ever. Her doubts about Alex still lingered, buzzing inside her head like a swarm of angry bees. Dragging herself out of bed, she took a fast shower and decided that the cloudless sky meant another sweltering day. Dressed in a cotton sundress, she went downstairs to find Alex in the morning room. Although he appeared engrossed in *The New York Times*, he put it aside when she walked through the door.

"Hi, sweetheart," he greeted her cheerfully. "You look a little happier. I knew a good night's sleep would work wonders."

"You were right," she lied, pouring a cup of coffee.

"I've decided to go into the office today. You'll be safe here with so many people around."

"You're going to Boston!" she exclaimed.

"No, my desk at Tom's. Although it isn't the greatest setup, I won't be needing it much longer."

"You've had a brainwave?" Linden asked eagerly.

"Not exactly, but I'm convinced we've overlooked something obvious. I want to go over Tom's files. I'm hoping that something will jump out at me with all the answers. What are you up to?"

Linden shrugged. "Probably stay here and relax. I could use a day doing nothing."

"Sounds good." Rising, he dropped a kiss on top of her hair. "See you later."

His footsteps echoed noisily in the quiet house and the gentle slam of the front door seemed to contain an air of finality. Filled with sudden foreboding, she raced outside and his face grew concerned as she hurried toward him.

"You didn't say when you'd be back." Her words tumbled out.

"Around four o'clock," he replied. "Maybe sooner. I don't want to be away from you any longer than necessary."

"This is our first real parting and I wanted to say goodbye properly. The others don't count. I didn't like you at the time."

"Then we better make this memorable."

Smiling, Alex pulled her to him and they kissed with growing desire until he pushed her away.

"Later," he whispered. "We'll pick this up later."

Shaken by the passion behind the kiss, Linden watched him get in his car. That, she decided, proved there was absolutely no way for him to be in league with the enemy. Yet as she watched Alex drive away, a little kernel of suspicion continued to gnaw at her. No matter how much her heart believed in him, her brain continued to think otherwise.

Torn between fury and guilt, she wandered back inside the house. Alex was so open about his feelings, she reminded herself, how could she not trust him? What made Peter's charges even slightly believable?

In need of more coffee, she headed for the morning room where Helena was seated at the table, a pile of unopened envelopes in front of her.

"Alex has gone to his office," Linden announced, pouring herself some coffee.

"I'm not surprised," the older woman said, taking a sip from her own cup. "He's very competent and extremely conscientious. Gives me frequent status reports."

Linden wished she could share her aunt's faith, but too much about Alex still remained an enigma. Pretending a brightness she didn't feel, she asked, "What are your plans for today?"

Helena sighed. "Visiting Gerry. Melanie wants me with her. I hope you're just going to stay home. You need some down time."

"I'll take it easy. First, though, I want to visit the cemetery. Since my car's still at the forensic lab, may I use the Volvo?" she ended.

"Of course, but it's time to let go," said Helena, eyes worried. "We all have to."

\* \* \*

No one was in sight when Linden pulled into the cemetery's sun-soaked parking lot, but three cars indicated the presence of other people. Although a majestic copper beech cast a giant shadow, a black Explorer hogged most of it, leaving only a tiny sliver of shade for the Volvo. After parking, Linden headed for the main pathway which she followed to the first turnoff. The narrow path was flanked by rows of headstones that ranged from shiny marble to lichen-covered granite, each one with its own story to tell. Her uncle's grave stood out from all the others in the carefully-tended grass, the exposed earth as raw as an open wound. Seeing a nearby bench, she sat in the sun-dappled shade and gave in to the grief that squeezed her heart like a noose.

*Though my soul will set in darkness, it will rise in perfect light*

For once, she couldn't find any comfort in either her uncle's favorite poem or in her memories. She felt totally alone.

Suddenly another emotion pierced her misery. She had the distinct feeling that someone was spying on her—and the sensation was neither kind nor even indifferent. Instead, she felt pure evil. The hairs on her arms quivered in alarm, but determined not to show fear, she remained motionless. Although the peace of the cemetery remained undisturbed, she had the overwhelming urge to protect herself.

Opening her purse, she groped for the pencils that accompanied her everywhere in case she had a sudden idea for a design. From experience, she knew it was best to sketch it out right then before she forgot it, so the pencils were always sharpened to a fine point. Jabbing them into someone might provide the distraction she needed to escape. If she were really lucky, her attacker could develop an infection from the cut.

As her fingers touched the smooth wood, she glimpsed movement amongst the trees and her grip on the pencils instinctively tightened. But the man who limped into sight definitely wasn't The Voice. Denim overalls flapped around his slight frame while a nimbus of iron grey curls topped his wrinkled face. A wide smile revealed perfect teeth, dazzlingly white against his mahogany skin. Linden tried to conceal her relief as she smiled back.

"Sorry to intrude," he said, hobbling over to the bench. "I need to sit down. Been walking for a while, checking out the area to make sure everything's okay."

"No problem," Linden responded. "I was just about to leave."

"Not such a bad idea. Don't pay to spend too much time here." Pointing an arthritic finger at the mound of earth, he asked, "Family?"

"Yes. My uncle. He and my aunt adopted me when my parents died."

"He was a good man?"

"The best."

"Been here over forty years and buried them all. Good and bad. Can't undo the past though. Just have to live with it and remember the good times."

"Easy to say but hard to do at the moment. It only happened last week."

Face serious, the man nodded. "Your uncle didn't die, you know. He's all around you, watching you. In the sunlight. Raindrops. A starry night."

"He loved the stars," said Linden. "Told me that's what my parents had become."

"Maybe he was right and now he's up there with them."

"If we really do turn into stars, that's where he is."

With a groan, the man stood up and massaged his right knee, his eyes sympathetic. "Think of the stars whenever you need a lift."

"I will. Thank you," she said, watching him lurch away.

Their conversation had eased some of her grief and she felt a little foolish for overreacting earlier. Much calmer, she strolled back to her car, but she checked the Volvo's rear before getting into the driver's seat. Keeping all the doors and windows locked, she switched on the air conditioner and checked her phone for messages. There were four missed calls, all from Peter Sinclair. Concerned he had bad news about Gerry, she dialed his number.

He picked up immediately and made no secret of his annoyance. "I've been trying to reach you for nearly an hour. Where the hell are you?"

"The cemetery. What's wrong?"

"I want to show you something. Meet me at Charlton Station."

"It won't be for at least ten minutes," she said.

"I'll wait."

Quickly, she put the car in gear and headed for the highway. Even though the lawyer didn't have bad news about her family, she was consumed with curiosity by the time she reached Charlton. Parked illegally outside the station's small waiting room, he followed her until she found a spot. Opening the passenger door of his Mercedes, he barely waited for her to buckle up before speeding off.

"Be prepared for a shock," he warned. "But this is something you need to see."

"What is it?"

"Alex," replied Peter harshly. "And a friend."

Too tense to talk, Linden sat stiffly in her seat while Peter roared along the country roads with little regard for safely. But when he pulled into Dylan's parking lot, apprehension swept over her with the force of an avalanche.

Once again, the dining room was almost deserted, with most diners preferring to eat out on the patio. Alex was seated at the table he and Linden had shared a few days earlier, deep in conversation with a male companion. Although the other man was hunched over the table with his back to the door, the sight of him caused the blood to drain from Linden's face.

"It's The Voice," she gasped.

The shade from the sun umbrella made it hard for Linden to get a clear look at him, but she could see that his suit jacket was stretched across his broad shoulders.

"I swear he's The Voice."

A satisfied smile crossed Peter's face. "I thought it might be."

"How?"

"Alex muscled his way into my office this morning

and asked if I knew anyone around six feet and built like a linebacker. At the time, no one rang a bell, but now . . ." Peter's voice trailed off.

"Get me out of here," she said. "I've seen enough."

Peter didn't argue and he sped away from Dylan's in silence until a familiar yellow arch came into view. Pulling into the drive-through, he ordered two coffees. At the pick-up window, he handed Linden hers.

"You look like you can use this."

"I could use something stronger but I guess this will do." She sipped the hot liquid, its cloying sweetness relieving some of her tension. "How did you find out about the scene back there?"

"Dumb luck." Peter's tone was wry. "My secretary was at lunch so I was looking for a client file myself. They're kept right outside Alex's office, and when his phone rang I couldn't help but hear his conversation. First, he asked, 'You have the money?' Next, he said, 'Look, I can't talk here. Let's meet somewhere'." Peter shrugged. "Naturally I was curious. Christ, everything about that man makes me curious so I followed him. At a discreet distance of course."

"And saw him meet The Voice," Linden stated flatly.

"Right." Expression grim, Peter said, "In a way I don't think I was surprised."

Linden couldn't contain her bitterness. "That man missed his calling. He should have been an actor. I never suspected it was all a pretense."

Peter took a sip of coffee before asking gently, "What do you want me to do?"

"Nothing for the moment. I have to think this through."

"Okay. But maybe I'll hire another private detective to watch Alex, someone guaranteed trustworthy. After all, we've no evidence Alex has done anything wrong."

"How ironic, a PI to watch the PI." A muscle throbbed in Linden's jaw. "How much longer can this go on?"

"Not very. Blair's starting to run out of time, and as the pressure mounts he'll begin to make mistakes."

"Well, I hope he makes them soon because I've had just about enough." She slumped in her seat. "Please take me back to my car. I want to go home."

# Chapter 23

Ominous clouds edged the horizon when she drove into the Lambert driveway twenty minutes later. The familiar surroundings brought her little comfort and even Garibaldi failed to appear. Leaving the Volvo outside the garage, she headed straight for the kitchen. Brunnings was nowhere in sight, and it was his wife who bustled into view from the laundry room.

"Where's Mr. B?" Linden's voice crackled with stress.

The image of him, always impeccably dressed in a dark suit, floated into her mind's eye. She'd never really thought about his solid body before or how his jacket always fit snugly across his shoulders.

A startled expression crossed the housekeeper's face. "Radford. He took the Jeep in for service."

"Why today?" Linden asked.

"No particular reason," Mrs. Brunnings replied. "With everyone gone for now, it seemed like a good time. He's been meaning to go for a few days, said the transmission was stiff. He has his cell phone if you need to reach him."

Linden regretted her sharpness. Mrs. Brunnings'

explanation was entirely reasonable. The butler's absence wasn't a reason for alarm.

"I'm sorry. My nerves are on edge. It also looks like we're also in for a storm, which doesn't help either."

"You don't need to apologize. I know the strain you've been under," Mrs. Brunnings sympathized. "Have you had lunch?"

"No, I wasn't hungry."

"Well, let me make something for you now. What would you like?"

"Nothing, thanks. It's too hot to eat."

"Maybe a nice Waldorf salad," Mrs. Brunnings coaxed. "You're too thin."

"I promise to eat all my dinner."

"You and Melanie are both alike, don't know what it is to have three meals a day." Her ample frame proved she did. "I know you didn't have any breakfast this morning. I could tell by the number of dirty dishes."

"Oh, Mrs. B, you're impossible." Linden couldn't help laughing. "Don't fuss, I'll be fine."

"I missed not having you to fuss over this last week. Never thought for a moment that you'd run off with those coins. And you better believe that's what I told Mr. Blair when he came to question us about you."

"When was this?"

"The day after your uncle died. I wasn't at all pleased, and let him know what I thought about everyone's accusations. I told him that not only did you adore your aunt and uncle, you'd never do anything to upset them."

"I bet he didn't buy it."

"He didn't," Mrs. Brunnings admitted. "But when I took him eggs this morning, know what he said? You were right, Mrs. B. Linden's quite a woman. And I said of course she is, and you better take care of her. And he said he wished he'd listened to me in the first place because he now knew you'd never hurt anyone on purpose. Exactly, I said," Mrs. Brunnings ended, beaming with delight.

"Alex has fooled you just like everyone else. He's used us, all of us, especially me." Linden was quickly becoming irrational. "And how do we really know who he is? He just turned up last week out of the blue."

"Honey, you're wrong. His uncle called him as soon as it became obvious you were missing."

Shocked, Linden stared at the housekeeper "How do you know?"

"I bumped into Tom Blair in Charlton on Tuesday and he told me."

"I'm so confused," Linden said. "I've heard things that make me suspicious. I really don't know much about him."

"Well, I can promise that he's completely trustworthy," Mrs. Brunnings stated firmly.

"Maybe you're right," Linden allowed. "But who was the man he was having lunch with? I . . . I saw him unexpectedly."

Mrs. Brunnings shrugged. "Doesn't need to be anyone bad, could even have been his father. After all, his parents live quite close by."

"Really!" Linden exclaimed, and then continued defensively, "See, there's so much I don't know about him."

"He'll tell you in his own good time," Mrs. Brunnings consoled. "Now, how about some lunch?"

"I'm still not hungry. Maybe I'll rest. I'm exhausted from all my running around."

"That sounds like a good idea. Then later you'll eat."

With a wan smile Linden dragged herself to the foyer, but instead of going upstairs she was drawn to her uncle's sick room. Sadness overwhelmed her as she walked inside, knowing she'd never see George again, hear his voice, watch him smile. Memories of his last few weeks surfaced, a kaleidoscope of shape-shifting images that finally crystallized into one sharp vision. It was the week before his death and she'd gone to say good night but he was asleep. She and Matt, the night nurse, had gazed down at him, his face clear of the pain that had become his recent companion.

"He's at peace now, but it won't last," Matt had told her. "He'll wake up in a few hours and become very restless."

"What do you do?"

"It's been so warm these last few nights we've gone out for a walk."

"In the dark!"

"We've been lucky. No clouds and a full moon. Plenty of light for a midnight stroll."

"Where have you gone?"

"Would you believe to the woods? Despite the moonlight, I still took a flashlight, just in case," Matt laughed. "We made it as far as the giant oak, too, although Mr. Lambert was wiped out by then. He had to rest before we could come back."

The memory faded, and going over to the French door, Linden stepped outside onto the marble terrace. Her eyes sought out the woods which she'd once imagined to be part of an enchanted forest where fairies lived and no one ever got hurt. Growing older, she'd known better, but it had still provided hours of fun for the family and neighboring children.

An air current tickled her ear and her uncle whispered, *"Remember the treasure hunts?"*

"You always found such inventive places."

*"I lived here my entire life. I knew them all."*

"You loved the giant oak best," Linden reminisced.

*"Remember my super-secret hidey hole?"*

She didn't need any prompting. "The giant oak."

For a moment she stopped breathing.

The giant oak.

Matt had said they'd gone there several times just before George died.

*For I love the stars too fondly to be fearful of the night.*

And with a cloudless sky, the moon and stars would be extra bright, giving George enough light to bury the coins.

Just as her gaze found the giant oak, a shaft of sunlight settled over it like a giant halo, bathing the leaves in a cloud of gold. She half expected to hear a choir of angels break into a heavenly chorus. Exoneration was so close she could almost taste it. And as with so many things in her life, she had her uncle to thank for it. Without his poem, the Hoard might have remained hidden for a lot longer. Still, at some point, she would have connected the dots—just as The Voice expected. Despite the heat, her blood seemed to turn to ice. Because, she realized, The Voice was someone who knew her very well.

She suddenly flashed back to the image of Alex and his lunch companion, and the glimpse she'd caught of the other man's dark hair and dark suit. She knew only one dark-haired man who consistently wore a dark suit.

*Brunnings.*

Granted, his shoulders weren't unnaturally broad, but he matched The Voice's profile in plenty of other ways. Most damning, both he and Alex were supposed to be in separate towns. Instead, they were at the same restaurant, huddled together like conspirators.

Yet how could Brunnings even be on her list of suspects, let alone at the top? Here was someone she'd known since childhood. He had been a trusted confidant as she grew up. There was absolutely no way he could be The Voice. Could he? He was the keeper of the family secrets. He had everyone's respect, trust . . . and access to the house at any time.

But most hurtful was the double betrayal. Alex's involvement was almost too painful to bear. She truly believed he was her soulmate—not a world-class louse. Or was she jumping to the wrong conclusion? Maybe Alex was just stringing the butler along in order to get incriminating evidence.

The prospect of vindication now tasted like ashes. She had to tell someone, though, and the only person she trusted was Detective Gorton.

Back inside the house, she headed straight for the library and Helena's desk. Given her aunt's passion for organization, Linden guessed the detective's card would be somewhere obvious. She found it at once: at the start of the G's in Helena's address book. Since the house phone was right next to her hand, she used it to call Gorton who answered on the first ring.

"Hi, this is Linden Travers," she announced. "My uncle hid the Judas Hoard and I just figured out where."

Gorton's interest was tempered with skepticism. "That's great news but why tell me? What about your PI buddy?"

"He's not around at the moment." As it wasn't a total lie, Linden managed to sound sincere. "And I also thought you'd want to be here when I retrieve it."

"You're right. I'd like to be a witness when the biggest coin theft in history becoming exactly that. History." Dropping all pretense of indifference, Gorton let his excitement show. "Give me fifteen minutes. Got a name for The Voice, too?"

"If only," she replied, trying to make it sound like a joke.

Totally dejected, she hung up the phone. The easy part was over. Her next problem was how to handle Brunnings whose wife, she realized, was standing in the doorway.

"I thought I heard your voice," the housekeeper said. "Was that Mr. Sinclair?"

"No, a friend. From college," she gabbled. "Julia."

"I remember her. Nice girl," Mrs. Brunnings commented. "Mr. Sinclair called about ten minutes ago but I couldn't find you. He said it wasn't important, just wanted to see how you were."

"I'll call him back." Linden felt like a traitor. "I have news for him anyway. I know where the Hoard is."

"That's wonderful." Mrs. Brunnings delighted smile abruptly faded. "You mean you did take the coins?"

"Uncle George decided to be very clever and hid them himself. I just figured everything out and I was about to tell Peter."

Expression troubled, Mrs. Brunnings caught Linden's arm as she reached for the phone. "Mr. B and I would never spy on you, but sometimes it's impossible to avoid hearing things. I've wanted to tell you this since yesterday. Remember Wednesday night, when you were having cocktails in the living room? Apparently Mr. Sinclair told you that he'd been here earlier."

Linden nodded. "Said he'd delivered some papers."

"Well, Mr. B was in the dining room and couldn't help but overhear the conversation. Later, he repeated it to me because Mr. Sinclair wasn't entirely truthful."

A spark of unease stirred in Linden's stomach. "Go on."

"He did stop by around lunchtime. There was a breeze so we'd left all the French doors open. It's quite safe because Garibaldi makes such a fuss if someone comes."

"Unless he knows the person." Linden's comment revealed none of her escalating concern.

"Well, Garibaldi didn't make a fuss that day," Mrs. Brunnings said. "We were in the kitchen and Mr. B was watching a ball game while I prepared dessert. Suddenly we heard a crash which seemed to come from the study. We rushed there to find Mr. Sinclair picking up an armchair. He said he'd arrived a few minutes earlier and rung the bell but no one answered."

"That doesn't sound very likely," Linden said.

Mrs. Brunnings gave an unhappy nod. "I'd been using the blender so it is possible that neither of us heard the bell."

"And Peter's been here often enough to know that you leave the French doors open in nice weather," Linden commented.

"So when Mr. Sinclair told us that rather than waste the trip he decided to see if the door to Mr. Lambert's study was open, it seemed quite normal. He said that he knocked over the chair while putting the envelope on the desk. We all laughed and accompanied him to the front door to let him out, only his car wasn't there. He said he'd parked it down at Moon Lake because he wanted the exercise."

"In other words, you've no idea when he actually arrived."

Looking even more distressed, Mrs. Brunnings said, "We don't know why he lied to you, but if it made him look good in front of your aunt, we didn't want to spoil it. However, it's been on my mind."

"Thanks, Mrs. B. I appreciate your telling me."

Face creased with worry, the housekeeper left the room and Linden closed her eyes against the weight of her snowballing suspicions. She'd never felt comfortable around Peter, and now those misgivings were justified. He was both devious and manipulative, especially the way he'd manufactured facts to play her for a fool. Well, here were some facts *he'd* missed. *Fact*: he could easily have arranged to have her apartment bugged. *Fact*: he certainly had sufficient time to search the attic. *Fact*: he'd created a rift between her and Alex by badmouthing him at every opportunity.

Peter's accusations barreled through her mind like a freight train. But she could now see they were nothing but lies . . . especially one innocuous comment that had slipped by her at the time. And not only was Alex the one person who could explain it away, it would prove exactly whose side he was on.

In too much of a hurry to find her cell phone, she flipped through Helena's address book. Alex's phone number was penciled in at the end of the B's. Dialing it, she pumped herself up with self-righteous indignation. Even though she knew her demand for answers would raise some ugly questions from him, her impatience grew with every unanswered ring. He finally picked up on the seventh.

"It's me," she bit out, skipping the pleasantries.

"Hi, sweetheart," he greeted her, a smile entering his voice. "I'm almost ready to leave."

"I know where the coins are," she stated harshly.

"Again," he teased.

"They were never in the attic. Uncle George had another favorite hiding place, one I haven't thought of in years."

"That's the best news I could have." Sounding genuinely thrilled, he asked, "Was it somewhere in the house as you suspected?"

"Not quite. Under the giant oak." With her mind spinning at warp speed, the words escaped before she could stop them. Still not entirely ready to trust Alex, she tried to downplay her discovery. "It's impossible to find unless you know where to look."

"We'll look together."

Linden kept her voice flat. "Mrs. Brunnings just told me something about Peter. He lied on Wednesday evening about giving the envelope to Mr. B. He actually came inside the house. Alone. They found him in my uncle's study."

"How did he get in unseen?"

"Told them no one answered the front door so he went to see if the French door to George's study was open. Brunnings usually leaves the doors open in nice weather so they weren't surprised to find him there. But Mrs. B said they'd no idea when he arrived." Hysteria tinged Linden's voice. "He could easily have gone to the attic to look for the coins. If so, then Peter's The Voice."

"That's a pretty heavy accusation," Alex said. "You're going to need proof."

Throat as dry as the Sahara, she could barely get the next words out. "When I saw Peter yesterday afternoon, he said you came to my apartment just as The Voice was about to drug me. I never told him that, did you?"

A taut silence greeted her question and Alex's voice was almost too-controlled when he finally spoke. "You saw Peter yesterday afternoon?"

She'd expected such a reaction. "Remember that call I got after lunch? It was Peter saying he wanted to talk to me and suggested we meet at Moon Lake."

"What made you agree to such a dumb idea?" Alex roared.

"Because both he and Gerry said things that made me doubt you," she shot back. "Like you weren't to be trusted."

"Thanks a lot," Alex retorted bitterly.

"You've not exactly been Mr. Open and Honest," she flared. "I really don't know much about you—like where you grew up; how long you've been in the PI business; or even if you're married."

"I'm not married," he snarled.

"Thanks for finally sharing," Linden scowled into the phone.

After another tense silence Alex said, "For the record I never talked to Sinclair about The Voice, but we sure need to do some serious talking. I'll be there shortly."

"Fine," she retorted. "And so will Detective Gorton."

# Chapter 24

Jamming the phone back into its charger, Linden thought her sudden chill was the result of the phone call until she looked out of the window. The wind had picked up dramatically and the oak tree dipped and swayed as if controlled by a malevolent puppeteer. As thunderheads billowed across the sky, she knew she had to get the Hoard before the storm hit. First, though, she needed to replace her sundress with jeans and a tee-shirt.

Racing to her room, she swiftly changed her clothes and headed outside. She was almost at the end of the lawn when Garibaldi bounded over, doggy grin widening at the prospect of a walk in the woods. Shrouded in early dusk, the trees twisted in the wind like souls in torment, making her thankful for the dog's company. A flashlight would have helped, but with the weather worsening by the minute, she didn't want to delay retrieving the coins. By the time she reached the oak tree, thunder rumbled in the distance. Reassuring Garibaldi with a tug at his ears, she knelt down.

Although a lattice of gnarled roots encircled the tree's trunk, she unhesitatingly stuck her hand into her uncle's favorite hiding place, the crevice indistinguishable from all the others. As if in protest, the old tree swayed violently and a loamy smell filled the air when she prodded the blanket of decaying leaves. Within seconds her fingers encountered the unmistakable slickness of plastic.

Excitement surged through her as she pulled out a wad of ziplock bags, which she quickly separated until reaching a fragile linen bag. With extreme care, she opened it and spilled the contents into the palm of her hand. The mere touch of the cold metal told her the Judas Hoard had survived unscathed. Beside her, Garibaldi sniffed the coins suspiciously, and she slipped them back into the linen bag.

"They don't seem to have suffered any," she remarked to the dog, packing them back in the ziplock bags.

"After all they've been through, being buried in plastic for a couple of weeks is nothing."

The words came out of nowhere.

Linden's head snapped up. Although the gloom made everything more sinister, the bulky figure towering over her was straight out of her nightmares. But she was *awake*. Here stood the man who had haunted her dreams, the vague image that appeared every time she tried to remember. Hackles rising, Garibaldi growled.

"I've waited a long time for this moment," Peter Sinclair added unemotionally.

"I was right. You are The Voice," she cried.

"Very clever," he sneered. "Not that it will do you much good now."

Linden scrambled to her feet. "You sadistic bastard! Just what the hell are you up to?"

"Diverting suspicion. Until today I wasn't quite ready to disappear. The last thing I needed was for you and Blair to team up or even worse, become a couple."

"You wanted to be the first person I called if I figured out the Hoard's hiding place," she stated.

"Damn right." He held out his hand. "Give me the coins."

Fury outweighing caution, Linden's fingers tightened on the plastic. "No. They're mine."

As a lightning bolt pierced the gloom, Garibaldi pressed against her legs with a pitiful whine. Automatically she patted his head and realized that salvation lay beneath her fingers. Thrusting the ziplock bag between his teeth, she pushed him away.

"Run, Gari," she whispered urgently. "Go get Mr. B."

Clearly sensing her tension, the dog bolted into the tangled undergrowth where he melted into the shadows. For an instant Peter seemed poised to follow but instead he rounded on Linden.

"You little bitch," he snarled, fingers curling around her arm like a manacle. "You've been nothing but trouble. I should've killed you right at the start. At least you're good for one last thing—my hostage. Neither Blair nor Helena take any chance on their precious Linden being harmed."

Frantically, Linden tried to escape his grasp. "They may not see it that way."

Peter pulled a gun from his pocket. "They will when they realize I have this, and I only need you until we get to Kennedy Airport. I was already on my way. Blair seemed to have me on his radar and my gut told me that it was time to leave. As much as I wanted the Judas Hoard, it was too risky to hang around any longer."

Twisting her arm, he shoved her viciously, but she refused to move. Eyes burning with murderous rage, he slowly aimed his gun at her head and pulled the trigger. As the sound of the shot faded away, Linden was amazed to find that being dead felt no different from being alive. Overhead, birds squawked furiously and, opening her eyes, she realized that the bullet had gouged a deep path through the adjacent tree trunk.

Peter slid a bullet into the gun's empty chamber while speaking in a voice devoid of emotion. "Linden, I am fast running out of patience. A dead hostage does me no good, but even wounded you can still be useful. The pain won't leave you totally incapacitated. Now, are you going to move or do you need further proof I'm not joking?"

The safety catch clicked loudly, convincing her not to waste any more time on resistance. With his gun at her back, Linden led the way along the narrow path, her brain working in overdrive. She'd played in the woods since childhood and knew each trail and tree, giving her a major advantage. The path forked in a few yards, and the left one veered toward the Vandergrafs' house where, with any luck, she could hide out.

Her other advantage was her tee-shirt which had once been hunter green. It was now so faded that it made her almost invisible in the early dusk while Peter, in his tan suit and a white dress shirt, stood out in the shadows like a beacon. A gnarled beech tree marked the fork and she plunged into the shrubbery around it. Taken by surprise, Peter stopped mid-step for a moment then charged after her with a loud roar. She raced along the path, following its curves automatically until a distant twinkle of light beckoned her to safety. Suddenly, she glimpsed whiteness where none belonged and Peter lunged at her from behind a tree.

"You fucking piece of shit," he screamed, grabbing a handful of her hair. "I'll get you for this."

Grinding the gun in her side, he dragged her through the trees, low hanging branches lashing at them like leather whips. Once they reached the lawn, he dropped his hand to her arm and yanked her toward the house, forcing her to keep up with his long-legged stride. As she stumbled up the steps to the terrace, she noticed that all the French doors were open. Since they were always locked during stormy weather, it was a very bad sign.

Grip tightening, Peter propelled her through the library and into the foyer where Linden's apprehension exploded into horror. Mrs. Brunnings was handcuffed to the staircase's carved wooden balustrade, the skin of her wrist chafed from struggling to free herself. With a furious glare at Peter, the housekeeper continued to twist her wrist.

"Get those cuffs off her," Linden yelled.

"I'm the one giving orders," Peter fired back.

"She can't do any harm, and Alex and the police are already on their way here."

"I know. That's why I don't have any time to waste." He waved his gun at her. "Move it."

In response to her defiant silence, a bullet embedded itself in the wall above the housekeeper's head. Aghast, Linden watched plaster fly in all directions.

"Missed," Peter smiled. "Need any more encouragement?"

"I'm so sorry," Linden whispered to the other woman.

Despite her pallor, Mrs. Brunnings's voice was steady. "It wasn't your fault, honey. And Mr. B will be here soon. He'll take care of us."

"Think I'm going to wait around for that to happen? We're out of here." Pointing to the security system, Peter ordered, "Open the gates."

Acutely conscious of the gun in her side, Linden pushed a button and the monitor showed a gap open up between the gates. Satisfied, Peter dragged her outside and shoved her into the passenger seat of his Mercedes.

Slamming the door, he hurried to the driver's side and told her, "We're going to Kennedy Airport. You're my security."

Although escape was too risky then, Linden left her seat

belt unbuckled, ready to take advantage of any opportunity. And she could still ask the questions that pounded at her like angry surf.

The gun remained in Peter's left hand as he careened down the driveway. After making the turn into Laurel Court, he stopped the car and dragged the gates shut. Back in the driver's seat, he ignored the seat belt chimes and headed in the direction of the Long Island Expressway.

Linden wasted no time in starting her interrogation. "Was your only interest in the coins financial?"

"Of course. Several years ago, I read an article about the Judas Hoard and became fascinated by the challenge. Here were six old coins that someone would pay millions of dollars to own. All I had to do was find that someone, sell him the coins and I'd be set for life."

"Except for one major obstacle—not having access to the Hoard."

"Good planning removes any obstacle," Peter replied crisply. "And my plan called for getting acquainted with the Lamberts. What easier way than through Tom Blair? Since we were members of the same professional organizations, I set out to cultivate him. It turned out we shared a love of golf, which soon led to us becoming regular partners. While out on the fairway, I let him know that corporate law didn't thrill me. The rest, as they say, is history."

"That's unbelievable!" Linden exclaimed.

"Okay, maybe it was more difficult than it sounds," Peter allowed. "It took a lot of work, but once I became his partner I quickly developed a friendship with the Lambert family. That's when I had to solve my final challenge: how to separate George from the Hoard."

"And the most direct way was through me," Linden said.

"As the only unmarried family member, I was the easiest to exploit. You set me up to take the fall."

"You've got it. You and the Judas Hoard were going to disappear together."

Shocked, Linden gasped, "You were going to *kill* me?"

"No, just keep you out of sight until I was safely out of the country. As soon as the police learned that you inherited very little from your uncle, you'd automatically be suspected of having secretly disposed of the coins. They'd consider you to be a scheming opportunist."

"And that's where the game plan fell apart. When you got me to open the safe, the coins were already gone."

Peter shot her a look of pure venom. "I almost killed you on the spot until I realized you were probably the only person to know where they were. Fortunately, I'd rented the house in Ashton in case of an emergency so I took you there. It's still a mystery how all that pentothal had almost no effect on you."

Signs indicated the entrance to the Long Island Expressway and after merging onto the highway, Peter edged into the center lane. His left hand rested on the bottom of the steering wheel, the gun pointed at Linden. Despite her limited options, she figured that if she could knock the gun out of his hand she might have a chance—especially with a little more room to maneuver. Surreptitiously she slid her seat an inch backwards.

"I sure messed up your plans by escaping," she taunted.

"I felt like going to the Sheraton and taking you out right there. At that point I didn't need the coins; they were just the icing on the cake."

"You'd already made yourself rich by looting my aunt's estate," Linden stated.

"I certainly won't have any money worries," Peter conceded, "but life would be even sweeter with the Judas Hoard, especially after all the effort I've put in. When you called Blair to tell him you'd figured out the Hoard's hiding place, there was no way I could *not* go after you."

Unable to keep silent, Linden said, "And what a monumental mistake that's turned out to be."

"Not the way I see it," Peter said, speeding up to overtake a truck. "I have you."

Although Linden had many of the answers, she still had questions. "Do you have a buyer?"

"Of course I have a buyer!" he exploded. "Tom kept a list of everyone who approached him about the Hoard. All I had to do was find someone who shared my sense of morality. I was lucky. My first choice agreed to my price with no hesitation."

"Why am I not surprised? I knew there were a number of collectors with no scruples. How much?"

"Five million dollars. Cash."

Surprised, Linden said, "That's a fire sale price."

Peter shrugged. "It wasn't the time to be greedy. Owning the Judas Hoard was this collector's dream, and since it was finally coming true there were other ways for him to show his gratitude. He gave me a very generous advance along with the promise to obtain anything to make my job easier."

"Like drugs," Linden observed, inching her seat back again. "And bugs. Bet you couldn't believe your ears when you heard me tell Alex about the Christmas decorations."

"Damn right. All those bugs I planted paid off big time. Fortunately I always had a good reason to visit Helena."

Linden's seat went back another fraction. "How did you manage to get into the house?"

Raindrops started to pelt the car and Peter slowed down slightly. Setting the windshield wipers on high, he said, "Dear Helena. She's been so helpful. She loved to show me her rose garden and around the grounds. The only thing that interested me, though, was the door in the wall. She even went as far as to tell me about the key. It wasn't hard to slip off one day and make an impression of it."

As she listened to Peter's boasts, Linden could barely stop from throttling him. Summoning up the last of her self-control, she said, "So now you had access to the house whenever you wanted, including my uncle's study. I guess you wormed the code out of her, too."

"I was so subtle that she probably never realized she told me."

Linden had heard enough. All she cared about was throwing Peter off balance. Grabbing the steering wheel, she yanked it to the right, but Peter never lost his grip on the gun. Instead, he swung the wheel to the left so the Mercedes swerved back into the center lane, barely missing the driver behind who blasted his horn in response.

"You try that again and, sure as hell, you'll be dead," Peter growled. "The closer we get to JFK, the less I need you, although I really expected your white knight to be charging after us by now."

Linden took a deep breath. She knew she had to stay calm and be rational if she wanted to come up with a plan. Although nauseated by the conversation, she realized her best shot at survival lay in letting Peter gloat about his cleverness.

"Did you also shoot Alex last week?"

Peter's lips curled cruelly. "Yes. He's another person who's caused nothing but problems. While we were in the rose garden, I saw him sneak toward the woods. After leaving you, I came back through the door in the wall to find him. Figured it would be a great chance to get him out of the picture. Too bad I failed."

"And my uncle." For the first time Linden's control cracked. "You said he was . . ."

"Yeah. He went just as I got there," Peter said dispassionately, "making it a whole lot easier for me to take the safe key from him and then put it back. Only a few people knew he wore it on a chain around his neck, which kept the list of suspects very short and you . . ."

The car jerked to a violent halt as he jammed on the brake. Several police cruisers were parked by the center median, their lights flashing like supernovas in the rain-darkened afternoon. Up ahead, the left lane was closed and several police officers were directing traffic over to the right, slowing traffic to a crawl. Periodically, light-colored cars were stopped and searched, which seemed to unnerve Peter.

Sliding the gun into his jacket pocket, he said, "Don't try and get smart, Linden. My gun's still aimed at you."

"I won't try anything," she replied, easing her seat back another inch.

They slowly reached the front of the line, but a police officer put up his hand before Peter could merge into the right lane. Although swamped by a too-big uniform, the man had the cold-eyed gaze of a hardened professional. His quick glance took in every detail of the car's interior.

Opening his window, Peter politely asked, "What's the problem, officer?"

"There's an Amber Alert," came the answer. "A little girl was abducted and witnesses said she was pushed into a light-colored sedan. Please step out of the car while we check your trunk."

Vividly aware that it was her only chance to escape, Linden threw open her door and hurled herself onto the highway. With a strength born of desperation, she crawled away from the car just as Peter hit the gas. Scraping the sides of the nearest cars, he shot into the deserted left lane, pushing the powerful car to its limit.

The police officer hauled Linden to her feet. "Are you okay?"

Ignoring the question, she panted, "We've got to stop that man. He murdered my uncle."

"It's all under control," said the man, flashing a photo ID. "Tony Delaney, FBI. I'm a friend of Alex. He's in that car there."

Just beyond the line of police cruisers, a black Crown Victoria roared after Peter's Mercedes. Tugging Linden past the police cruisers, Tony shoved Linden into the rear of a silver Taurus where a red-haired man was already seated behind the steering wheel. As Tony catapulted into the front seat, the driver slammed his foot on the accelerator and the car shot forward.

Pointing to the driver, Tony said, "This is Don Saunders."

Straining to see through the rain-splattered windshield, Don acknowledged the introduction with a distracted nod. Tony pulled out his cell phone and speed dialed a number.

"We're behind you," he announced, putting his phone on speaker. "Linden's safe. She's in the car with us."

"Thank God," a man responded fervently.

"Who's that?" Linden asked.

"Ben McGuire," Tony answered.

"Another friend of Alex?"

There was a brief silence. "I guess you could call him that."

"Sinclair's driving like a maniac." Ben spoke again. "Doesn't have any place to go, though. The highway's blocked."

Despite the slashing windshield wipers, the torrential rain had reduced visibility to a few yards. Abruptly, the glass cleared to reveal the Crown Victoria hard on the Mercedes's tail. For a moment Peter's lead increased but suddenly his brake lights flickered. Up ahead, three police cars barricaded the highway, red and amber lights swirling like sparks in a wildfire.

"Holy shit," Ben's voice crackled over the phone, "he's going to make a U-turn."

Perched on the edge of the back seat, Linden clung to the armrest between Don and Tony, trying to make out shapes through the blurred glass. Another deluge of rain drenched the car, but Don kept his foot on the gas until Ben finally broke the tense silence.

"He won't make it," he informed them tautly.

As if controlled by an unseen switch, the rain lessened as the Mercedes swung into a gap in the center median. Peter's speed allowed no margin for error, and although his car only grazed the edge of the concrete divider, it flipped over. With a dull thud the fuel tank exploded and flames enveloped the car.

Although vehicles on both sides of the highway screamed to a halt, Don veered onto the right shoulder and continued driving the short distance to the wreck. Leaping from the car, Linden ran toward the inferno but a tall figure blocked her path.

"Stop," commanded Alex, grabbing her arm. "Don't get any closer. Nothing can be done for him."

"He's inside?"

"There was no time to escape."

Impervious to the heat and drizzle, she watched the flames slowly die until just twisted metal remained. As she stared at the last wisp of smoke, reaction to the strain of the last hour set in and violent tremors spread through her body. Pulling off his wind-breaker, Alex gently placed it around her shoulders.

"Are you all right?" another man asked, joining them. "You had us pretty worried while Sinclair had you hostage."

Recognizing Ben's voice, Linden started to smile but it froze on her lips. The brawny man was unmistakable. He was Alex's lunch companion.

"Too bad it had to end this way," Ben continued, staring at the charred remains. "A lot of questions still need answers."

Linden looked at him in confusion, and watching her, Alex's own expression turned sheepish. "Ben isn't just a friend. He's also my boss."

"Boss," she echoed.

"I'm no more a private investigator than you are," he admitted. "I work for the FBI."

# Chapter 25

Stunned, Linden looked from one man to the other. "Why is the FBI involved?"

"The local police weren't equipped to handle a theft as big as this," Alex replied. "They asked us for help since we have better resources, almost all of which we just used to rescue you from Sinclair. He was The Voice?"

Linden's eyes briefly rested on the wrecked Mercedes. "Yes. Too bad he went so fast, but at least he won't be calling me anymore." Frowning at Alex, she said, "I still can't believe you're an FBI agent. Why didn't you tell me?"

"I wanted to, but Ben overruled me. Even though you seemed to be innocent, we couldn't risk blowing my cover."

"In other words, you didn't trust me."

"I was in a tough position, especially as we became . . . friends." For a moment, Alex dropped his professional mask. "I had a job to do, which was to find the Judas Hoard. But I also had to keep you safe and that was always my priority."

Linden was about to brush him off until her conscience pointed out that he had been there for her every day. "Thanks," she said grudgingly. "I never want to be held hostage ever again. It could have ended very differently for me."

The earsplitting sound of sirens stopped any chance of further conversation. As fire trucks and ambulances converged on the scene, Ben joined the crowd of uniformed officials gathered around the burned-out wreck.

Handing Linden a phone, Alex said, "I have to go. Use this to call Helena and let her know you're safe. She's been frantic."

Without another word, he hurried away, leaving Linden alone. Seconds later she was talking to her aunt who was almost incoherent with relief. After being brought up to date, Helena insisted that Linden return home immediately.

Disconnecting the call, Linden realized that leaving wasn't so easy. Although everyone had claimed to be worried earlier, they were now totally focused on the crash site. Exhausted, she slumped against the trunk of Ben's car, still upset that Alex hadn't been honest with her. What else, she wondered, had he lied about?

The minutes ticked by slowly, and just as she was convinced her day from hell would never end, Tony and Don walked over. With his borrowed police uniform covered by an FBI windbreaker, Tony looked more like a typical clean-cut agent.

"We're no longer needed here so we'll take you home," he said.

Deep in conversation with Detective Gorton, Alex appeared to have forgotten about her.

"Thanks," she replied. "Seems I'm no longer needed either."

Too drained to make conversation, Linden sat in silence during the five-mile drive to her aunt's house, but she remembered her manners sufficiently to invite the two men inside for a drink. Both declined, and leaving the car, she stepped straight into Helena's arms.

"Thank God it's over," the older woman whispered, hugging Linden tightly.

"And hopefully Peter's rotting in hell."

"That's no way to speak of the dead," Helena chided.

"He deserves it—and a whole lot more," Linden retorted, but her anger faded as she asked, "How could Alex mislead us the way he did?"

"He must have had a perfectly good reason for everything," Helena said.

"Maybe I'll find out tomorrow. I'm to meet with his boss at ten o'clock. He wants to interview me at the local police precinct."

"We'll go together," Helena promised. "And I'm sure Alex will call tonight."

"Don't bet on it. He was pretty angry when he heard I met Peter yesterday. Like Alex is some sort of saint," Linden ended defensively.

"It will all work out," Helena comforted, slipping an arm around her niece's shoulders. "Everyone's in the living room and very anxious to hear what happened. We've all been so worried."

They were about to walk inside when Garibaldi bounded up. With an ecstatic woof, he licked Linden's hand.

"The Judas Hoard!" Linden exclaimed. "What happened to it?"

"Garibaldi brought it to Brunnings," Helena smiled. "Not only is it locked in the safe, but two armed guards from our security company are spending the night in George's study for extra protection."

Although in no mood for company, Linden went with Helena to the living room. Seated on the sofa and seemingly unfazed by her ordeal, Mrs. Brunnings was chatting with Melanie and Elizabeth, while Brunnings, Tom Blair and Roger talked by the window. Noting that everyone held a drink, Linden felt like a late arrival at a cocktail party. If they were concerned, she thought sourly, they hid it well.

Spotting her, Melanie let out a squeal of joy and flung herself at Linden.

"Oh, Lindy, it's so good to have you back," she sobbed.

"Yeah, your calls made me feel real welcome," Linden said.

"It's been very traumatic for all of us," Melanie sniffed. "Mrs. B told us how brave you were, standing up to Peter. I never trusted him, right from the start."

As usual, Linden couldn't remain mad at her cousin for long, and a vodka and tonic helped relax her further. But even as she updated everyone on the day's events, she became increasingly annoyed at Alex.

It wasn't long before the media picked up the story, setting off a fire storm of phone calls from friends anxious for details. Only Alex showed no curiosity, and at eleven o'clock Linden went to bed, too bone-weary to wait for his call.

Instead of nightmares, a healing slumber carried her though to dawn when further sleep proved elusive. Her eyes kept returning to the window seat where she'd left Alex's windbreaker. All she could see was the huge FBI logo, the florescent letters an unnecessary reminder of his deception. During their love-making, when he'd whispered how much he loved her, she was convinced that she'd finally met the man of her dreams. How could she have been so wrong? It was obvious he'd seduced her just to further his own agenda.

Yet as much as she tried to forget, memories continued to torture her until she couldn't stand the torment any longer. After a rapid shower, she went downstairs and took Garibaldi for a long walk, avoiding the media camped out in Laurel Court by going through the woods at the rear.

The trees were old friends. Not even yesterday's experience could taint them.

* * *

Accompanied by her aunt, Linden arrived at the local police precinct precisely on time. Inside the drab reception area, an overweight police officer sat behind a scarred Formica counter covered with clipboards and flyers. Tony Delaney was waiting for them, and he led the way to a conference room where six executive chairs were squeezed around the oval table. Ben sat in one, a blank scratch pad in front of him. Seated in the adjacent chair was Alex, his usual jeans and sneakers replaced by a charcoal business suit and wing tipped shoes. They both rose as Tony ushered the two women inside, and although Alex greeted Helena warmly, Linden just received a bleak smile.

"Thanks for coming," Ben said. "We need to get your account for the record."

"All done," Linden responded, holding out two sheets of papers. "I woke up early and put something together."

With a smile Ben reached for them. "Excellent. This will save some time."

Linden braced herself for a barrage of questions, but neither man displayed any emotion while reading through the handwritten pages. Alex was the first to speak, his face impassive as he looked at Linden.

"So Sinclair took the job with my uncle for the sole purpose of stealing the Judas Hoard. Why involve you?"

"To take the blame. He figured if the coins and I vanished together, everyone would think I was a scheming opportunist." Her voice shook with anger. "Those were his very words."

"Except it didn't quite happen that way," Ben said. "To paraphrase Robert Burns, even the best laid plans of mice and men can go awry."

"When he discovered the coins were missing, he was positive I knew where they were. He was super-organized and already had contingency plans in place. He'd rented the house in Ashton, and even had various drugs, courtesy of his buyer. It was no big deal to take me there to work on me."

"Another wasted effort, since Mr. Lambert had hidden them himself," Ben commented.

"The poem was my only clue. Thank God Uncle George wrote it down," Linden finished in a heartfelt voice.

"And you were able to connect the dots," Alex said. "Did Sinclair reveal his buyer's name?"

Linden shook her head. "No, just the price. Five million dollars. He'd already received a large advance."

"Certainly worth all the risks he took," Ben observed. "Well, I think this does it. Once your statement's typed up and signed, you can leave."

Striding across the room, he opened the door and spoke to someone out of view. Alex studiously inspected the brilliant shine on his black shoes while Linden stared out of the window at the barrier of trees the separated the complex from the highway. Gaps in the bushes allowed a glimpse of the passing cars, streaks of sunlight bouncing off their windshields like flaming arrows. Lost in her own thoughts, Helena seemed unaware of the uncomfortable silence that stretched between Linden and Alex. When Ben returned a few minutes later, the tension lessened slightly, and everyone watched with more interest than necessary as he perched on the edge of the credenza.

"We'll issue a press release about the Judas Hoard's return. That should put an end to all the gossip flying around the neighborhood," he smiled. "And we'll make sure it emphasizes all your help, Linden."

"Where are the coins?" Alex asked.

"We dropped them off at the bank on our way here," Helena replied. "They spent the night in George's safe, but the bank's the best place for them. After being thoroughly vetted, all prospective buyers will have to go there to see them, and we'll have security guards present."

"I hope you won't hold Alex's deception against him, Mrs. Lambert," Ben said. "Naturally we'll refund your retainer. He had to cash it to maintain the pretense."

Flashing Alex a fond smile, Helena said, "I must admit the truth came as quite a shock, especially since I'd specifically requested that the FBI not be involved." Displaying a rare show of irritation, she added, "There was already too much publicity."

"The robbery was too high profile for the local police department," Ben explained. "I understood why you wanted to hire a private investigator, but I felt that the case was too big to entrust to someone outside of government. Since Tom Blair's been your family lawyer for decades, we'd been working with him and he'd told us about Alex right from the start. Although he worked out of the field office in Boston, we knew Alex would be a good fit."

"There was just one problem," Alex smiled. "I'd resigned from the FBI and was down to my final week's notice."

"With the promise that he could set his own terms, we persuaded him to stay on as a favor. His talent for finding people who didn't want to be found made him too valuable to lose. As of today, though, he's officially on his own," Ben laughed.

"But not as a private investigator," Alex stressed. "Ten years of irregular hours are enough. After taking some refresher courses in finance, I'm joining my father's CPA firm. I was an accounting major in college, but most of what I learned is long forgotten."

"Yet even with all your resources, Peter still managed to slip through the cracks," Helena said, returning to the previous conversation. "How did you miss him?"

"He was a very clever man, and extremely cautious," Ben replied. "Everyone was a suspect at first, but he initially came up clean so we dropped him to the bottom of the list."

"What about the funds he transferred from my account?" Helena exclaimed.

"We had no cause to monitor your finances," Alex pointed out. "The red flags didn't go up until after Thursday's meeting with Sinclair when Linden voiced her concerns. By then, though, we were too late; the money was gone. We have found an electronic paper trail and have people working on it. It could even lead us to Sinclair's buyer."

"Our search of his condo last night turned up some very sophisticated listening equipment," Ben disclosed, pausing to scrawl a note on the legal pad. "Which reminds me: we must send someone over to debug both your residences."

"Forensics detected trace evidence of a similar setup in his car," Alex added. "He obviously listened in when Linden called to say she'd figured out the Hoard's hiding place. I guess he just couldn't pass it up, not after all the trouble he'd gone through."

"As soon as Alex hung up with you, he called me," Ben told Linden. "I wanted to be there in person when you produced the Hoard and also to hear why you thought Sinclair was The Voice. Alex and I reached Laurel Court almost simultaneously and found Gorton waiting for us."

"That's when we realized we were in big trouble," Alex continued grimly. "We couldn't get anyone to open the front gate or answer the house phone. Fortunately, we had Brunnings' cell phone number and he gave us the code to the gate. Took me less than ten seconds to make it up the drive. I didn't even bother with the front door; just went straight for the nearest open window, expecting the worst."

Now, Ben could smile. "It was almost a relief to find Mrs. Brunnings just handcuffed to the banister. She was spitting nails but unhurt, and she told us that you were both in Sinclair's car, which we soon had under surveillance. Since we couldn't take the risk of interception, we used an Amber Alert in order to close down the highway. Considering how little time we had, it was very effective."

A knock at the door interrupted him and Tony entered the room with a sheaf of papers. Accepting it with a nod of thanks, Ben scanned the top two sheets before passing them to Linden.

"If you've nothing further to add, please sign and date each page at the bottom," he said. "Then your involvement's over."

Although the sheets were the formal version of her statement, Linden found it hard to accept that the document represented a chunk out of her life. The last week had already taken on a surreal quality. Hugely relieved, she signed the last sheet.

"Well, that about does it," Ben said. "And you need to put it behind you, Linden. Take a trip, visit friends in another city, anything to start the healing process."

"Thanks for the advice," she said, shaking his outstretched hand.

Alex gave a preoccupied smile and returned to reading her statement.

Linden refused to let herself get upset, especially since she was now free to return to her old life. But she wasn't about to forgive Alex so quickly

Tony guided the two women to the front door, and after thanking him for his help, they walked outside. Leaden clouds were fast obscuring the clear blue sky of earlier and they hurried across the parking lot to the Bentley. Spotting them at the last minute, Martin put down his newspaper and opened the car's rear door.

"You'll be glad to know that the whole affair is now closed," Helena announced. "The FBI will issue a press release that explains everything and exonerates Linden."

"We never believed her guilty in the first place," Martin declared.

Linden laughed. "Unfortunately, you were in the minority."

"What do you want to do now, my dear?" Helena asked. "Come with me to visit Gerry?"

"I'd rather go back to Laurel Court," Linden said. "It's already been quite a day. I'm really not up to making small talk in a hospital."

"After yesterday, you deserve time for yourself, just doing nothing."

"I agree," a familiar voice called. "I can also give Linden a lift."

Turning, Linden saw Alex coming toward them, prompting a warm smile from Helena.

"Alex to the rescue as usual," she said, settling herself into the Bentley's rear seat. "In fact, you've been marvelous all along, even if you did deceive us. However, it seems to be a classic case of the end justifying the means. I'd be very grateful if you could take Linden home. Radford's the opposite direction to New York,"

"No problem," Alex replied easily.

As Martin headed for the exit, Alex punched a button on his key ring and the lights of a nearby Toyota Camry flickered in response. Face set in stern lines, Alex stalked over to it and opened the passenger door.

"Get in," he ordered.

Linden complied without a word and the silence continued as Alex drove away.

"Are you angry with me?" she finally ventured.

"Damn right," he snapped.

"Why?"

He shot her a cold look. "Work it out for yourself."

Lips compressed into a thin line, she lapsed into silence, able to be equally juvenile. Several miles passed before she spoke again.

"You made a wrong turn. This isn't the way to Aunt Heni's."

"I don't need directions," he snarled.

Linden's slow burn ratcheted up a couple of notches. For the second time in as many days she was an involuntary traveler in the company of an irate male. A few miles later, Alex pulled into the driveway of a weather-beaten Cape Cod, stopping just short of a garage door with a large dent in the center.

Leaving his seat, he said, "Come with me."

Sullenly, Linden followed him along a cracked path flanked by an unruly mass of wild flowers and tangled weeds, vivid evidence of long-term neglect. The rainstorm erupted as Alex unlocked the front door. Pushing it open, he ushered Linden into a shadowy entrance hall and then led the way to an unfurnished living room. Daylight trickled in through French doors and onto a wall of fieldstone with a fireplace in the center. A fine layer of ash lay beneath the cast iron grate.

Alex let a few minutes of uncomfortable silence pass before speaking.

"A lot has to be done yet, but this is my home. I bought it after

I handed in my notice. It's not too far from my father's office." He glared at Linden. "Well, do you have anything to say?"

Linden shrugged. "Are you upset because I believed Gerry and Peter?"

"Now why would I think that?" he retorted.

"Don't blame me because you didn't have the guts to 'fess up," she flared. "How was I to know you were really an FBI agent in disguise? Telepathy?"

"You could have just trusted me," he pointed out.

"Except for a few brief moments, I did trust you," she responded, "despite everything Gerry and Peter said. And believe me, Peter made a very convincing case against you."

Alex grabbed her shoulders. "I could wring your neck for that."

No longer fooled by his pretense of anger, she added, "Gerry, too."

A smile lurked in Alex's eyes. "I noticed he didn't make the written statement you gave to Ben."

"I decided he'd suffered enough," she chuckled. "Since his name never came up, I guess you didn't bring up his involvement either."

"Like you, I took pity on him, although it's more than he deserves. Miserable rat," Alex muttered. "But I'll probably be seeing a lot of him in the future, so maybe I shouldn't be too hard on him."

"What are you talking about?"

His face broke into a tender smile. "I love you and want to be with you."

Linden wasn't about to have her dreams smashed twice in two days. "You certainly move fast. We've known each other for less than two weeks and you didn't exactly come across as my knight in shining armor at first."

"True, but within just a few days I was crazy about you."

Linden's eyes flashed angrily. "You sure fooled me over the last twenty-four hours. I could have used a few words of comfort last night."

"Me, too. I was still stewing over your secret meeting with Sinclair. It took a good night's sleep to restore my sense of perspective." All traces of humor disappeared as he caught her to him. "When I woke up, I realized what you meant to me, just how much I love you."

Linden rested her head on his chest. "I love you, too. So very much. But we still have a lot to learn about each other."

Releasing her, he glanced around the living room. "And this house is a good place to start. What do you think?"

"Perfect—except it's rather bare."

"Upstairs is better," he said.

Taking her hand, he led her up the narrow staircase to a square landing with four doors. The nearest opened onto an airless room furnished with just a queen-sized bed.

Linden immediately opened the windows. "This room could definitely use a woman's touch."

Ripping off his jacket and tie, Alex dropped them on the floor. "Right now, I know another place that needs a woman's touch more. Especially from this woman."

Pushing her down onto the bed, his mouth descended hungrily on hers while his hands sought favorite pleasure points. It was enough to reassure Linden that she had finally made the right choice. There was a future for them. Consumed by desire, they gave themselves to each other.

Bodies entwined, they slowly returned to the present. After lying in contented silence for a long time, Linden opened her eyes to find the room bathed in sunshine. There was no trace of the heat and humidity of the last few days and the fragrance of honeysuckle hung in the warm air.

With a languorous sigh, she said, "I take it I'm forgiven."

"Not completely," replied Alex, pulling her to him again. "But you've made a good start and this is as good a time as any to continue."

# # #

Made in the USA
Coppell, TX
17 January 2022